Fantastic Four

FAMILY OF HEROES

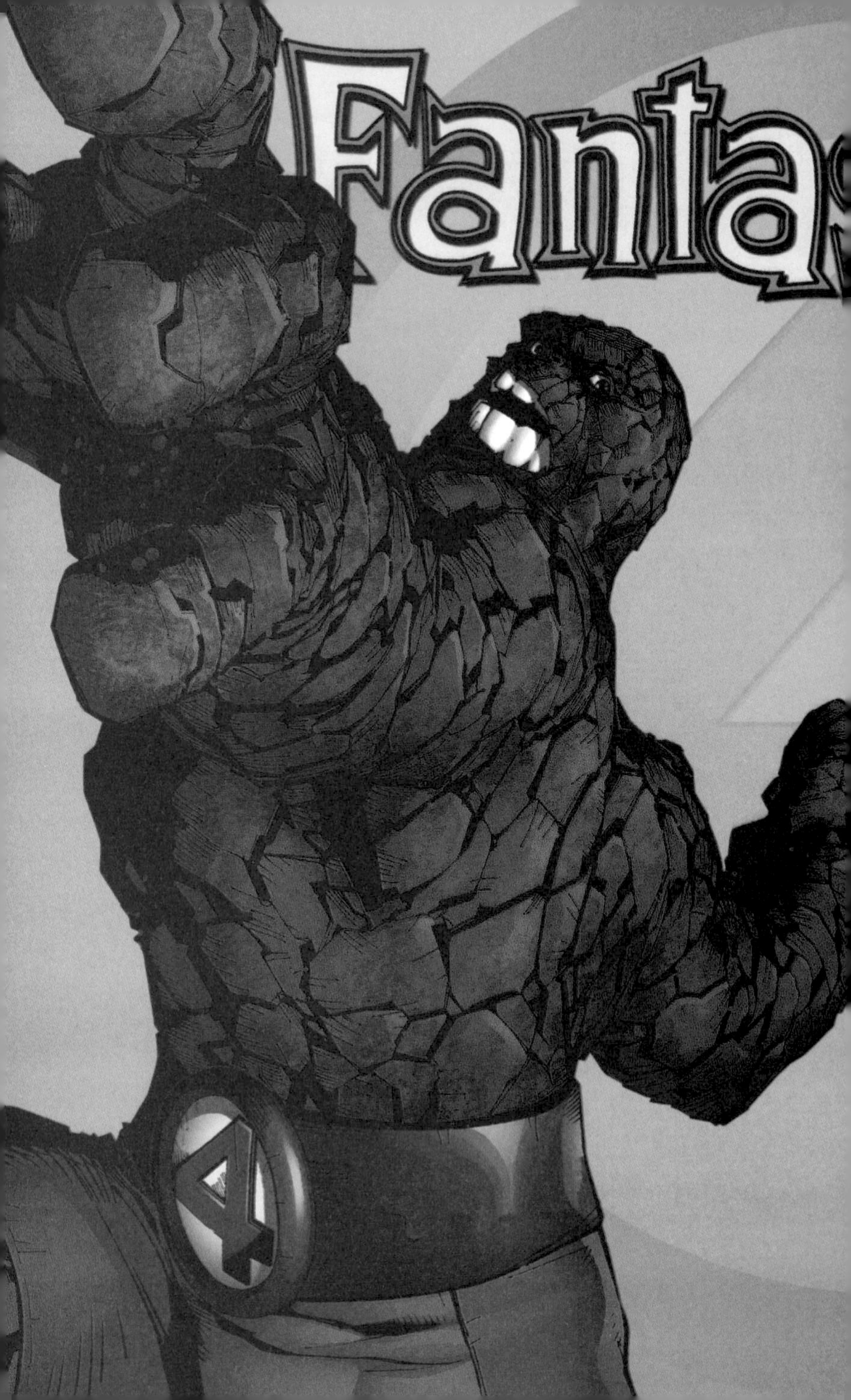

Fantas

tic Four

FAMILY OF HEROES

Writers:
Jeff Parker & Akira Yoshida
Pencils:
Carlo Pagulayan & Juan Santacruz

Inks: **Jeffrey Huet & Raul Fernandez**
Colors: **Sotocolor's A. Crossley**
Letters: **Dave Sharpe**
Cover Art: **Michael Ryan**
Assistant Editor: **Nathan Cosby**
Editor: **Nicole Wiley**
Consulting Editors: **MacKenzie Cadenhead & Mark Paniccia**

Collection Editor: **Jennifer Grünwald**
Assistant Editor: **Michael Short**
Senior Editor, Special Projects: **Jeff Youngquist**
Director of Sales: **David Gabriel**
Book Designer: **Jhonson Eteng**
Creative Director: **Tom Marvelli**

Editor in Chief: **Joe Quesada**
Publisher: **Dan Buckley**

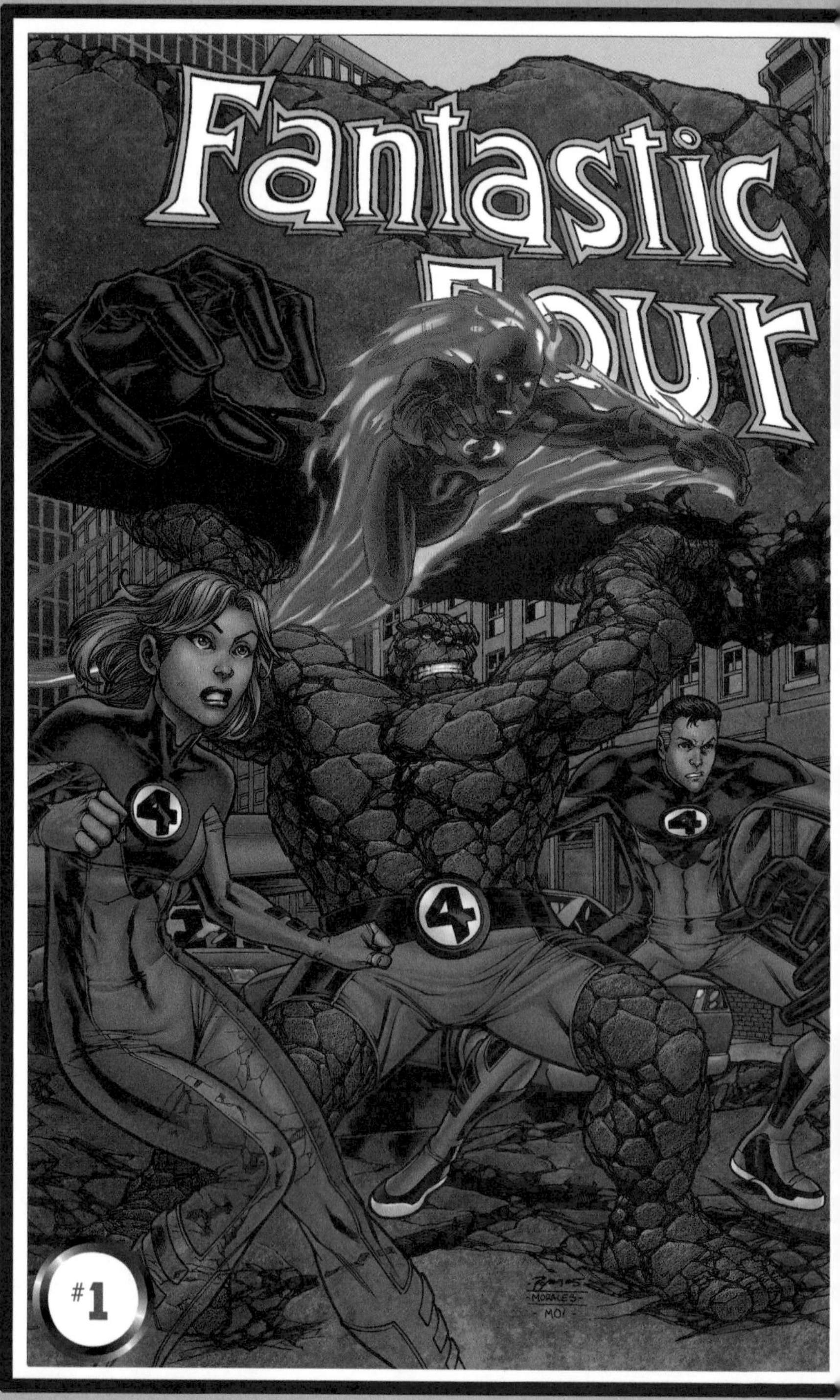
Fantastic Four
#1

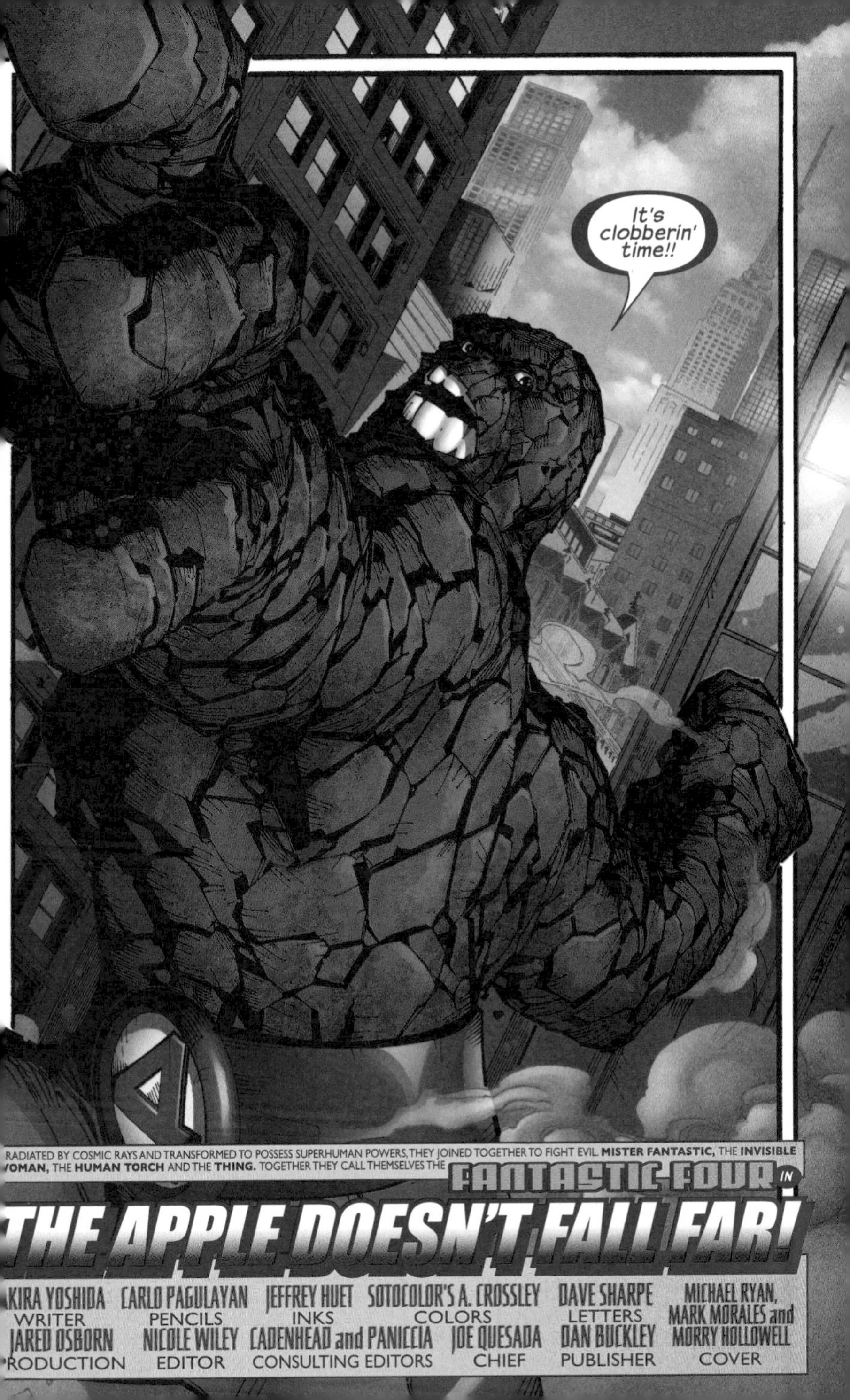
It's clobberin' time!!
RADIATED BY COSMIC RAYS AND TRANSFORMED TO POSSESS SUPERHUMAN POWERS, THEY JOINED TOGETHER TO FIGHT EVIL. MISTER FANTASTIC, THE INVISIBLE VOMAN, THE HUMAN TORCH AND THE THING. TOGETHER THEY CALL THEMSELVES THE FANTASTIC FOUR IN
THE APPLE DOESN'T FALL FAR!
KIRA YOSHIDA WRITER
CARLO PAGULAYAN PENCILS
JEFFREY HUET INKS
SOTOCOLOR'S A. CROSSLEY COLORS
DAVE SHARPE LETTERS
MICHAEL RYAN, MARK MORALES and MORRY HOLLOWELL COVER
JARED OSBORN RODUCTION
NICOLE WILEY EDITOR
CADENHEAD and PANICCIA CONSULTING EDITORS
JOE QUESADA CHIEF
DAN BUCKLEY PUBLISHER

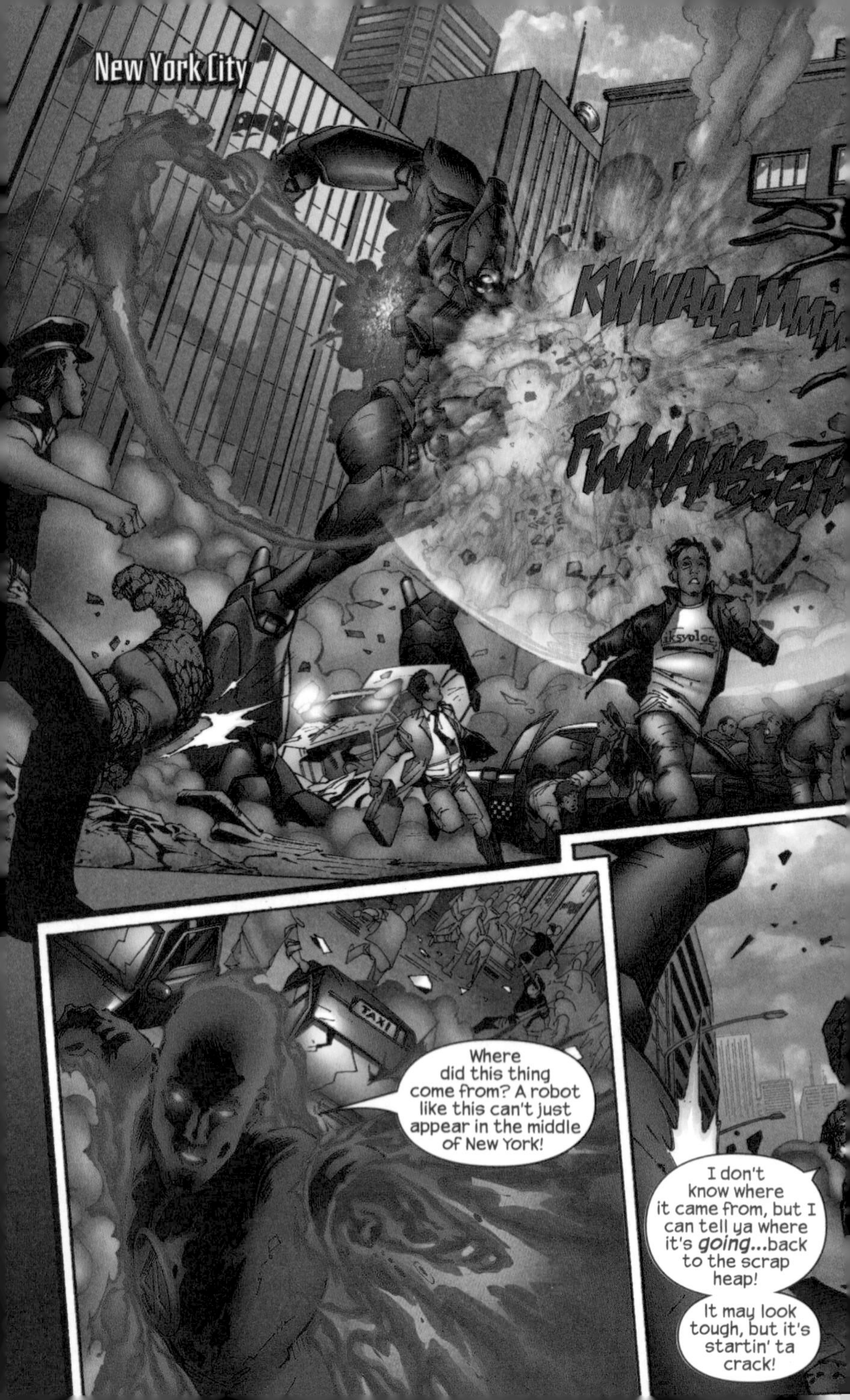

New York City
KWWAAAMMMM
FWWAASSSH
Where did this thing come from? A robot like this can't just appear in the middle of New York!
I don't know where it came from, but I can tell ya where it's *going...*back to the scrap heap!
It may look tough, but it's startin' ta crack!

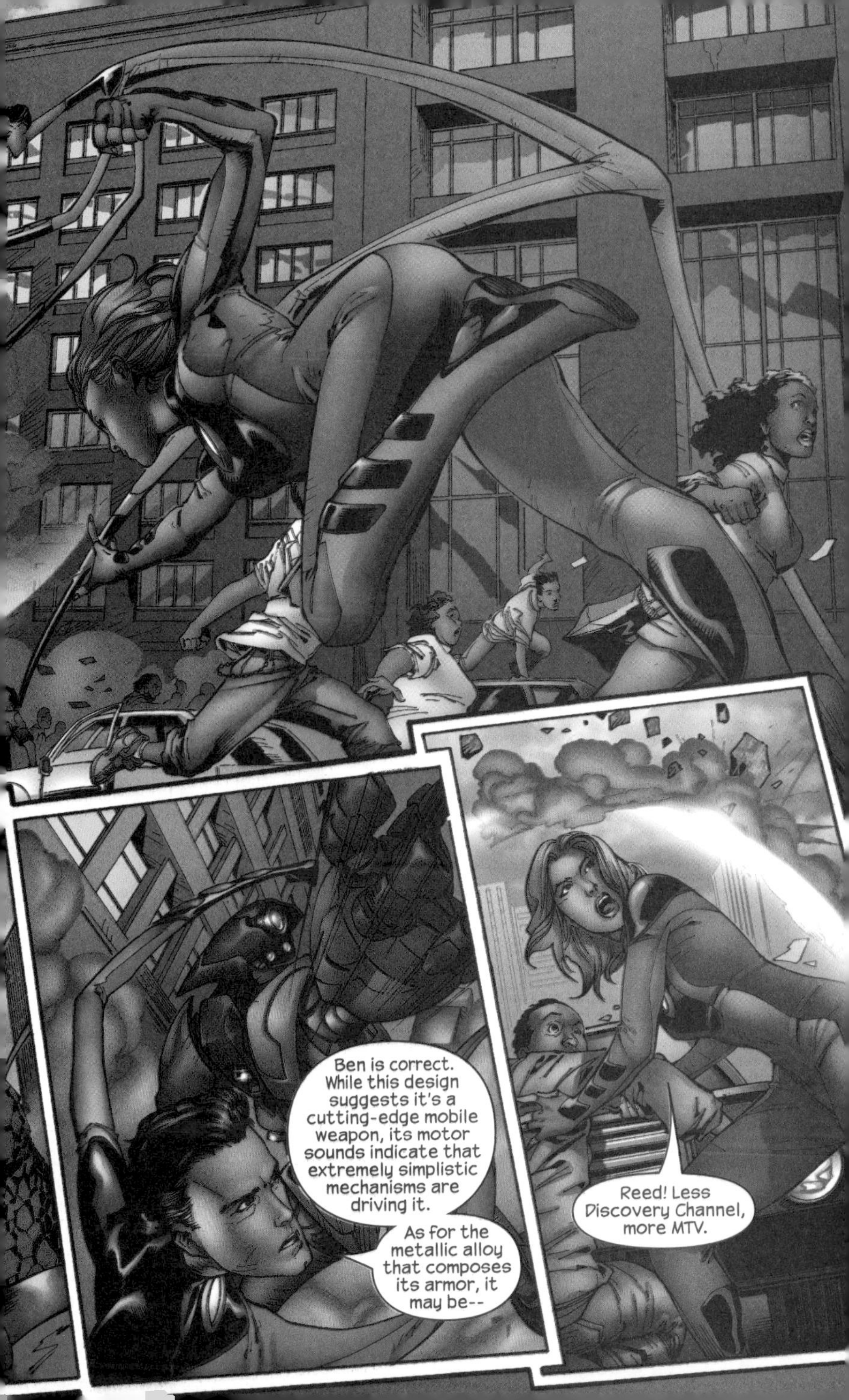
Ben is correct. While this design suggests it's a cutting-edge mobile weapon, its motor sounds indicate that extremely simplistic mechanisms are driving it.
As for the metallic alloy that composes its armor, it may be--
Reed! Less Discovery Channel, more MTV.

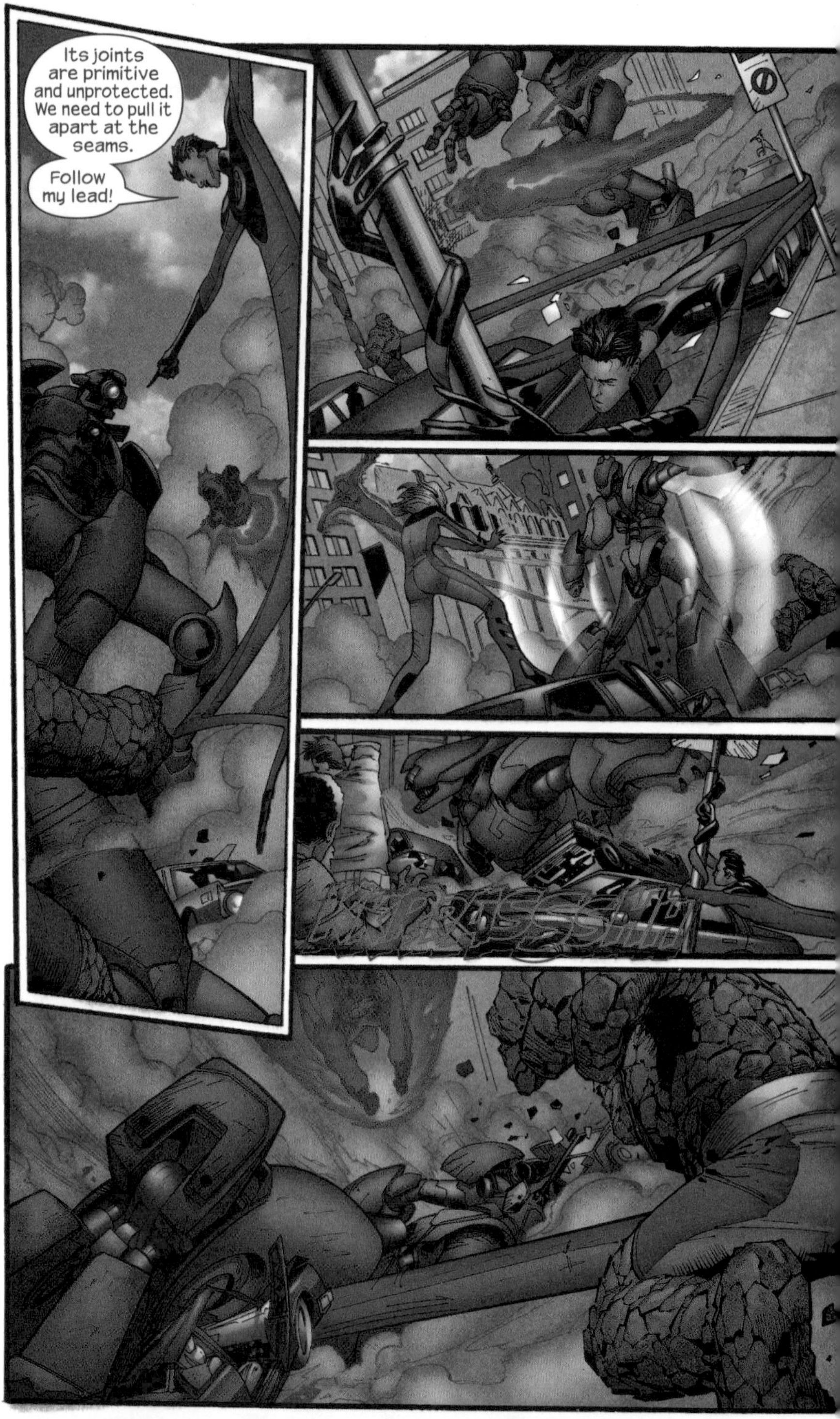
Its joints are primitive and unprotected. We need to pull it apart at the seams.
Follow my lead!

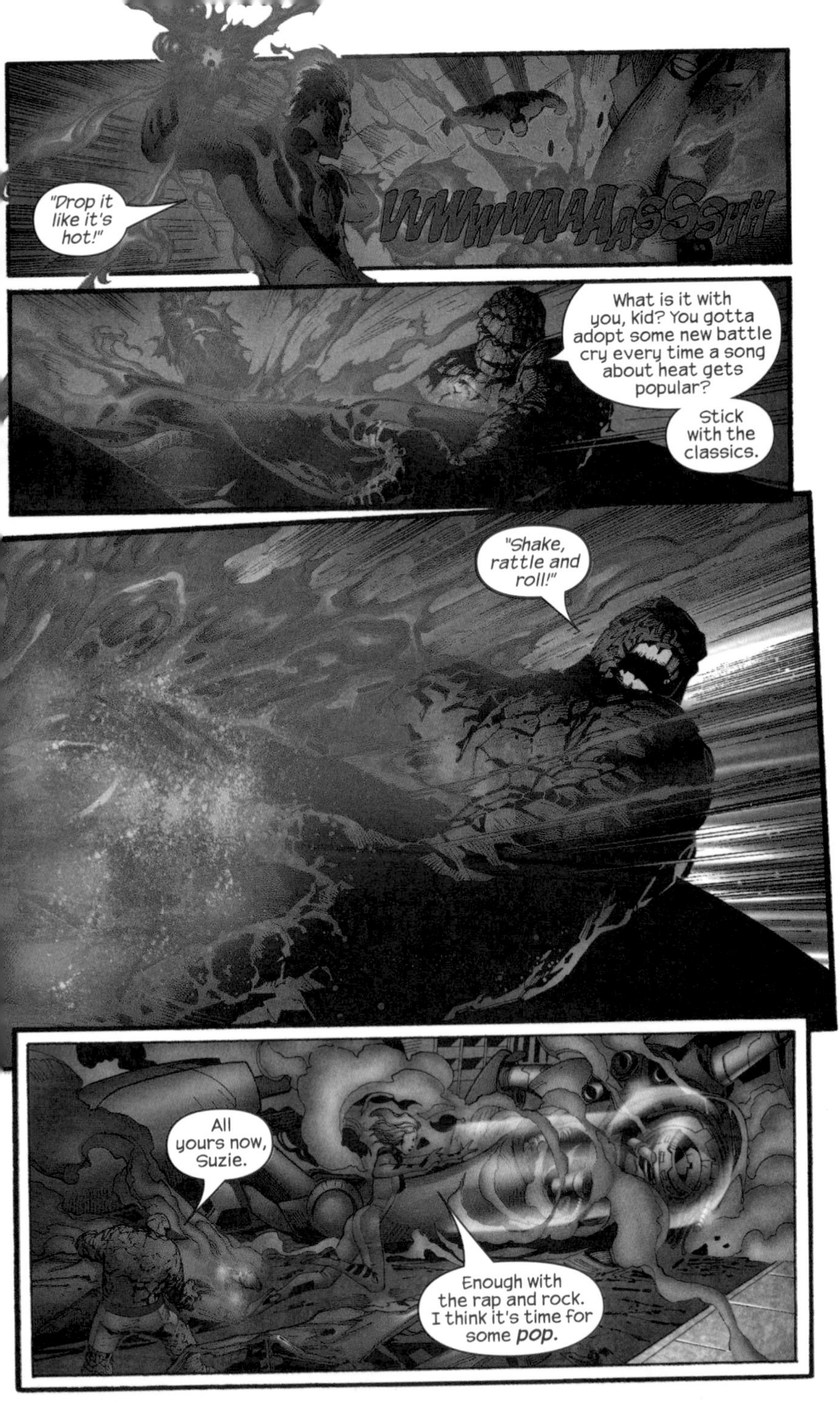
"Drop it like it's hot!"
VWWWWAAAAASSSHH
What is it with you, kid? You gotta adopt some new battle cry every time a song about heat gets popular?
Stick with the classics.
"Shake, rattle and roll!"
All yours now, Suzie.
Enough with the rap and rock. I think it's time for some *pop*.

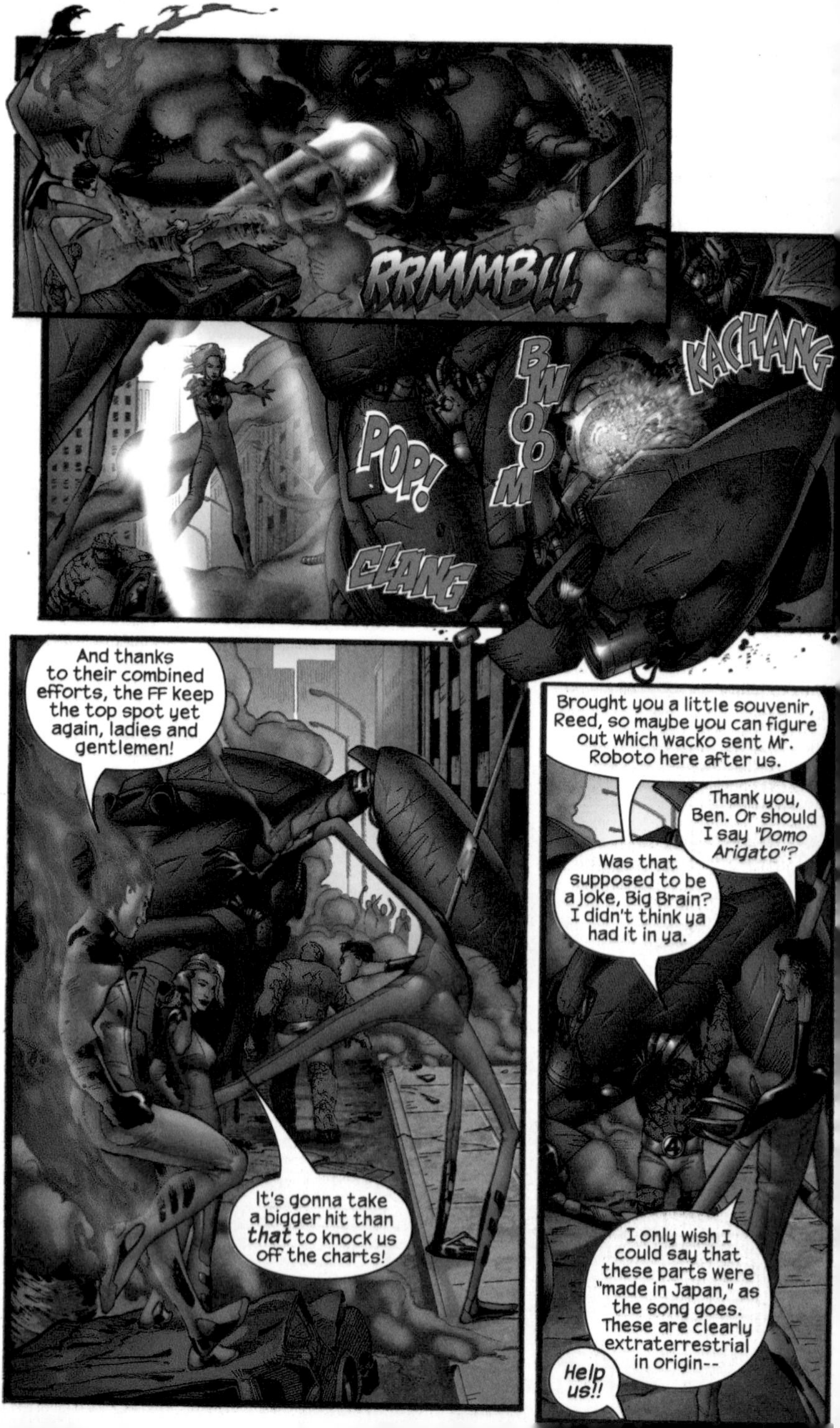
RRMMBLL
POP!
CLANG
BWOOOM
KACHANG
And thanks to their combined efforts, the FF keep the top spot yet again, ladies and gentlemen!
It's gonna take a bigger hit than *that* to knock us off the charts!
Brought you a little souvenir, Reed, so maybe you can figure out which wacko sent Mr. Roboto here after us.
Thank you, Ben. Or should I say *"Domo Arigato"*?
Was that supposed to be a joke, Big Brain? I didn't think ya had it in ya.
I only wish I could say that these parts were "made in Japan," as the song goes. These are clearly extraterrestrial in origin--
Help us!!

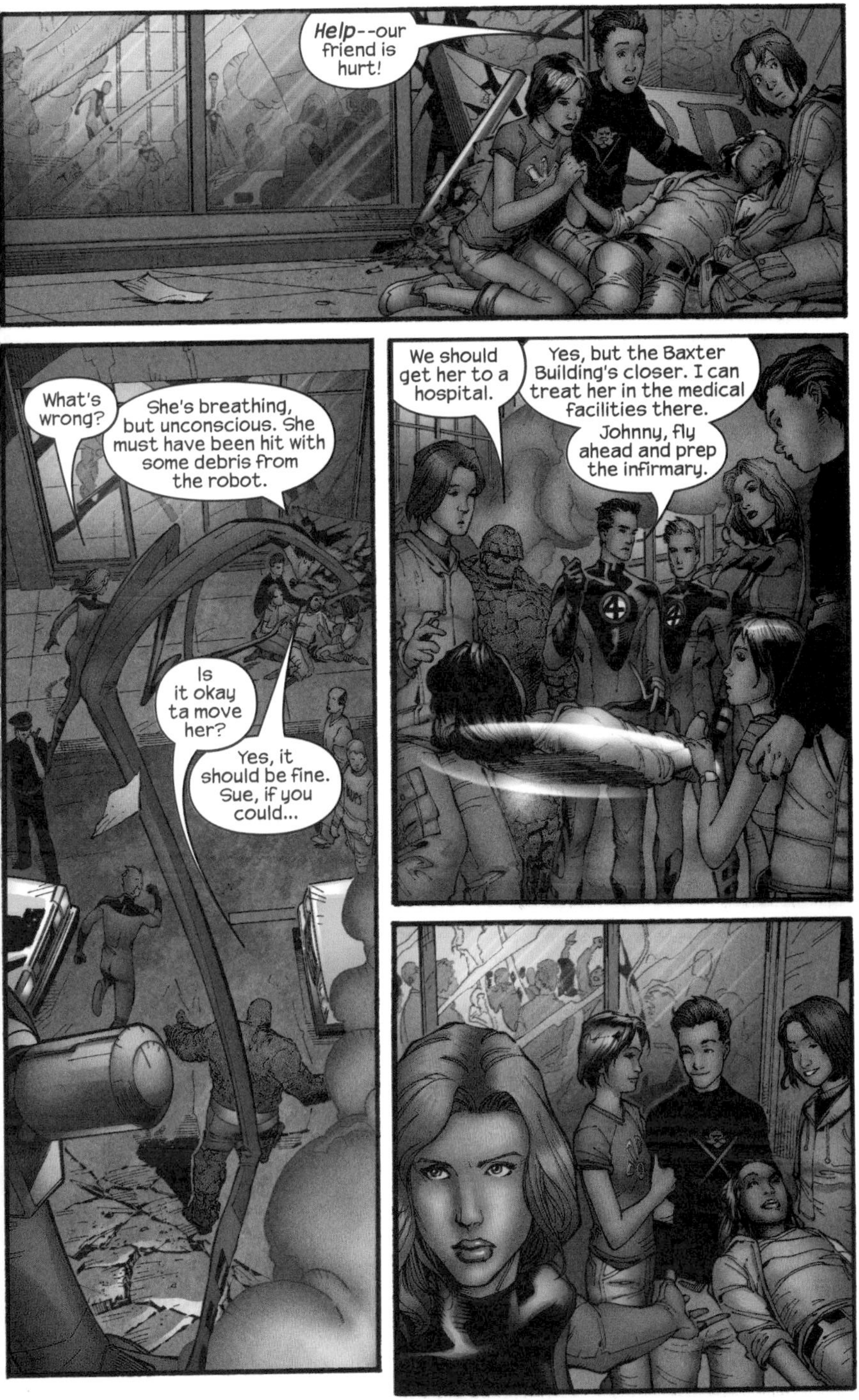
Help--our friend is hurt!
What's wrong?
She's breathing, but unconscious. She must have been hit with some debris from the robot.
Is it okay ta move her?
Yes, it should be fine. Sue, if you could...
We should get her to a hospital.
Yes, but the Baxter Building's closer. I can treat her in the medical facilities there.
Johnny, fly ahead and prep the infirmary.

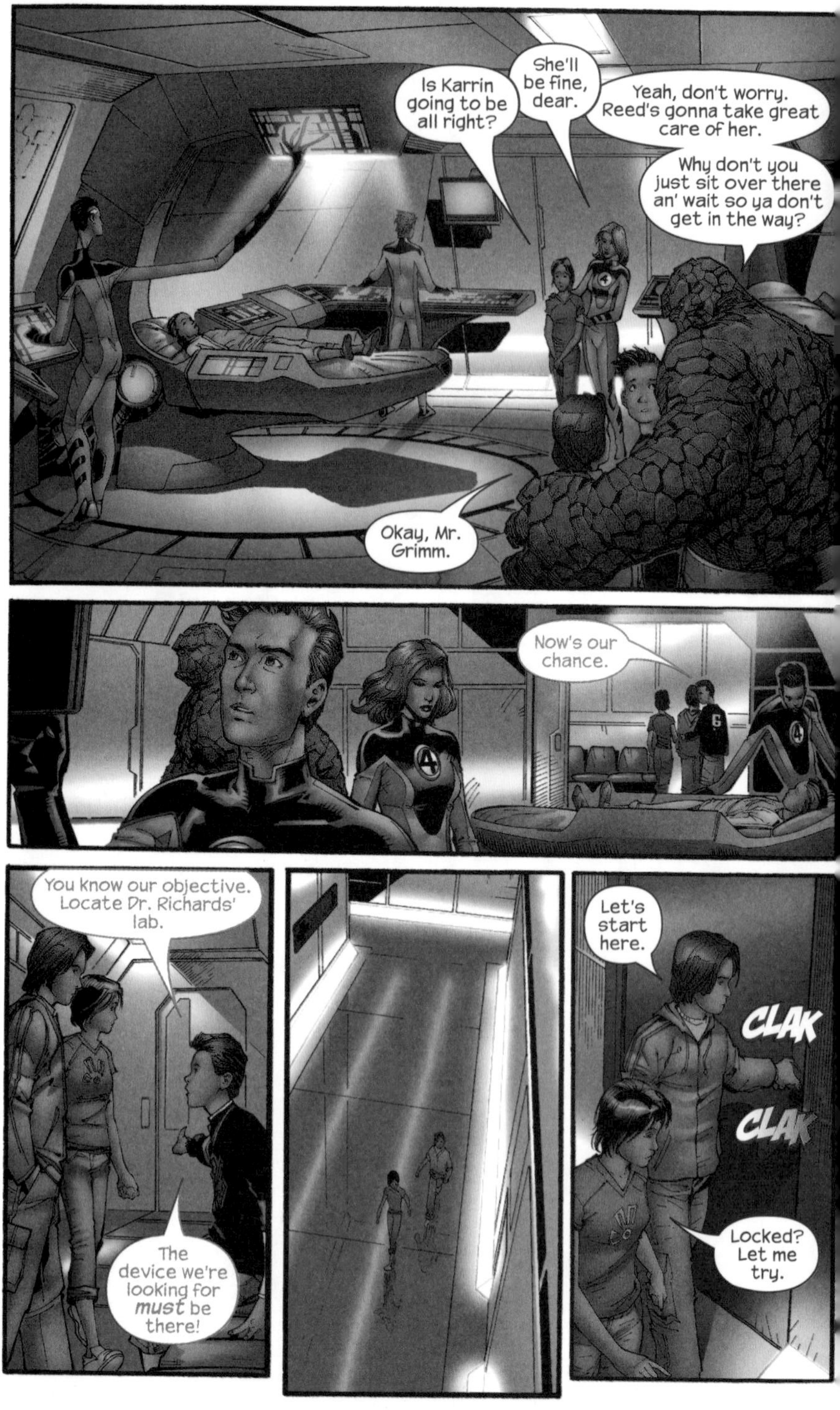
Is Karrin going to be all right?
She'll be fine, dear.
Yeah, don't worry. Reed's gonna take great care of her.
Why don't you just sit over there an' wait so ya don't get in the way?
Okay, Mr. Grimm.
Now's our chance.
You know our objective. Locate Dr. Richards' lab.
The device we're looking for *must* be there!
Let's start here.
CLAK
CLAK
Locked? Let me try.

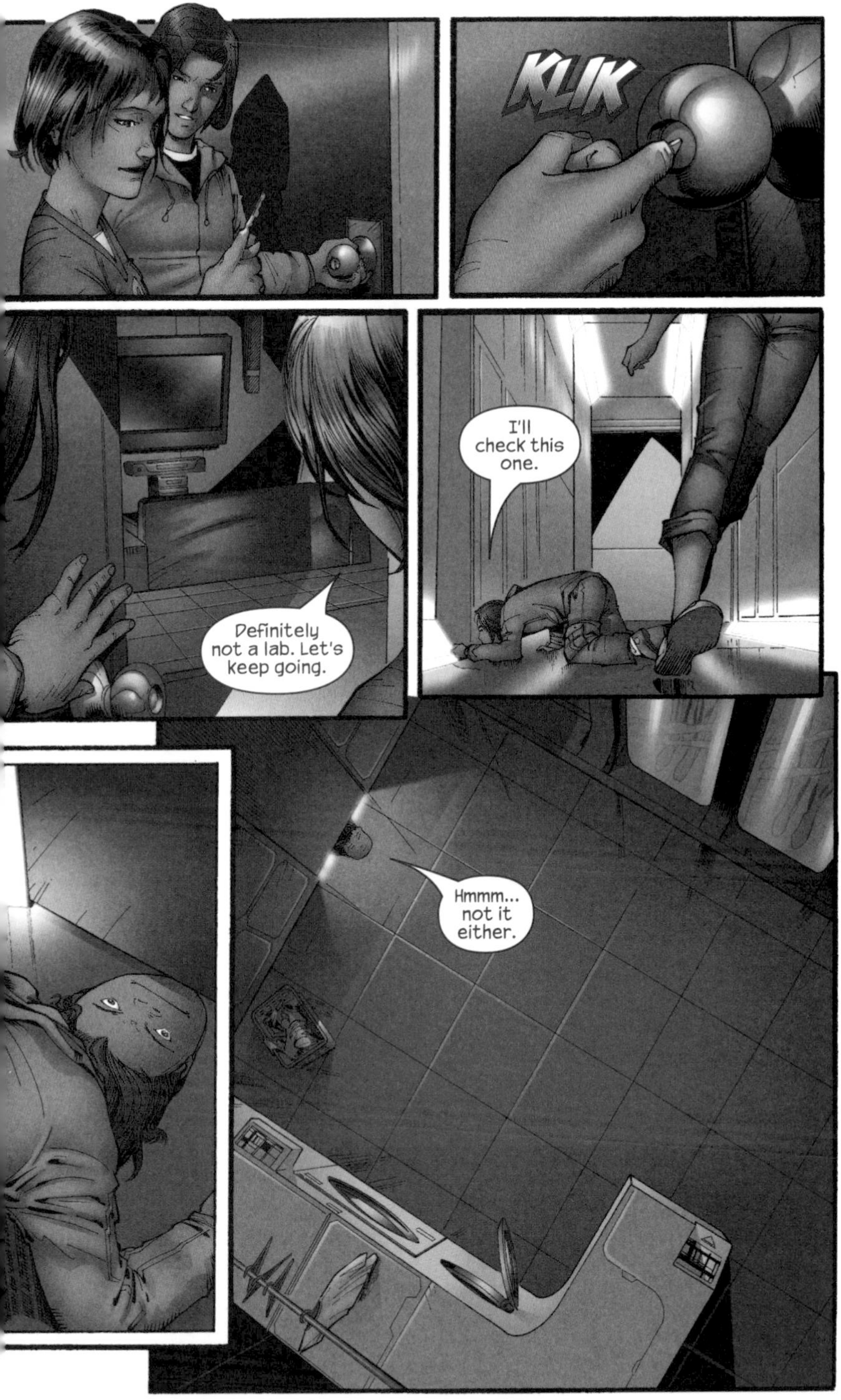
KLIK
Definitely not a lab. Let's keep going.
I'll check this one.
Hmmm... not it either.

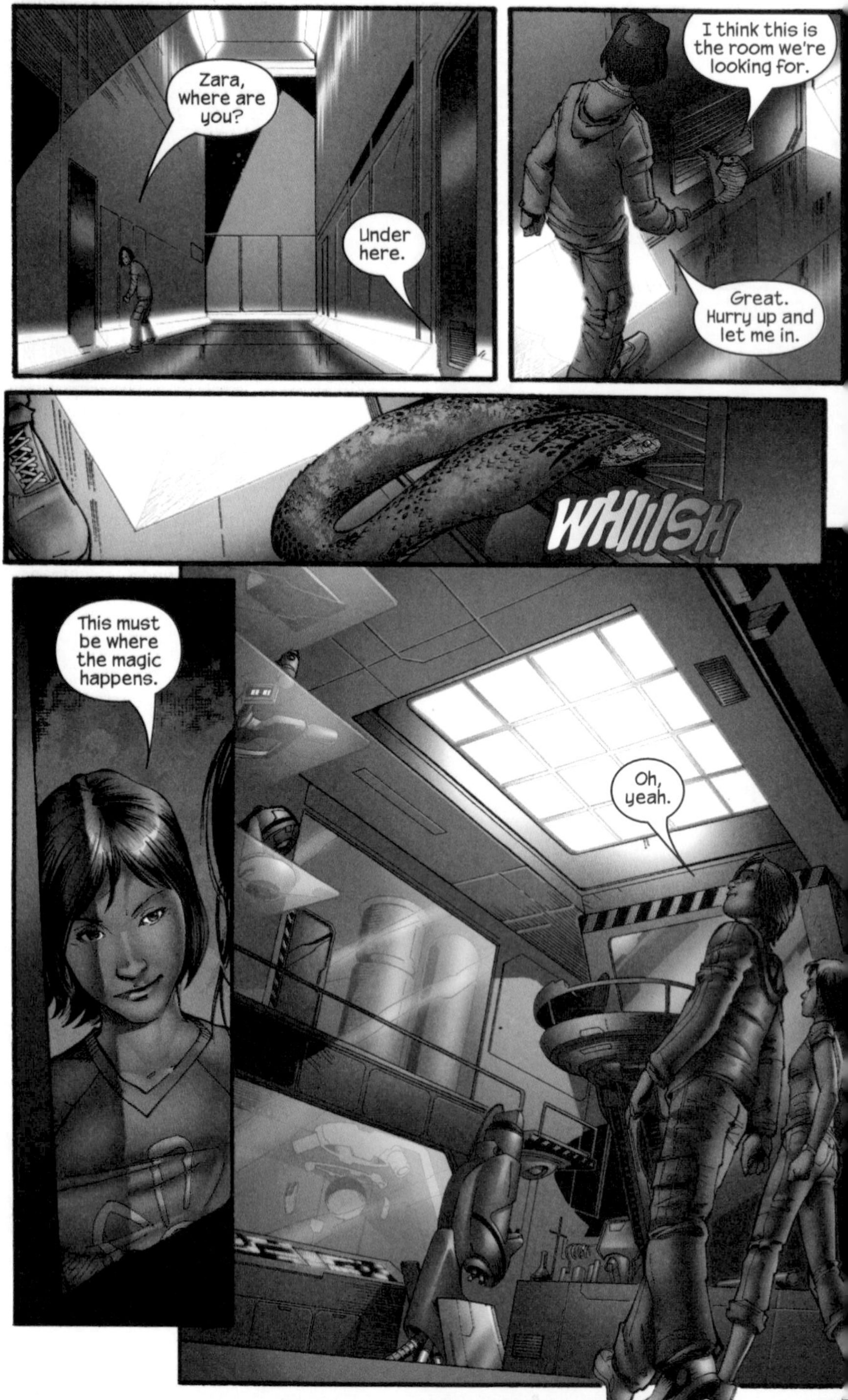
Zara, where are you?
Under here.
I think this is the room we're looking for.
Great. Hurry up and let me in.
WHIIISH
This must be where the magic happens.
Oh, yeah.

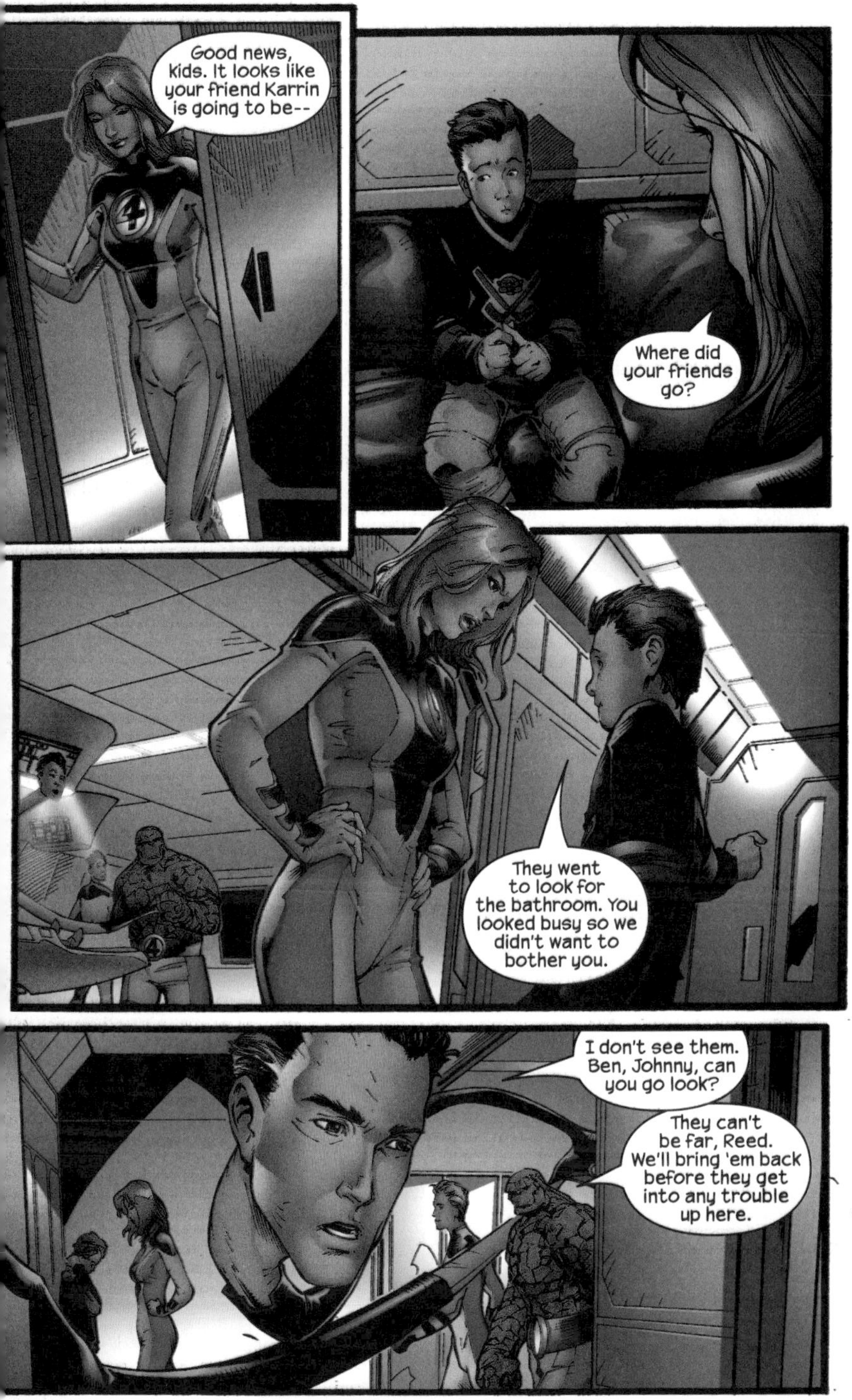
Good news, kids. It looks like your friend Karrin is going to be--
Where did your friends go?
They went to look for the bathroom. You looked busy so we didn't want to bother you.
I don't see them. Ben, Johnny, can you go look?
They can't be far, Reed. We'll bring 'em back before they get into any trouble up here.

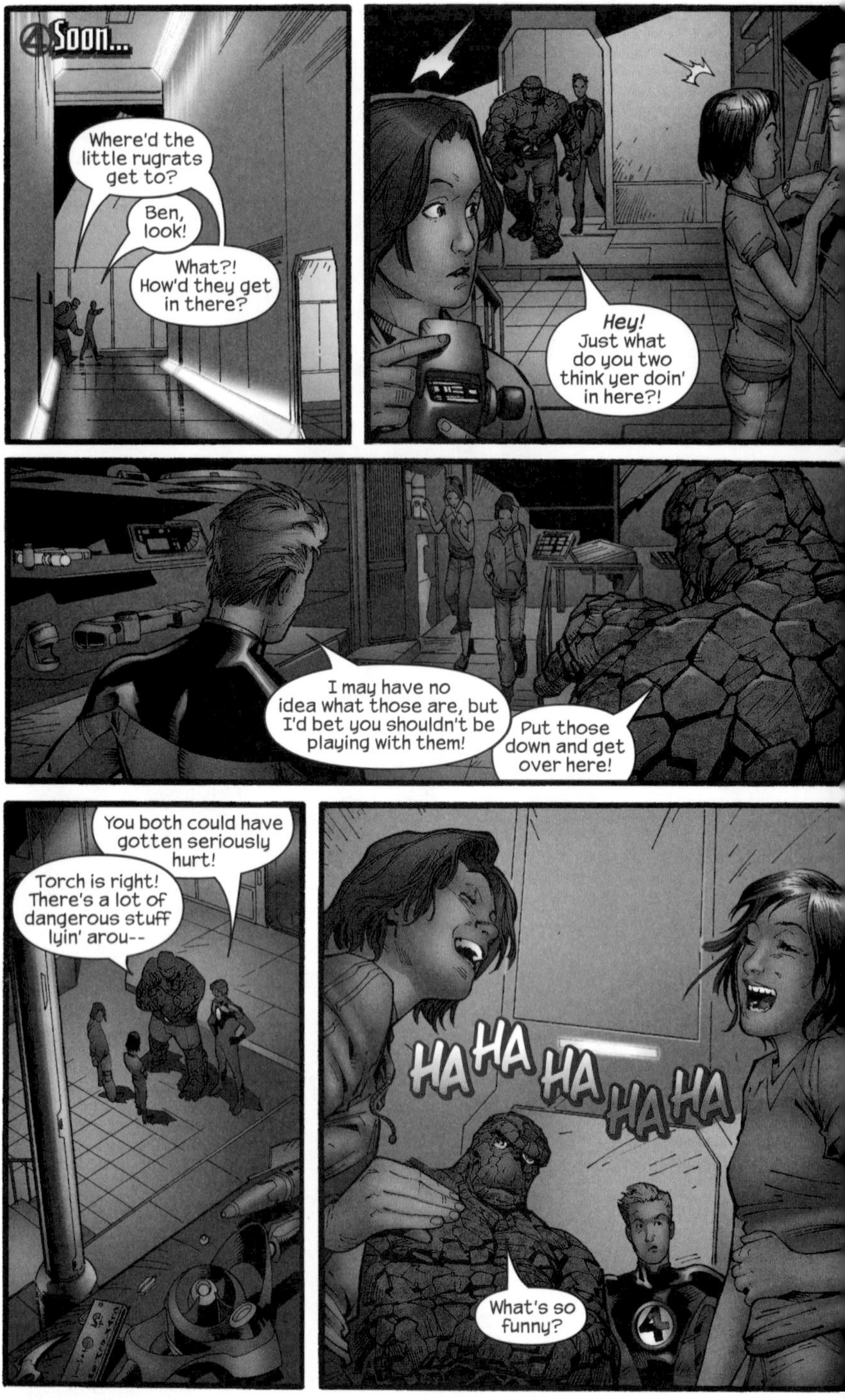
Soon...
Where'd the little rugrats get to?
Ben, look!
What?! How'd they get in there?
Hey! Just what do you two think yer doin' in here?!
I may have no idea what those are, but I'd bet you shouldn't be playing with them!
Put those down and get over here!
You both could have gotten seriously hurt!
Torch is right! There's a lot of dangerous stuff lyin' arou--
HA HA HA HA HA HA
What's so funny?

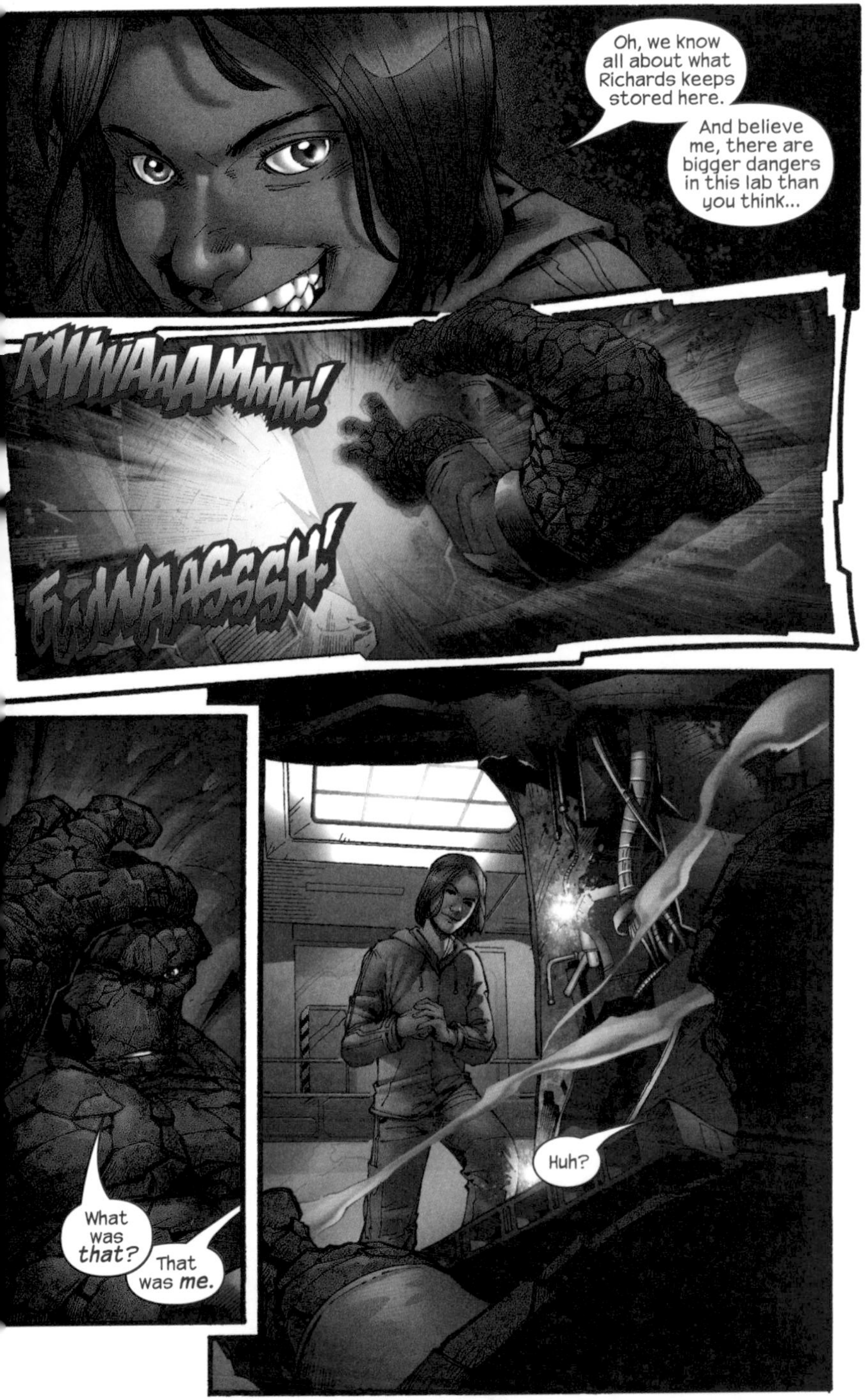
Oh, we know all about what Richards keeps stored here.
And believe me, there are bigger dangers in this lab than you think...
KWWAAAMMMM!
FTWAASSSH!
Huh?
What was *that?*
That was *me.*

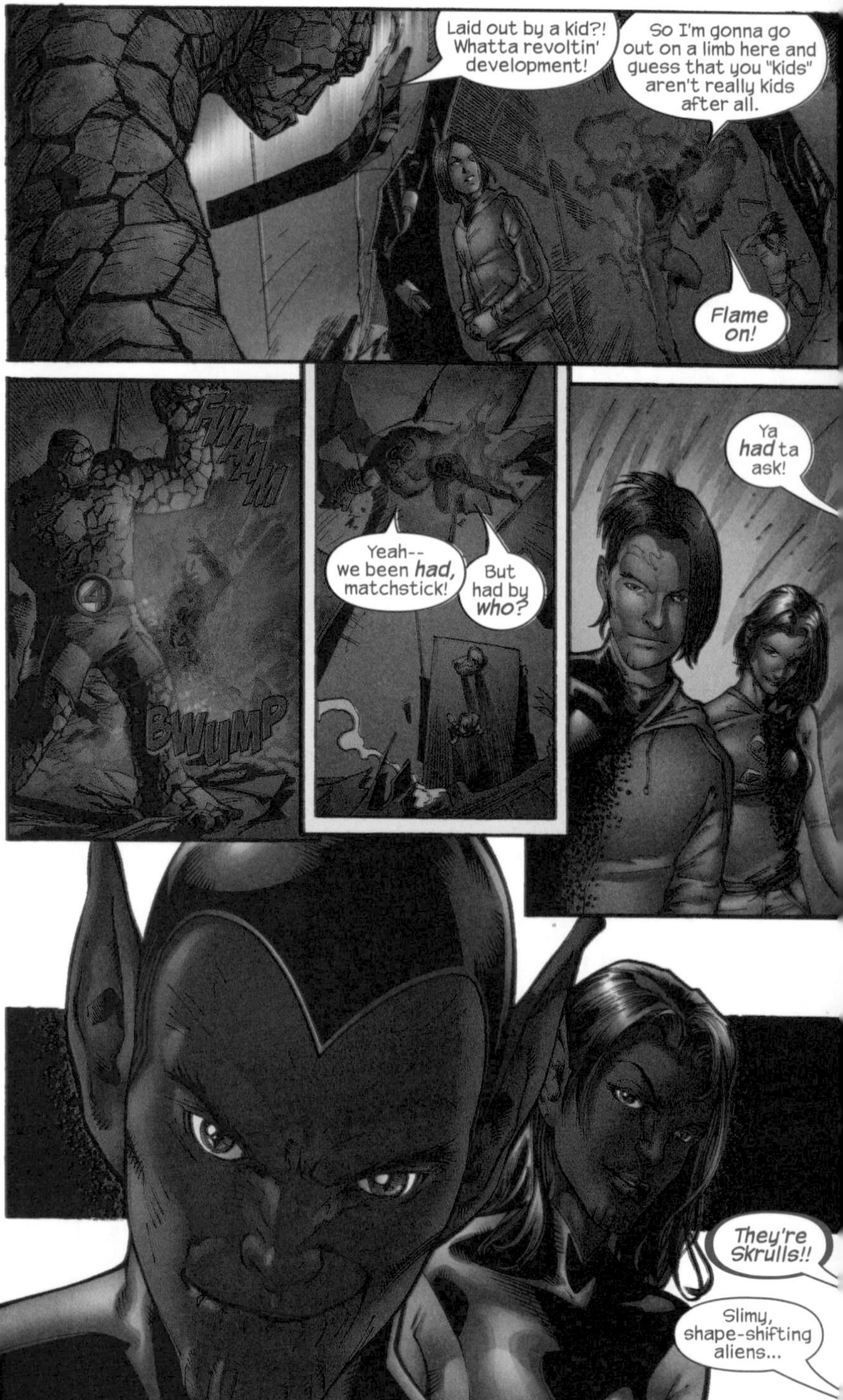
Laid out by a kid?! Whatta revoltin' development!
So I'm gonna go out on a limb here and guess that you "kids" aren't really kids after all.
Flame on!
FWAAM
BWUMP
Yeah-- we been had, matchstick!
But had by who?
Ya had ta ask!
They're Skrulls!!
Slimy, shape-shifting aliens...

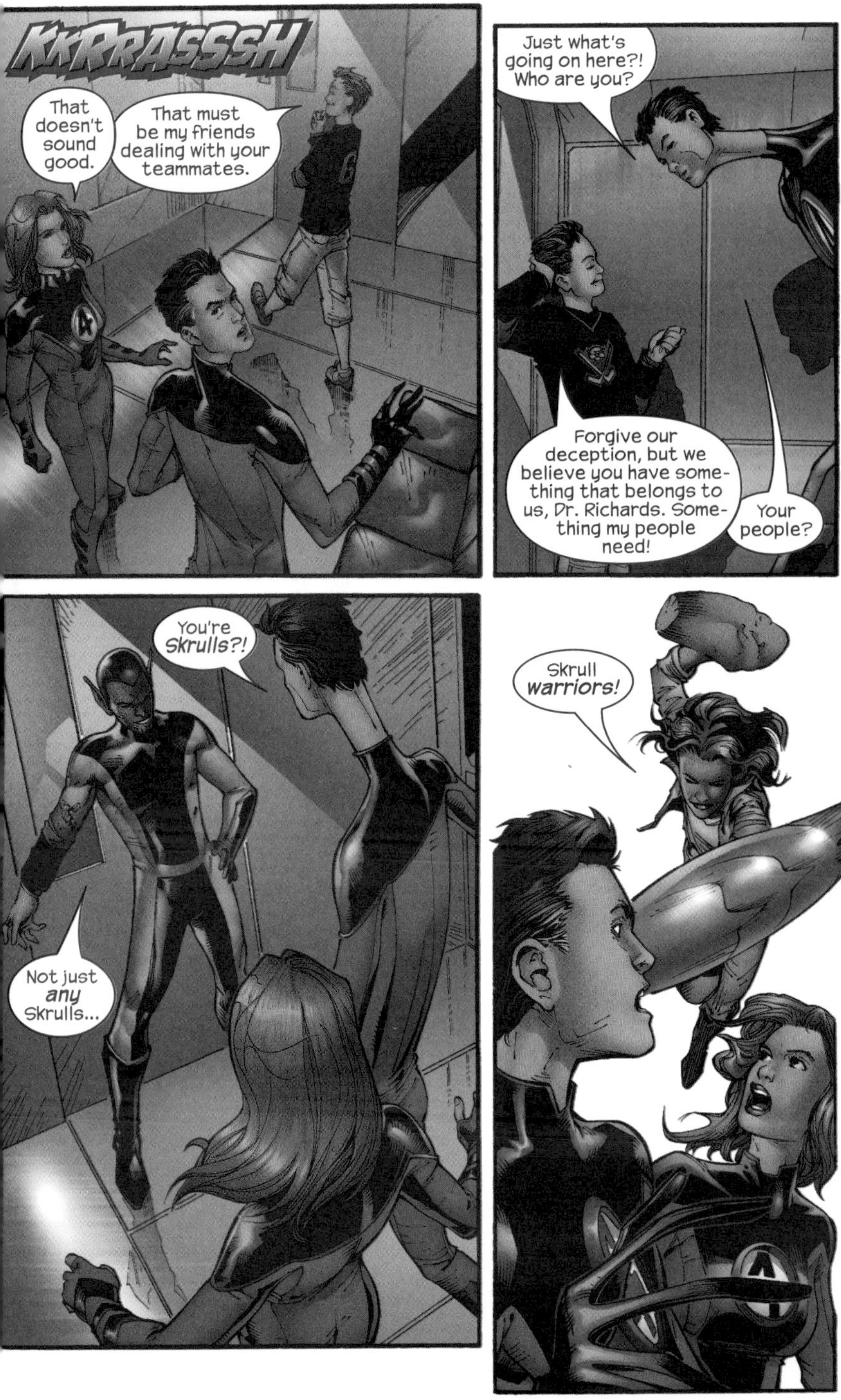
KKRRASSSH
That doesn't sound good.
That must be my friends dealing with your teammates.
Just what's going on here?! Who are you?
Forgive our deception, but we believe you have something that belongs to us, Dr. Richards. Something my people need!
Your people?
You're Skrulls?!
Not just any Skrulls...
Skrull warriors!

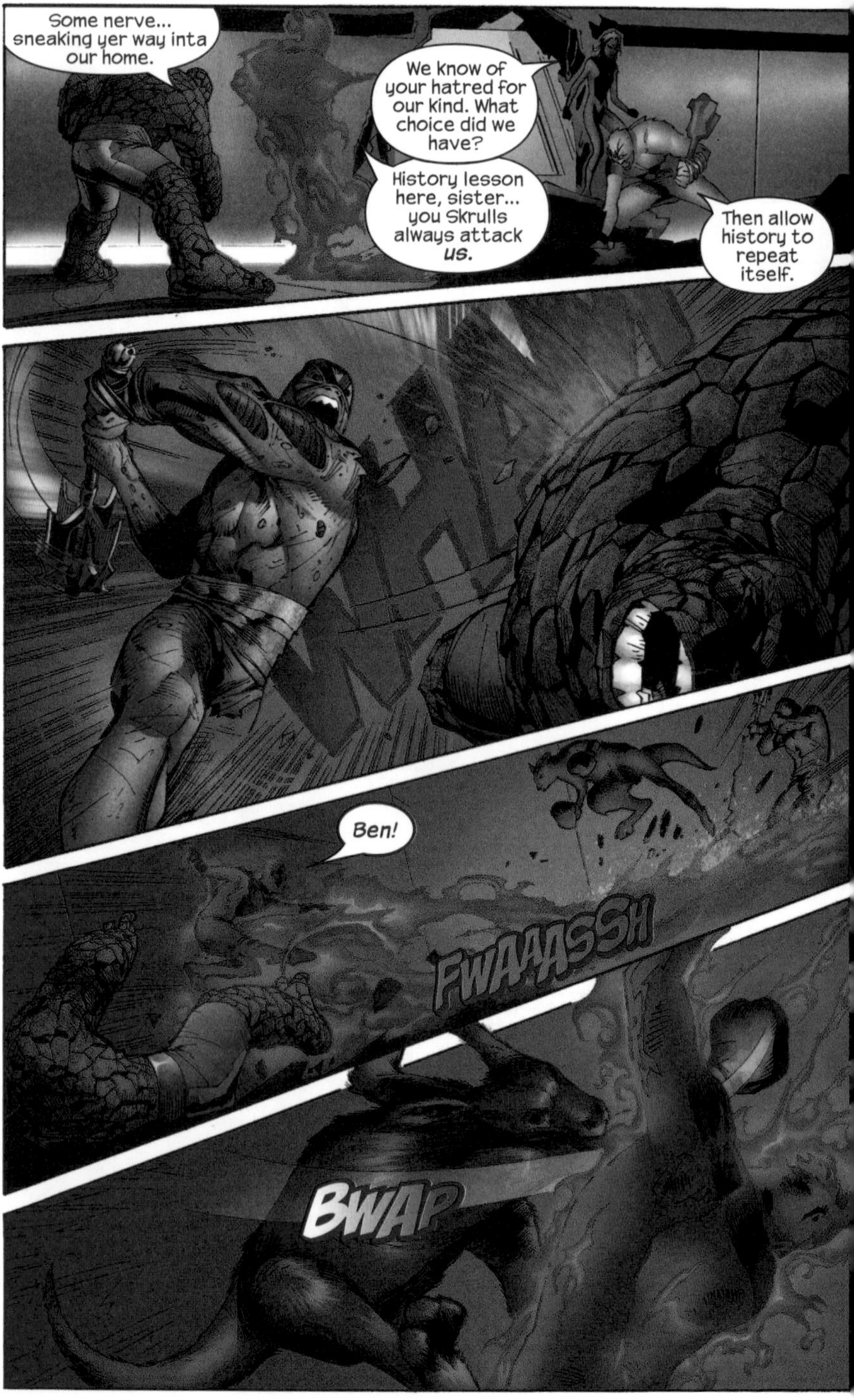
Some nerve... sneaking yer way inta our home.
We know of your hatred for our kind. What choice did we have?
History lesson here, sister... you Skrulls always attack *us.*
Then allow history to repeat itself.
Ben!
FWAAASSH
BWAP

Brute force is useless against the Invisible Woman. She'll simply repel your attacks! Try something else.

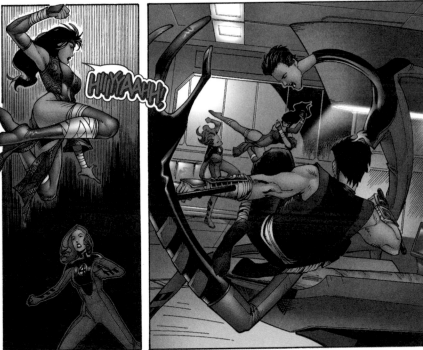

HIIYAAHH!

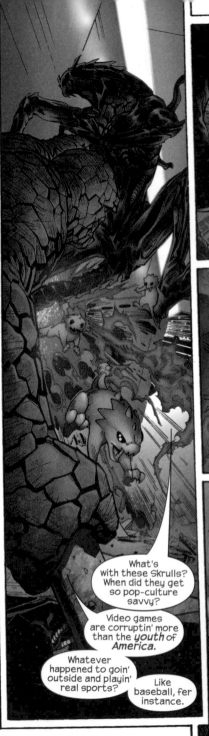

WHAAP

Or football.

Hey, Ben-- catch!

What's with these Skrulls? When did they get so pop-culture savvy?

Video games are corruptin' more than the *youth* of *America.*

Whatever happened to goin' outside and playin' real sports?

Like baseball, fer instance.

Touch-down!

But I'd guess you don't want me to spike you, eh?

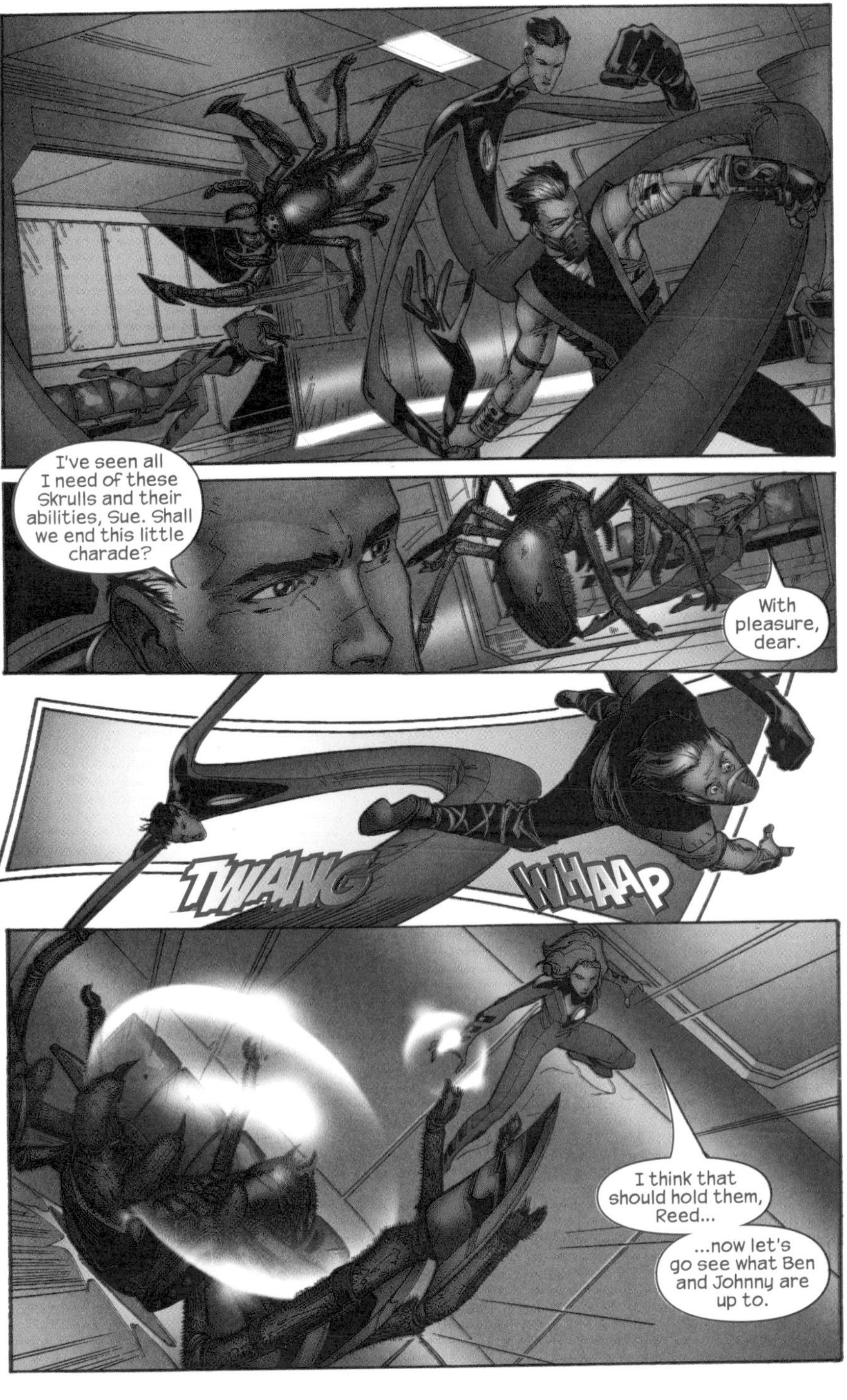
I've seen all I need of these Skrulls and their abilities, Sue. Shall we end this little charade?
With pleasure, dear.
TWANG
WHAAP
I think that should hold them, Reed...
...now let's go see what Ben and Johnny are up to.

Shortly...

Given your shape-shifting, your inexperience, and the forms you chose, I'm going to guess that you're not Skrull warriors, but Skrull *children*?

Yes--

No, Karrin, tell them nothing!

Why not, Darko?! Your plan failed, what other choice do we have?

While by your human calendar we're older than most of you, in Skrull years we would be considered adolescents.

We originally came to Earth with our parents who disappeared shortly after our arrival.

And you've been on your own ever since?

Yes, using our powers to assimilate into your culture and survive...

While trying to locate our parents.

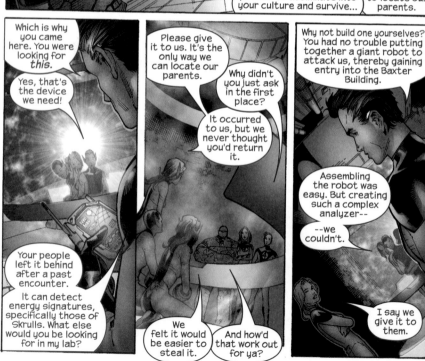

Which is why you came here. You were looking for *this*.

Yes, that's the device we need!

Your people left it behind after a past encounter.

It can detect energy signatures, specifically those of Skrulls. What else would you be looking for in my lab?

Please give it to us. It's the only way we can locate our parents.

Why didn't you just ask in the first place?

It occurred to us, but we never thought you'd return it.

We felt it would be easier to steal it.

And how'd that work out for ya?

Why not build one yourselves? You had no trouble putting together a giant robot to attack us, thereby gaining entry into the Baxter Building.

Assembling the robot was easy. But creating such a complex analyzer--

--we couldn't.

I say we give it to them.

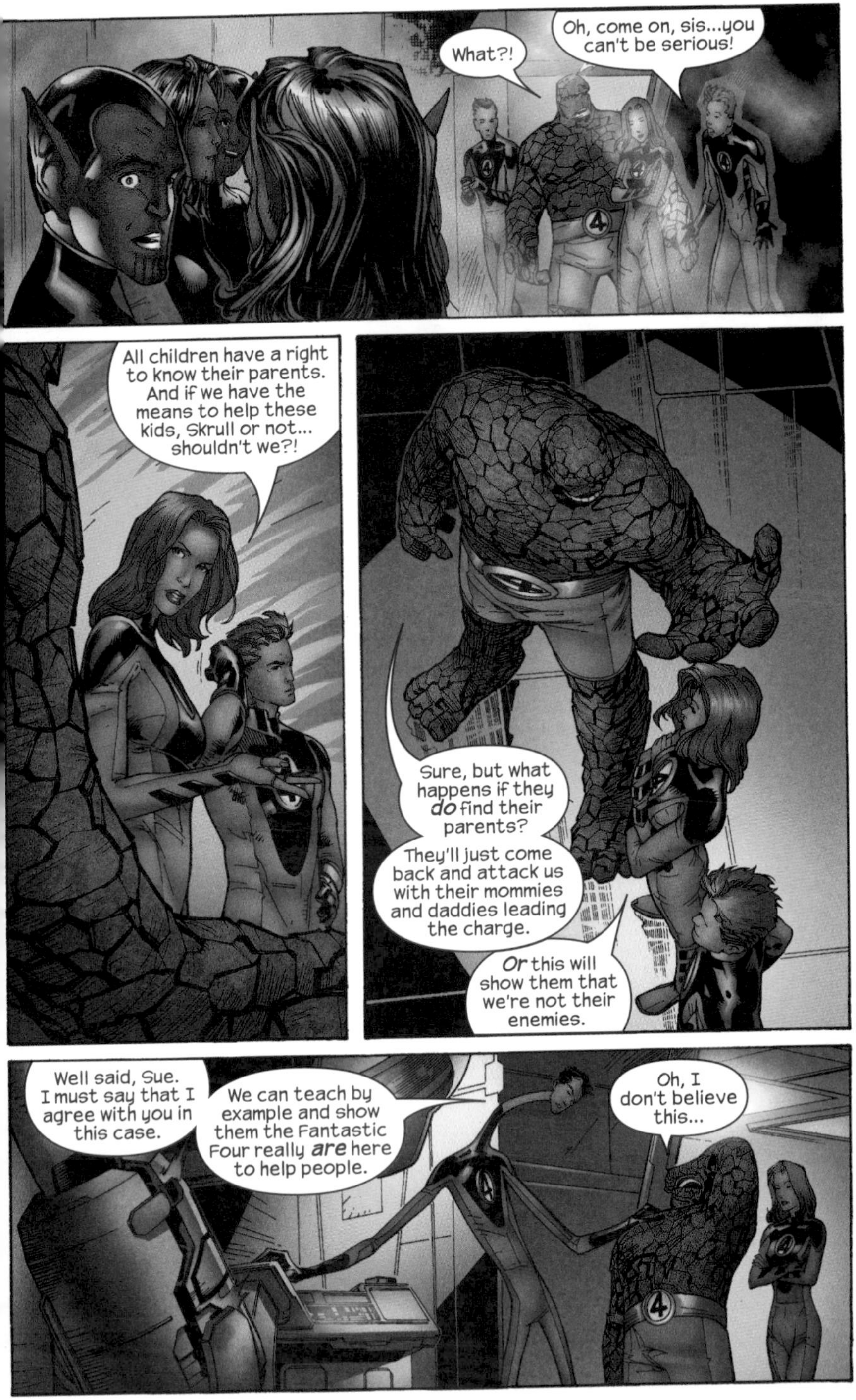
What?!
Oh, come on, sis...you can't be serious!
All children have a right to know their parents. And if we have the means to help these kids, Skrull or not... shouldn't we?!
Sure, but what happens if they *do* find their parents?
They'll just come back and attack us with their mommies and daddies leading the charge.
Or this will show them that we're not their enemies.
Well said, Sue. I must say that I agree with you in this case.
We can teach by example and show them the Fantastic Four really *are* here to help people.
Oh, I don't believe this...

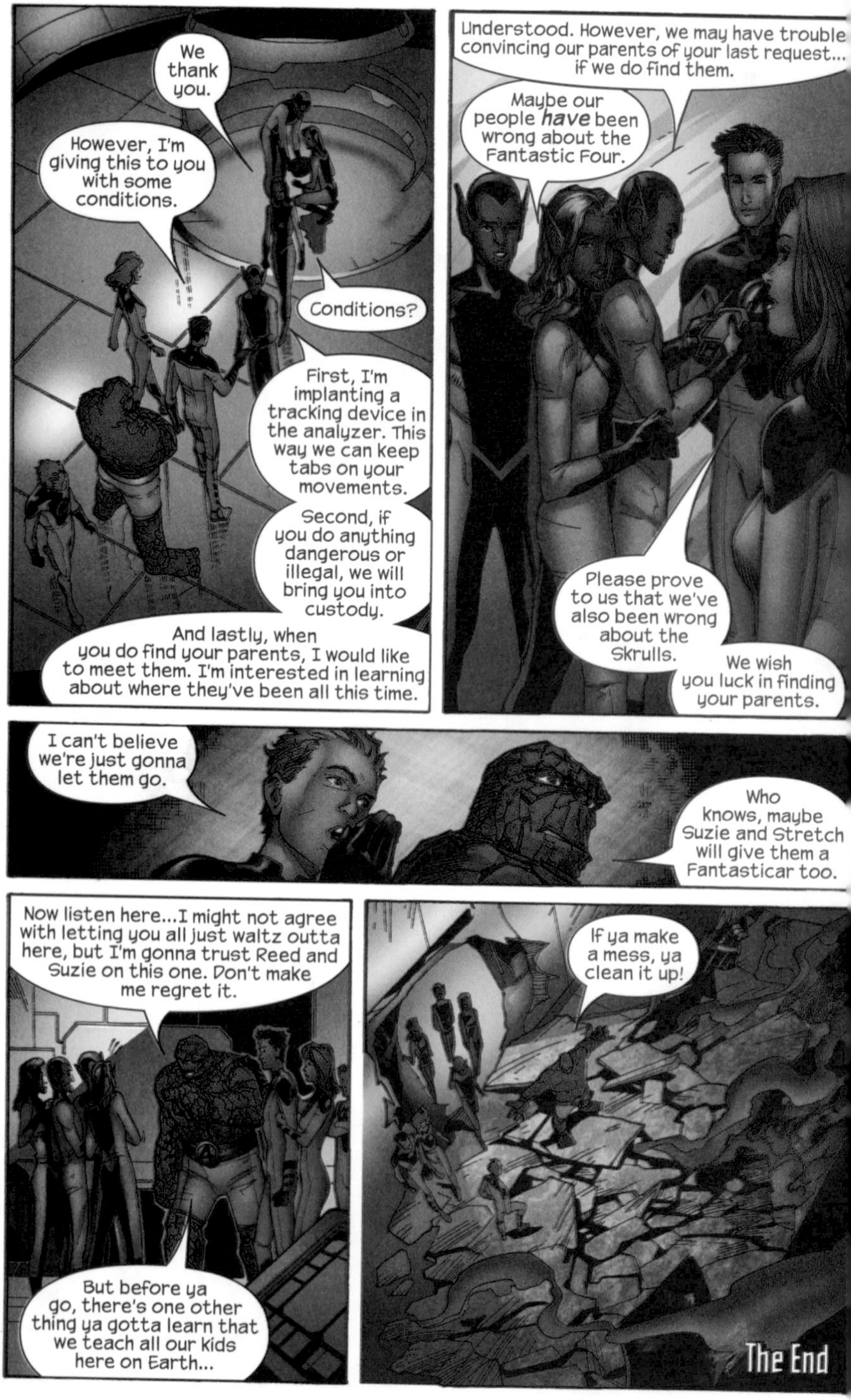
We thank you.
However, I'm giving this to you with some conditions.
Conditions?
First, I'm implanting a tracking device in the analyzer. This way we can keep tabs on your movements.
Second, if you do anything dangerous or illegal, we will bring you into custody.
And lastly, when you do find your parents, I would like to meet them. I'm interested in learning about where they've been all this time.
Understood. However, we may have trouble convincing our parents of your last request... if we do find them.
Maybe our people *have* been wrong about the Fantastic Four.
Please prove to us that we've also been wrong about the Skrulls.
We wish you luck in finding your parents.
I can't believe we're just gonna let them go.
Who knows, maybe Suzie and Stretch will give them a Fantasticar too.
Now listen here...I might not agree with letting you all just waltz outta here, but I'm gonna trust Reed and Suzie on this one. Don't make me regret it.
But before ya go, there's one other thing ya gotta learn that we teach all our kids here on Earth...
If ya make a mess, ya clean it up!
The End

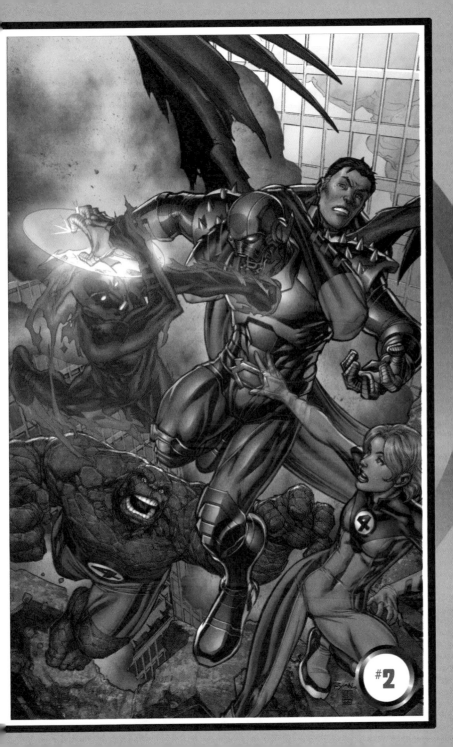

#2

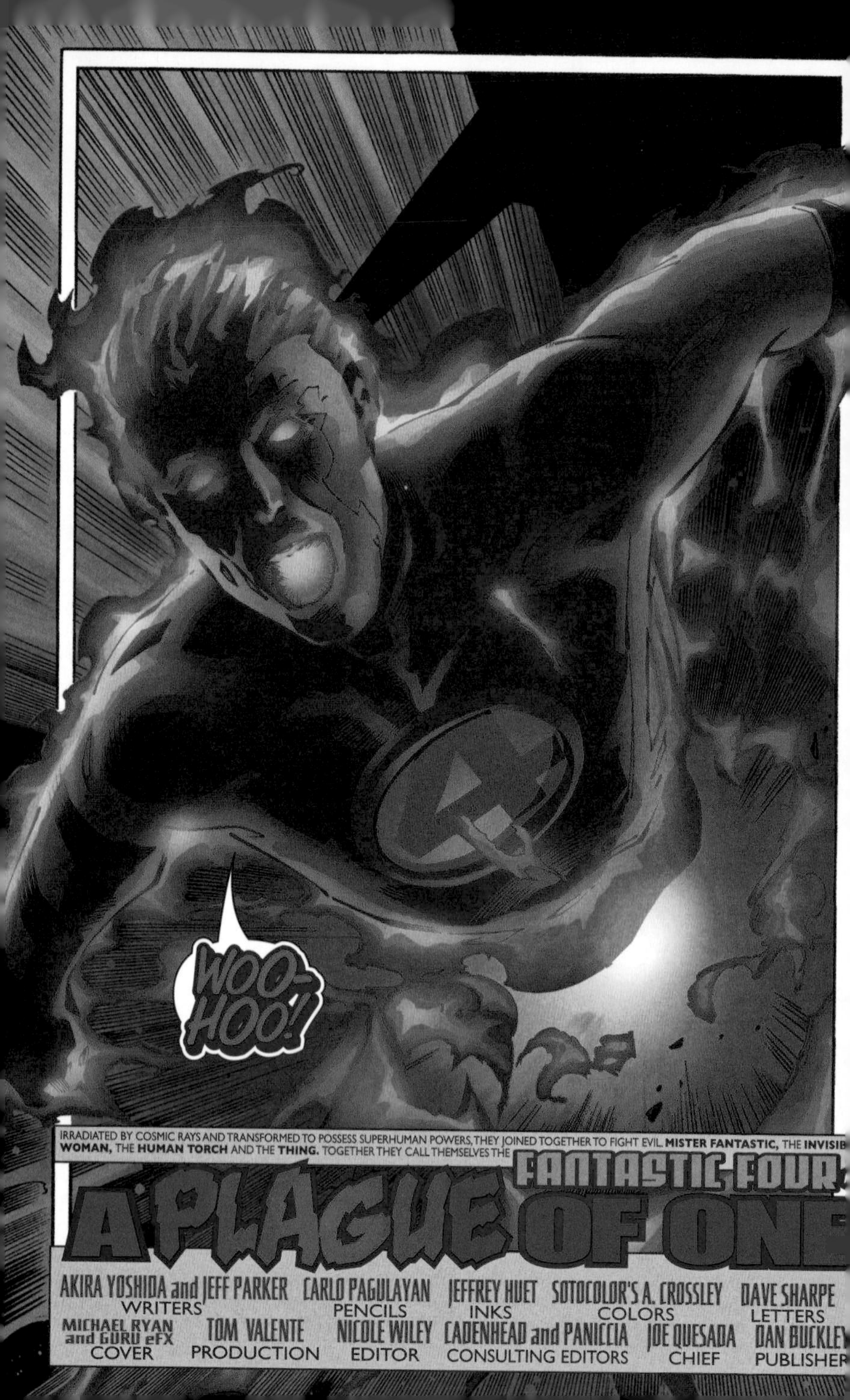
WOO-HOO!
IRRADIATED BY COSMIC RAYS AND TRANSFORMED TO POSSESS SUPERHUMAN POWERS, THEY JOINED TOGETHER TO FIGHT EVIL. MISTER FANTASTIC, THE INVISIB WOMAN, THE HUMAN TORCH AND THE THING. TOGETHER THEY CALL THEMSELVES THE
FANTASTIC FOUR
A PLAGUE OF ONE
AKIRA YOSHIDA and JEFF PARKER WRITERS
CARLO PAGULAYAN PENCILS
JEFFREY HUET INKS
SOTOCOLOR'S A. CROSSLEY COLORS
DAVE SHARPE LETTERS
MICHAEL RYAN and GURU eFX COVER
TOM VALENTE PRODUCTION
NICOLE WILEY EDITOR
CADENHEAD and PANICCIA CONSULTING EDITORS
JOE QUESADA CHIEF
DAN BUCKLEY PUBLISHER

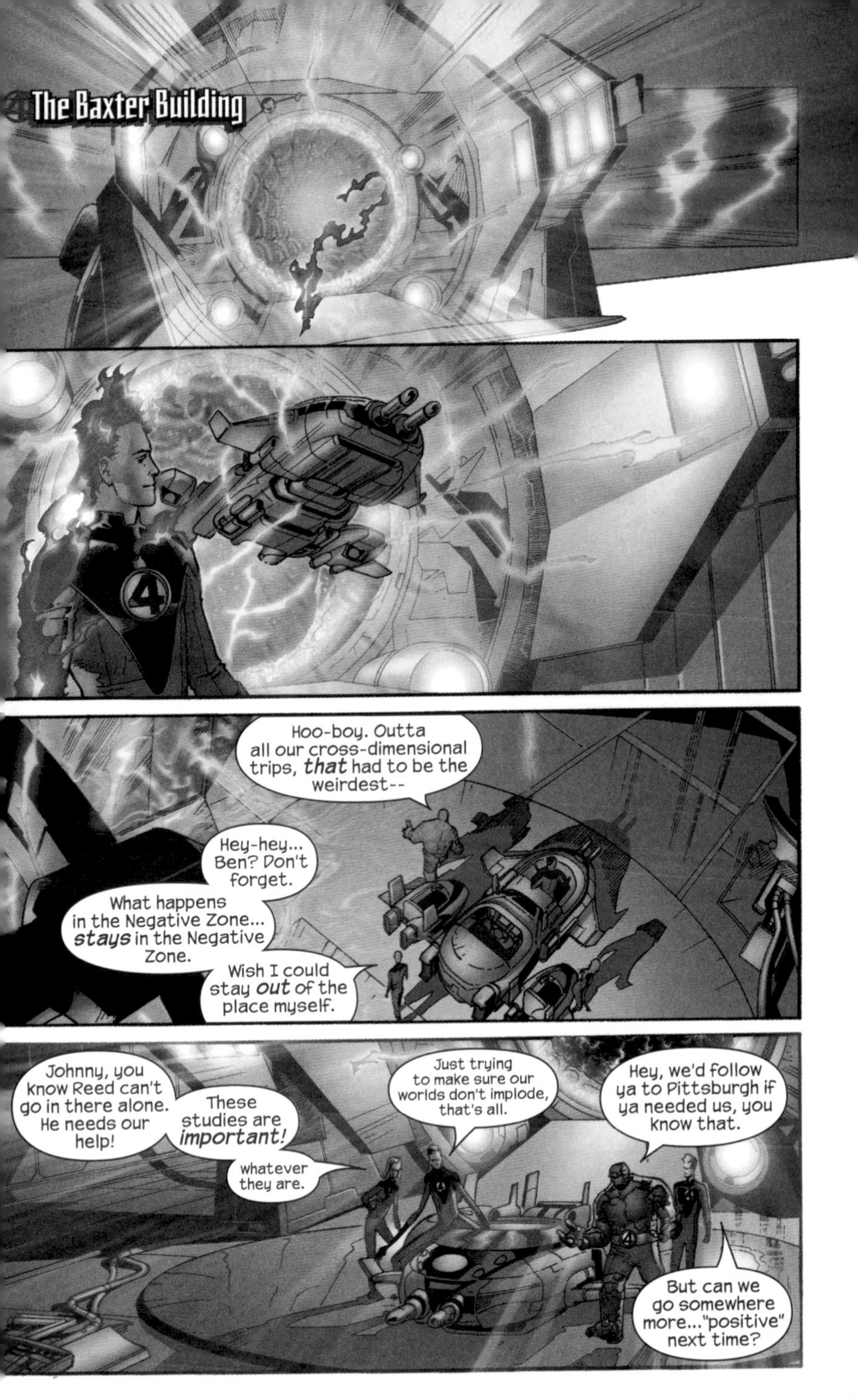
The Baxter Building
Hoo-boy. Outta all our cross-dimensional trips, *that* had to be the weirdest--
Hey-hey... Ben? Don't forget.
What happens in the Negative Zone... *stays* in the Negative Zone.
Wish I could stay *out* of the place myself.
Johnny, you know Reed can't go in there alone. He needs our help!
These studies are *important!*
whatever they are.
Just trying to make sure our worlds don't implode, that's all.
Hey, we'd follow ya to Pittsburgh if ya needed us, you know that.
But can we go somewhere more..."positive" next time?

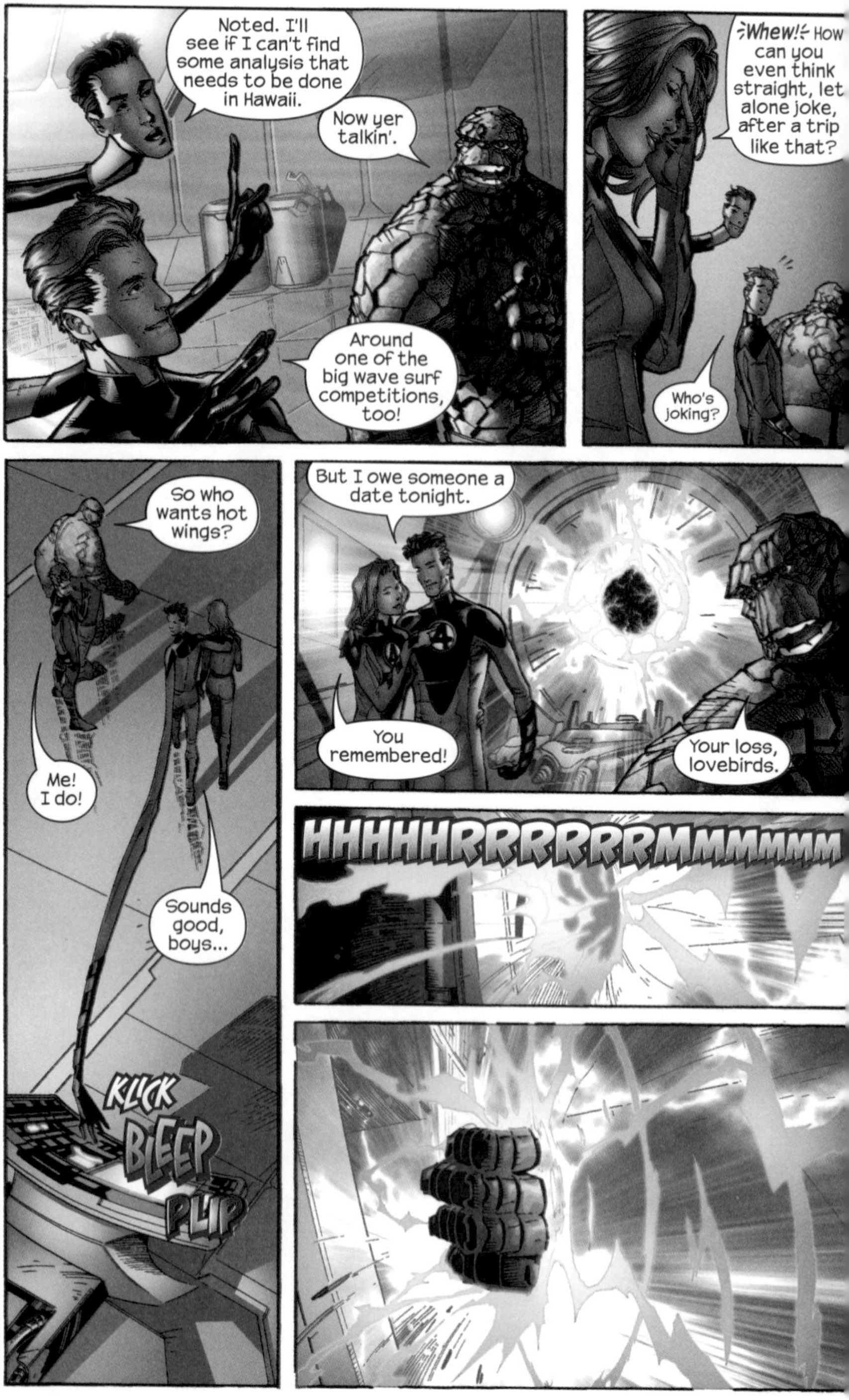
Noted. I'll see if I can't find some analysis that needs to be done in Hawaii.
Now yer talkin'.
Around one of the big wave surf competitions, too!
Whew! How can you even think straight, let alone joke, after a trip like that?
Who's joking?
So who wants hot wings?
Me! I do!
Sounds good, boys...
KLICK
BLEEP
PLIP
But I owe someone a date tonight.
You remembered!
Your loss, lovebirds.
HHHHHRRRRRRMMMMMM

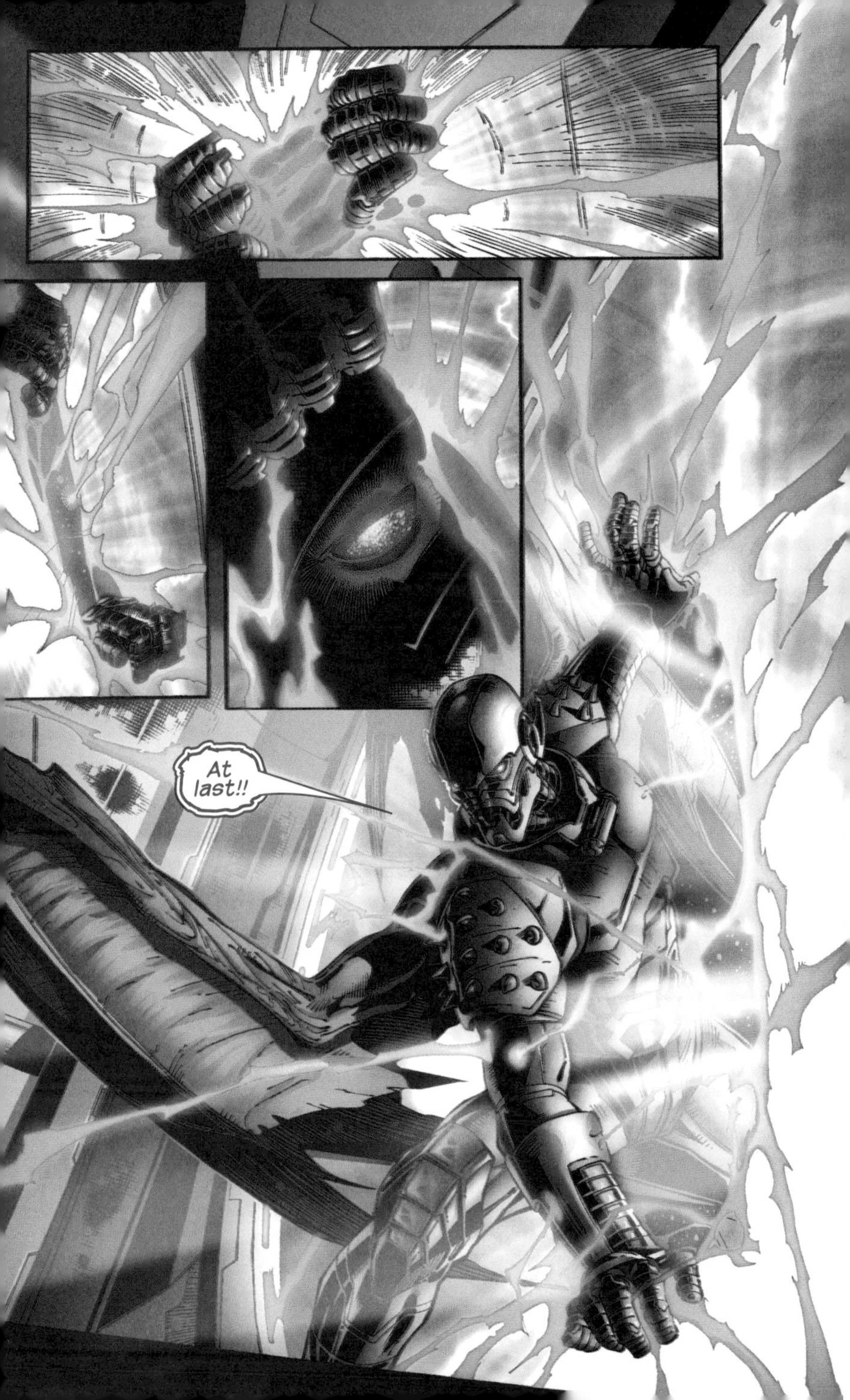
At last!!

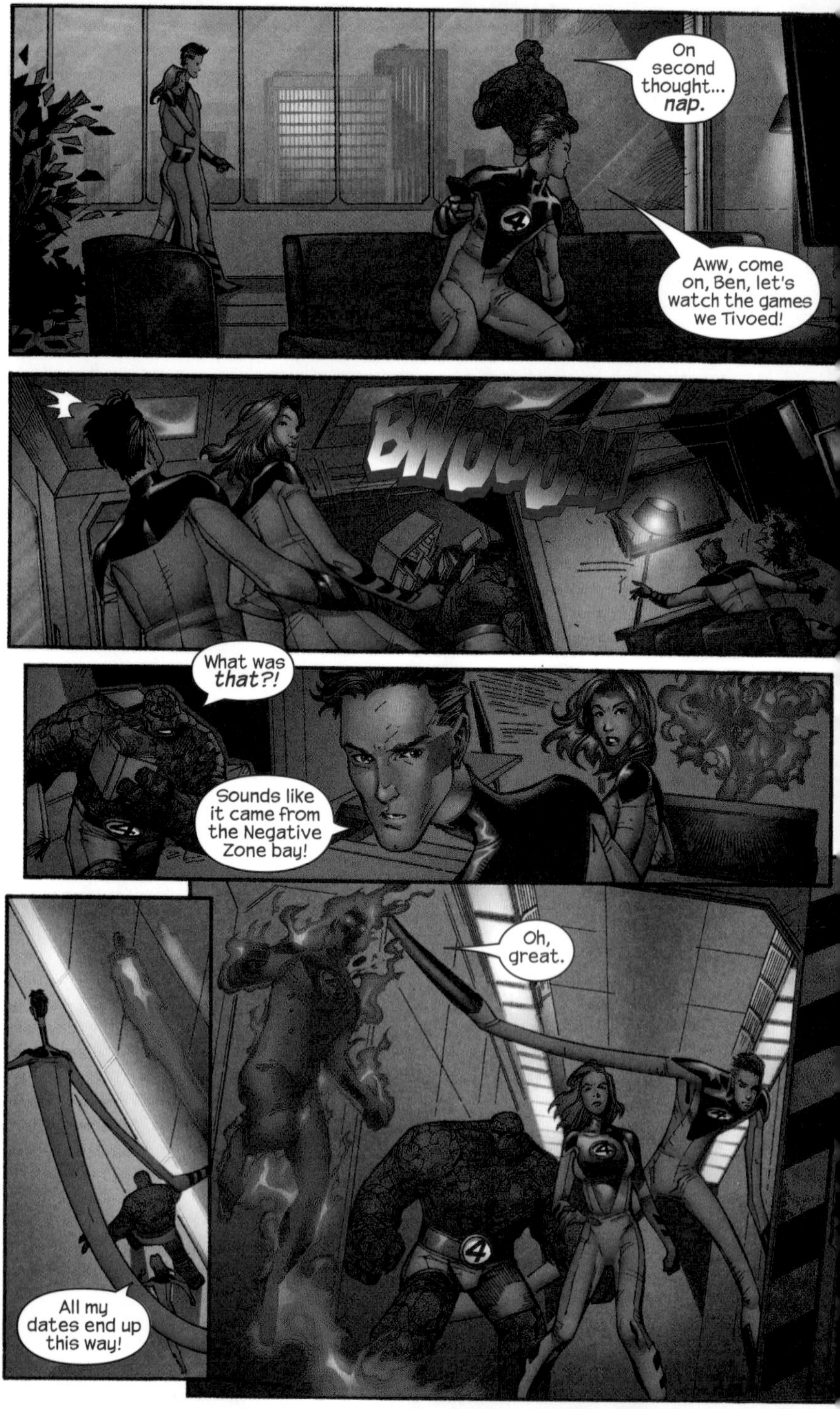
On second thought... nap.
Aww, come on, Ben, let's watch the games we Tivoed!
BWOOOOM
What was that?!
Sounds like it came from the Negative Zone bay!
Oh, great.
All my dates end up this way!

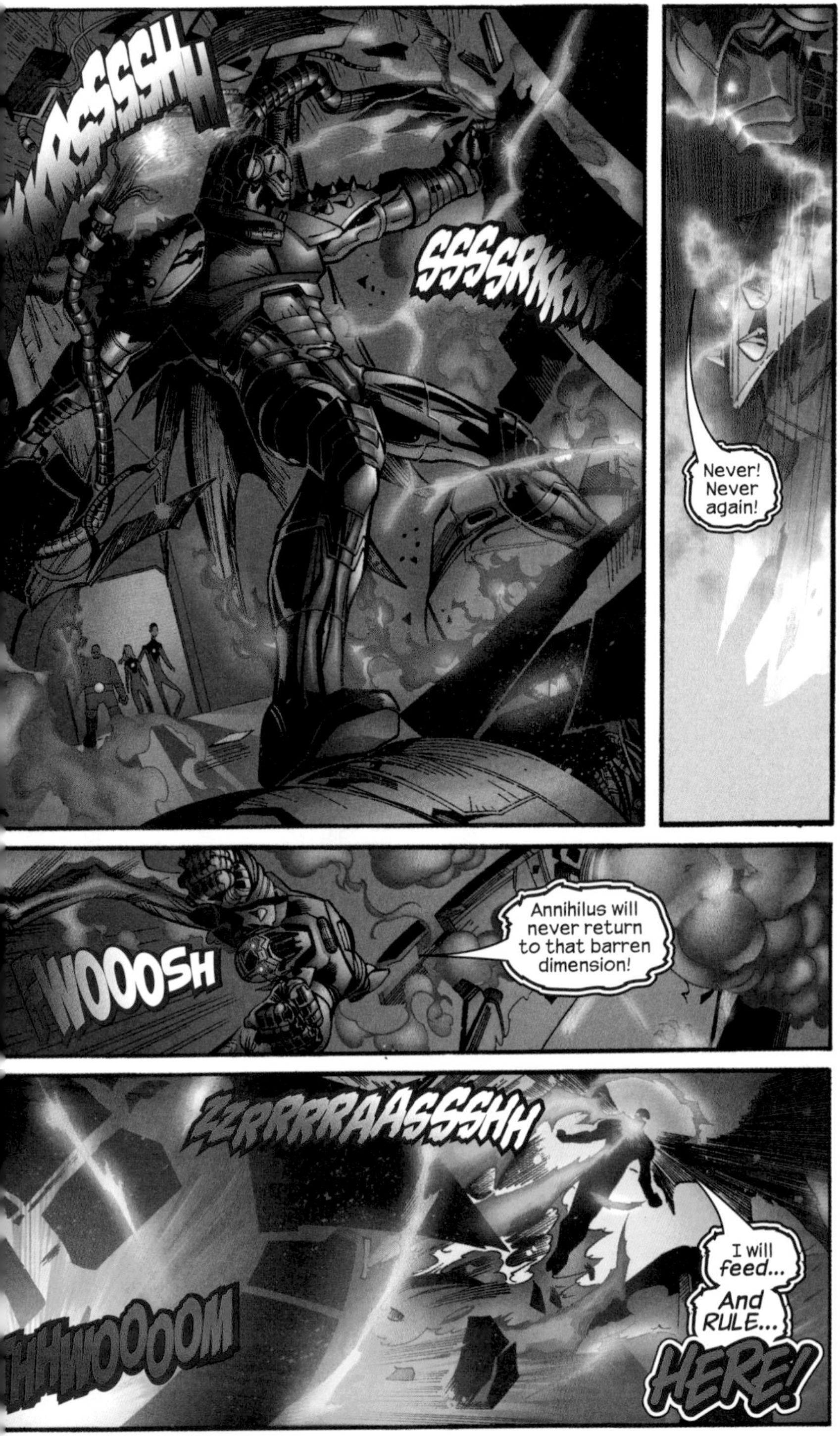

KRASSSSH
SSSSRKKK
Never! Never again!
WOOOSH
Annihilus will never return to that barren dimension!
ZZRRRRAASSSHH
THHWOOOOOM
I will feed...
And RULE...
HERE!

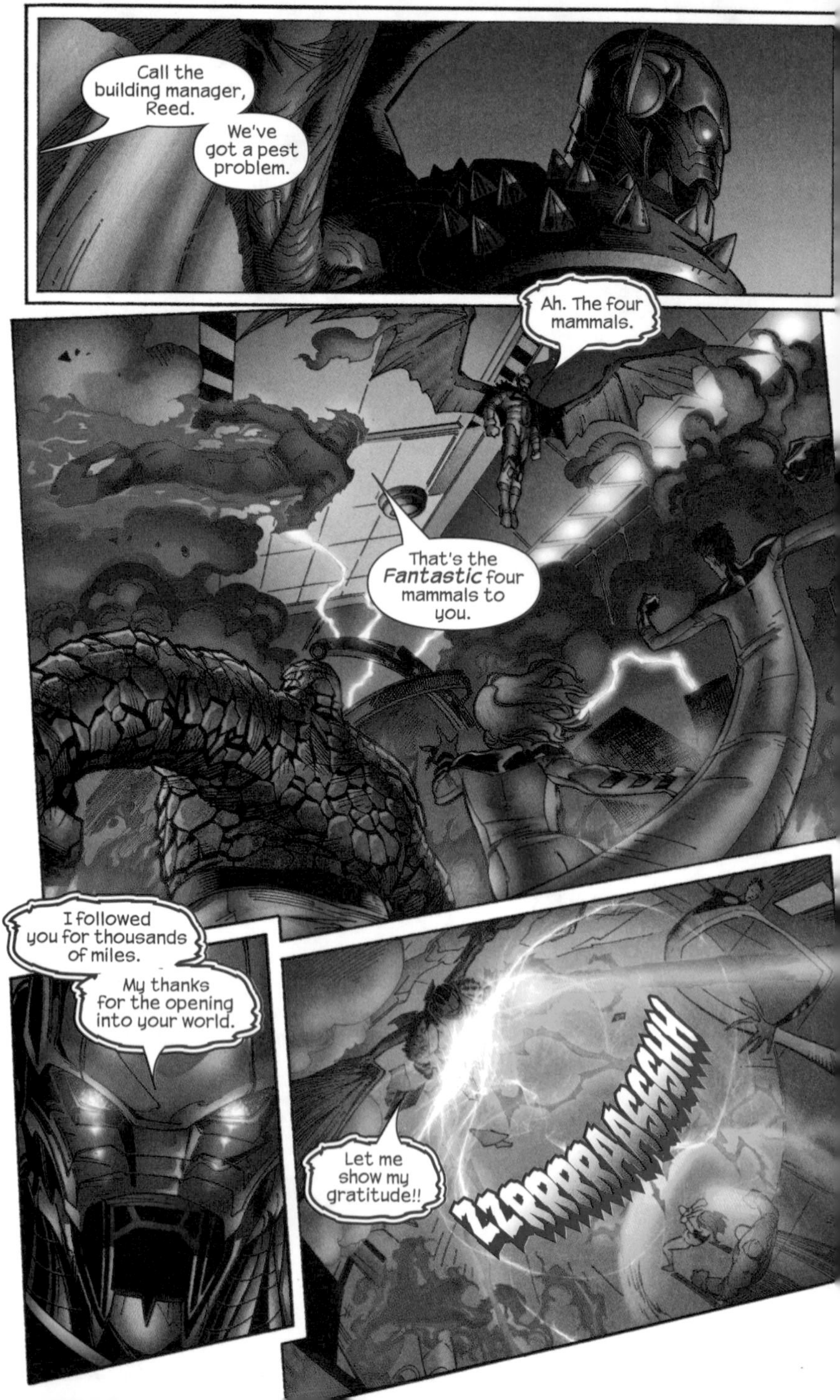
Call the building manager, Reed.
We've got a pest problem.
Ah. The four mammals.
That's the *Fantastic* four mammals to you.
I followed you for thousands of miles.
My thanks for the opening into your world.
Let me show my gratitude!!
ZZRRRRAKSSHH

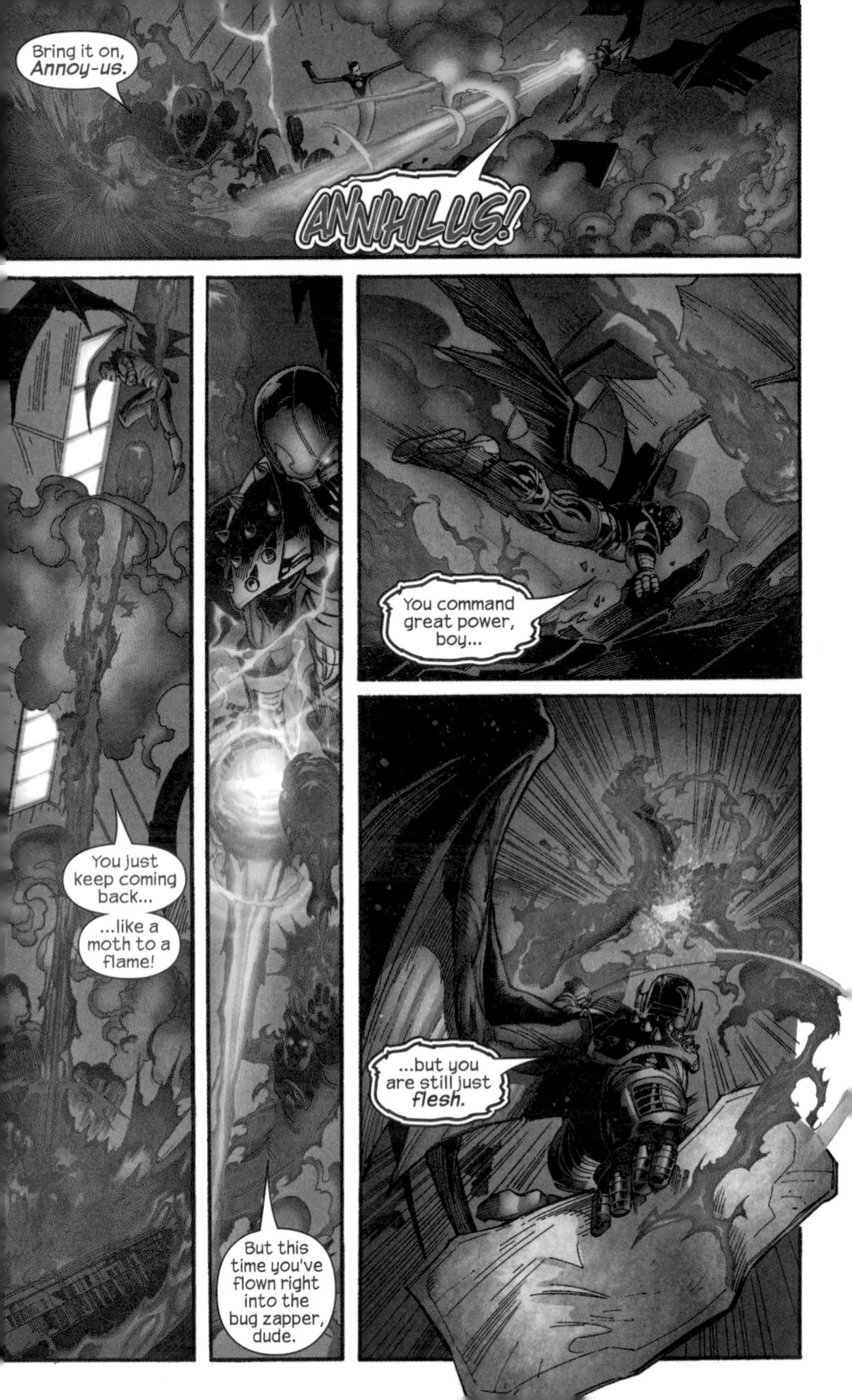
Bring it on, Annoy-us.
ANNIHILUS!
You just keep coming back...
...like a moth to a flame!
But this time you've flown right into the bug zapper, dude.
You command great power, boy...
...but you are still just flesh.

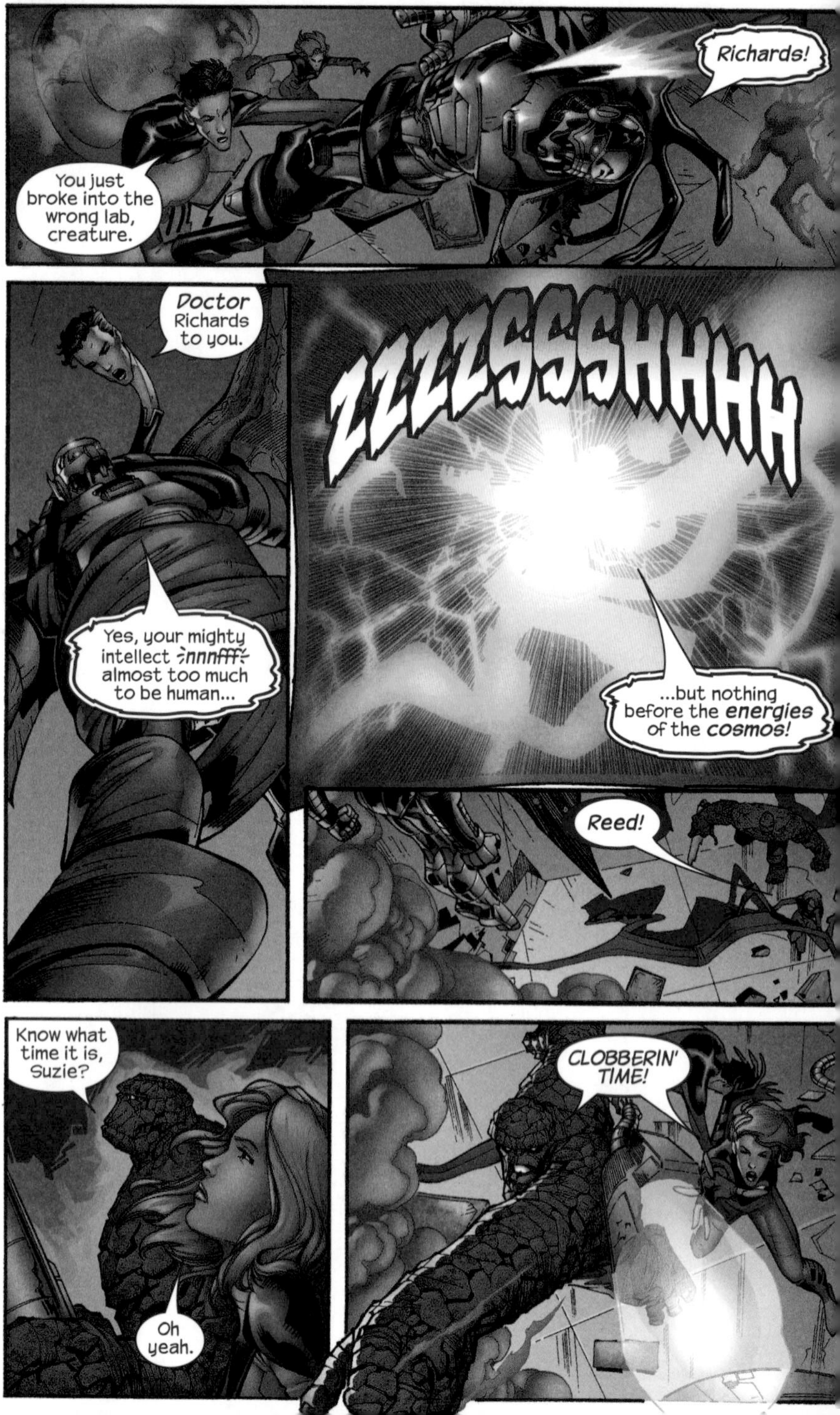
Richards!
You just broke into the wrong lab, creature.
Doctor Richards to you.
ZZZZSSSHHHH
Yes, your mighty intellect -nnnfff- almost too much to be human...
...but nothing before the energies of the cosmos!
Reed!
Know what time it is, Suzie?
Oh yeah.
CLOBBERIN' TIME!

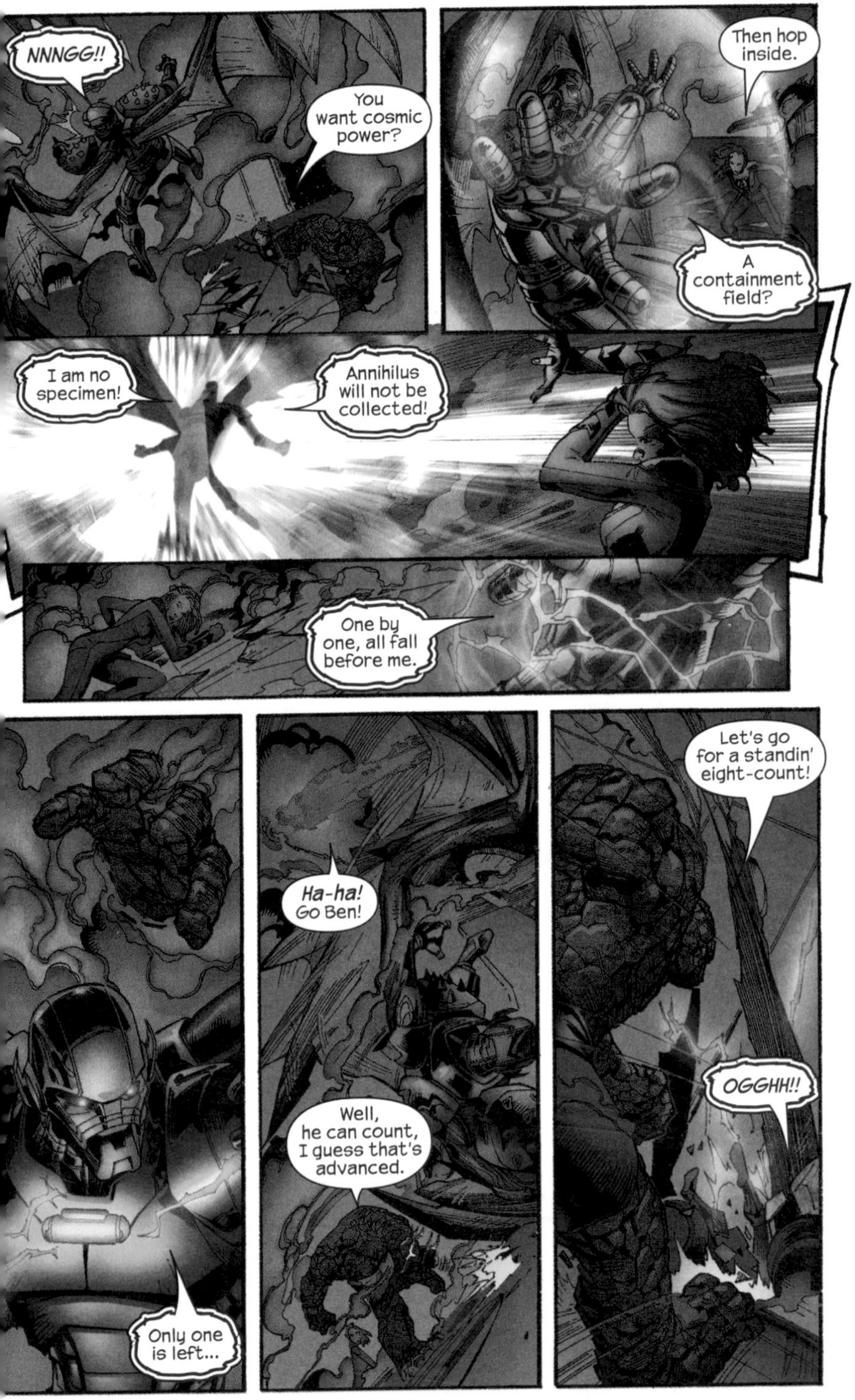
NNNGG!!
You want cosmic power?
Then hop inside.
A containment field?
I am no specimen!
Annihilus will not be collected!
One by one, all fall before me.
Only one is left...
Ha-ha! Go Ben!
Well, he can count, I guess that's advanced.
Let's go for a standin' eight-count!
OGGHH!!

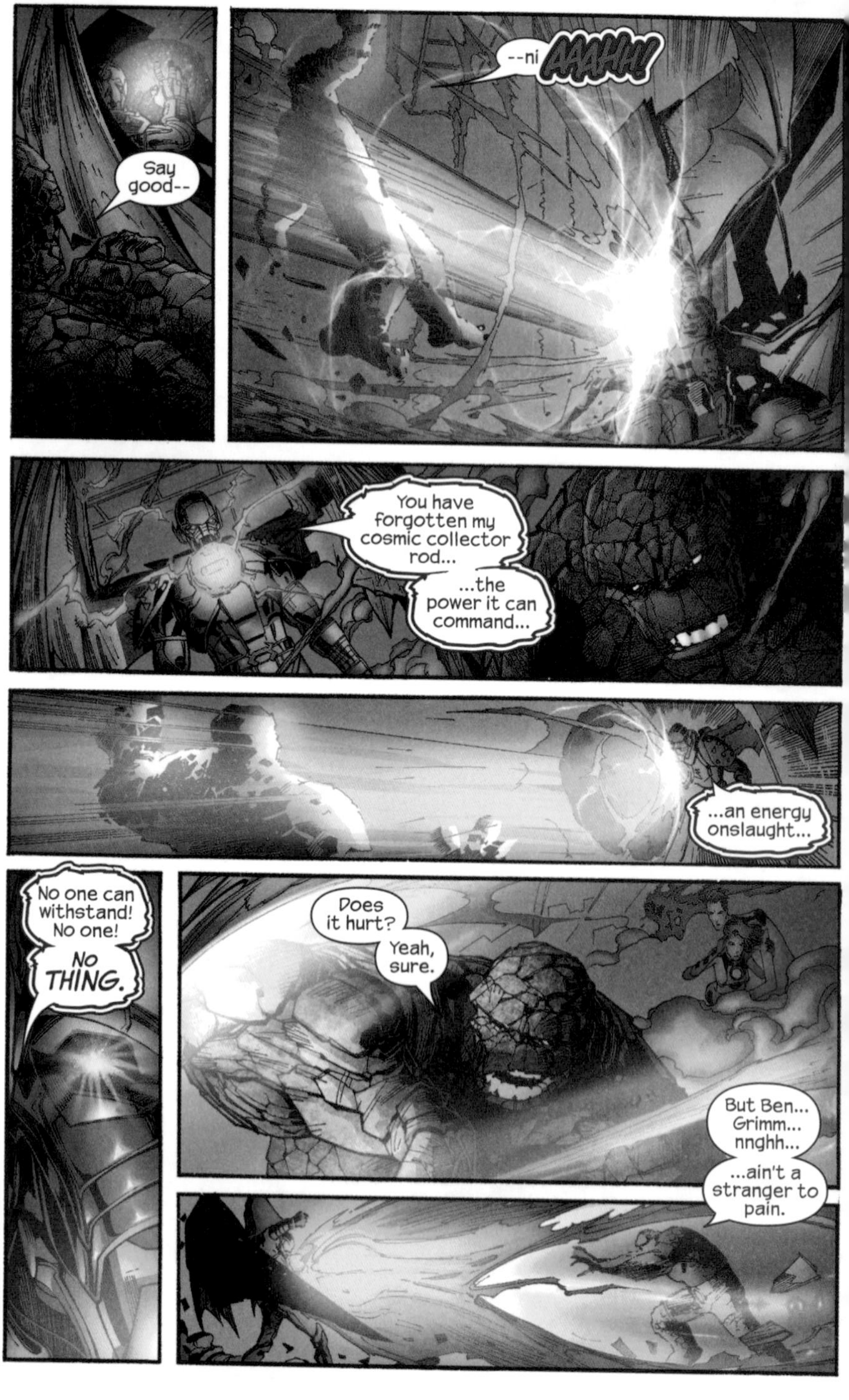
Say good--
--ni AAAHH!
You have forgotten my cosmic collector rod...
...the power it can command...
...an energy onslaught...
No one can withstand! No one!
NO THING.
Does it hurt?
Yeah, sure.
But Ben... Grimm... nnghh...
...ain't a stranger to pain.

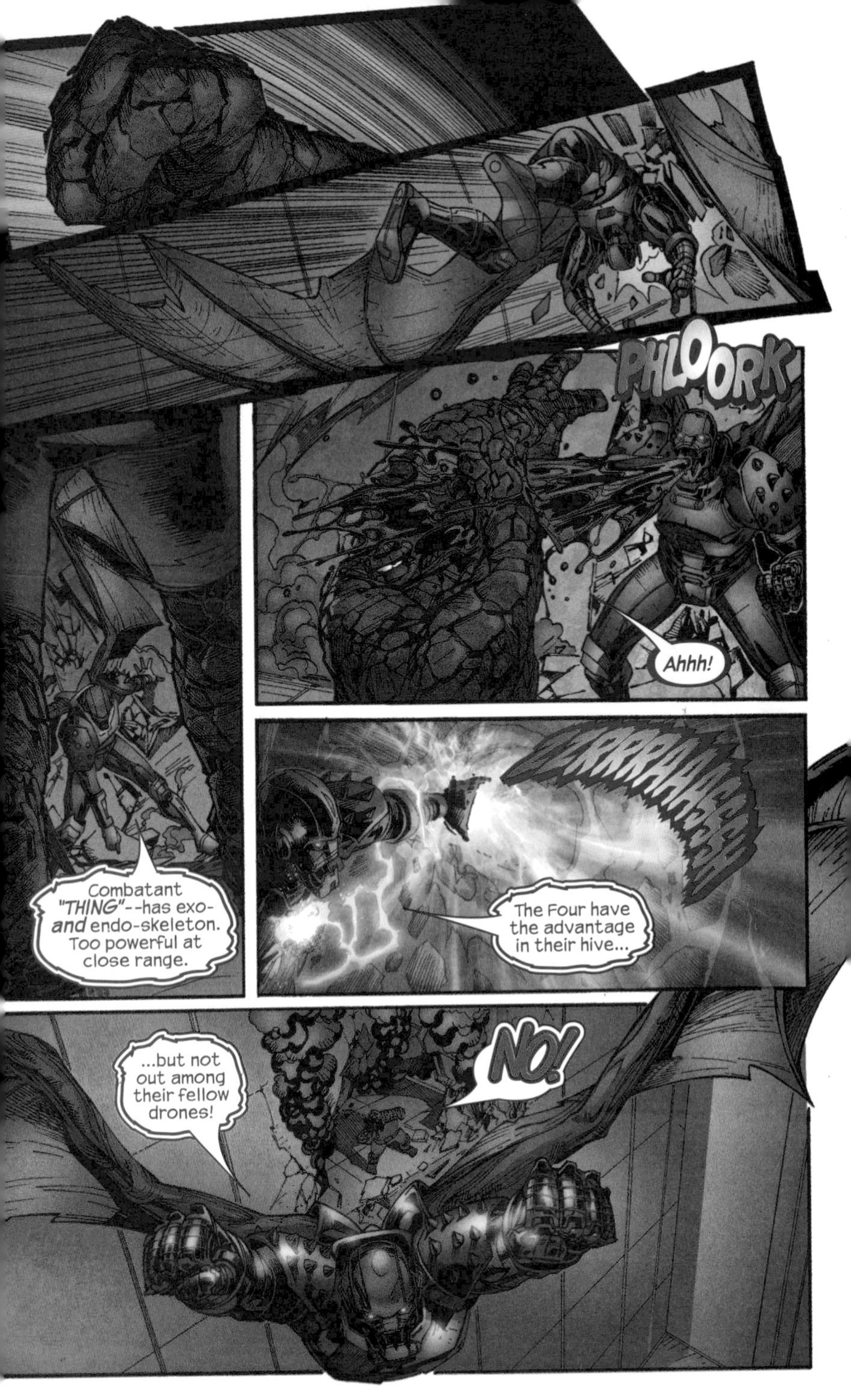
PHLOORK
Ahhh!
Combatant "THING"--has exo- and endo-skeleton. Too powerful at close range.
The Four have the advantage in their hive...
...but not out among their fellow drones!
NO!

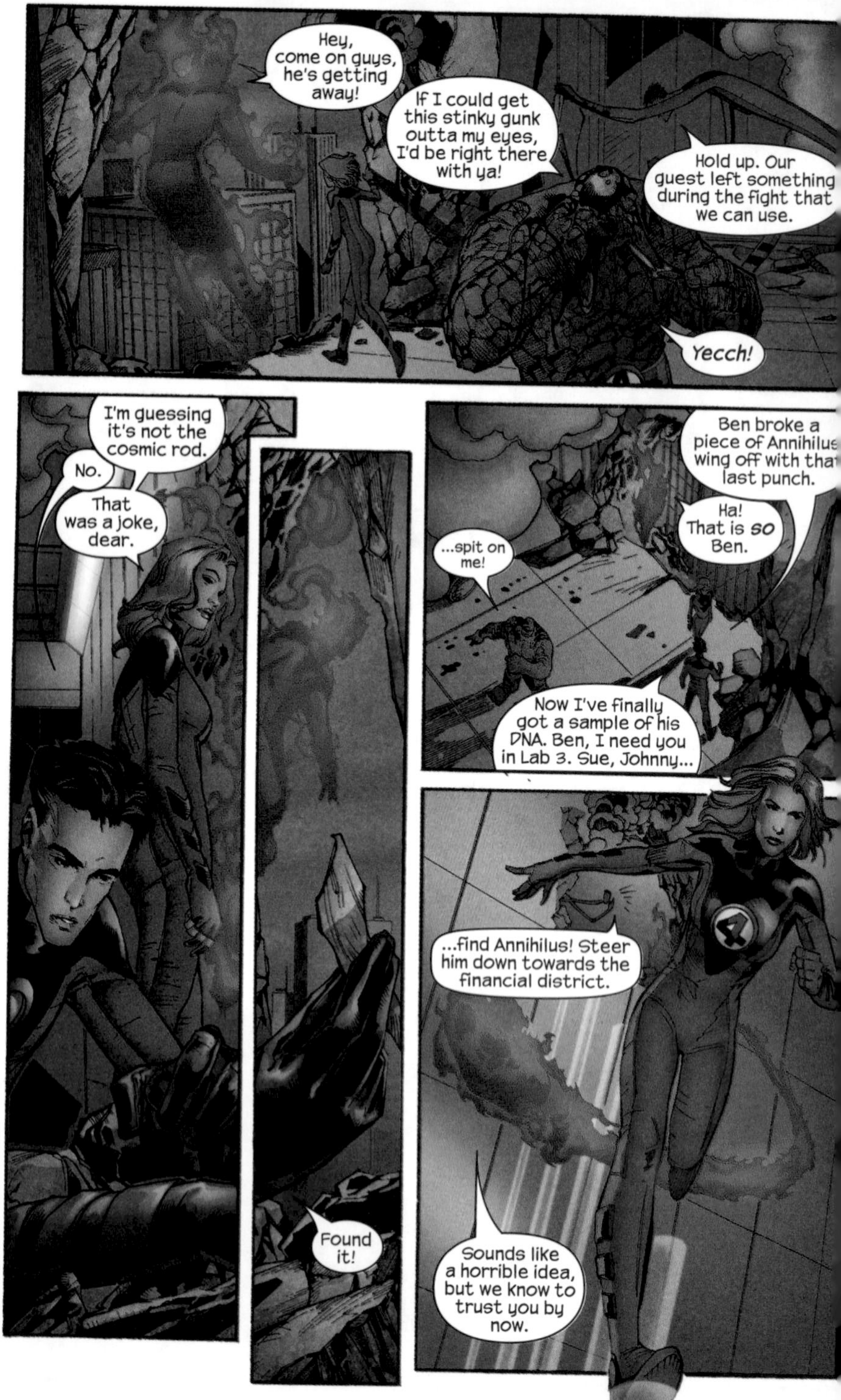
Hey, come on guys, he's getting away!
If I could get this stinky gunk outta my eyes, I'd be right there with ya!
Hold up. Our guest left something during the fight that we can use.
Yecch!
I'm guessing it's not the cosmic rod.
No.
That was a joke, dear.
Found it!
Ben broke a piece of Annihilus wing off with that last punch.
Ha! That is so Ben.
...spit on me!
Now I've finally got a sample of his DNA. Ben, I need you in Lab 3. Sue, Johnny...
...find Annihilus! Steer him down towards the financial district.
Sounds like a horrible idea, but we know to trust you by now.

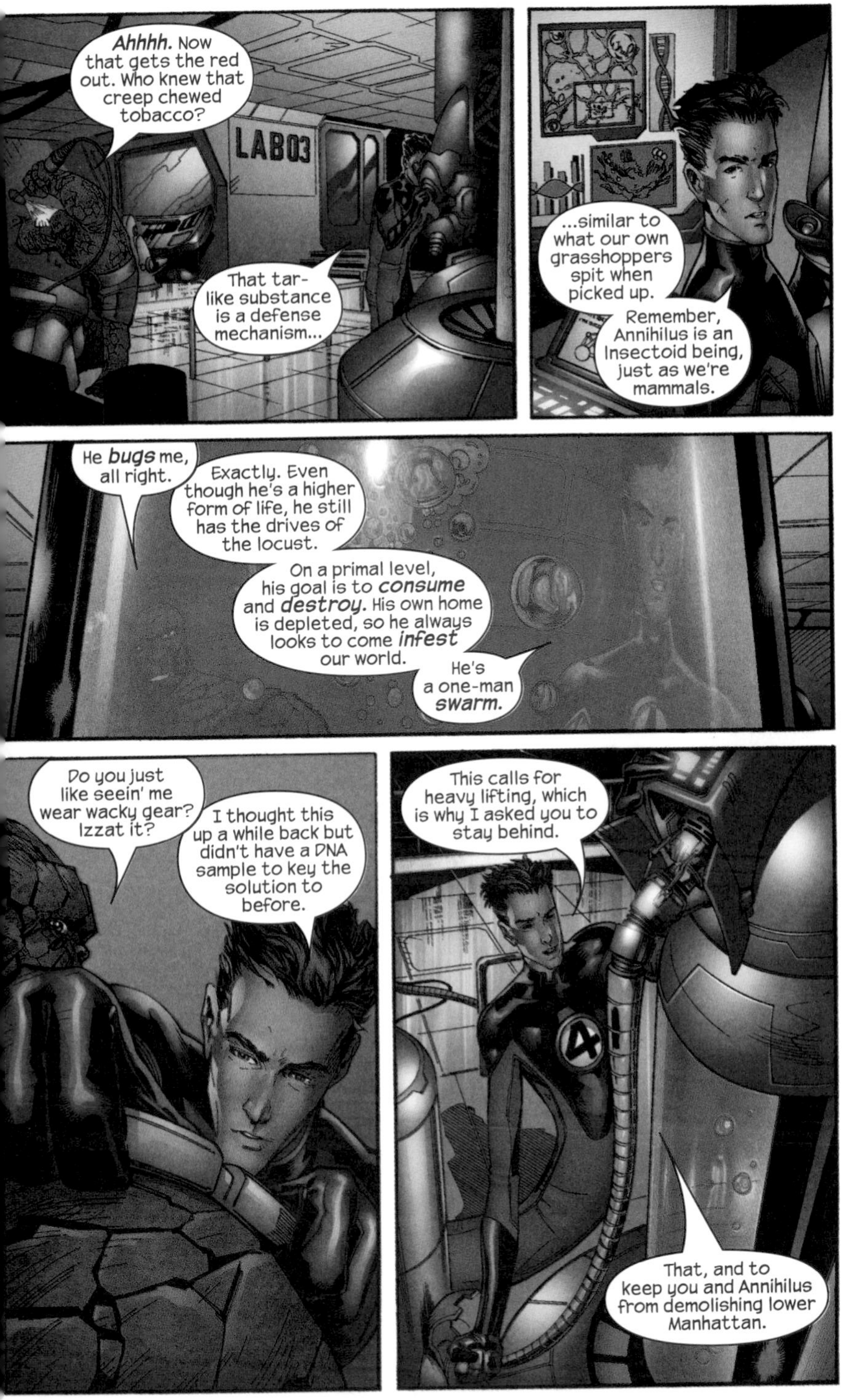
Ahhhh. Now that gets the red out. Who knew that creep chewed tobacco?
LAB03
That tar-like substance is a defense mechanism...
...similar to what our own grasshoppers spit when picked up.
Remember, Annihilus is an Insectoid being, just as we're mammals.
He bugs me, all right.
Exactly. Even though he's a higher form of life, he still has the drives of the locust.
On a primal level, his goal is to consume and destroy. His own home is depleted, so he always looks to come infest our world.
He's a one-man swarm.
Do you just like seein' me wear wacky gear? Izzat it?
I thought this up a while back but didn't have a DNA sample to key the solution to before.
This calls for heavy lifting, which is why I asked you to stay behind.
That, and to keep you and Annihilus from demolishing lower Manhattan.

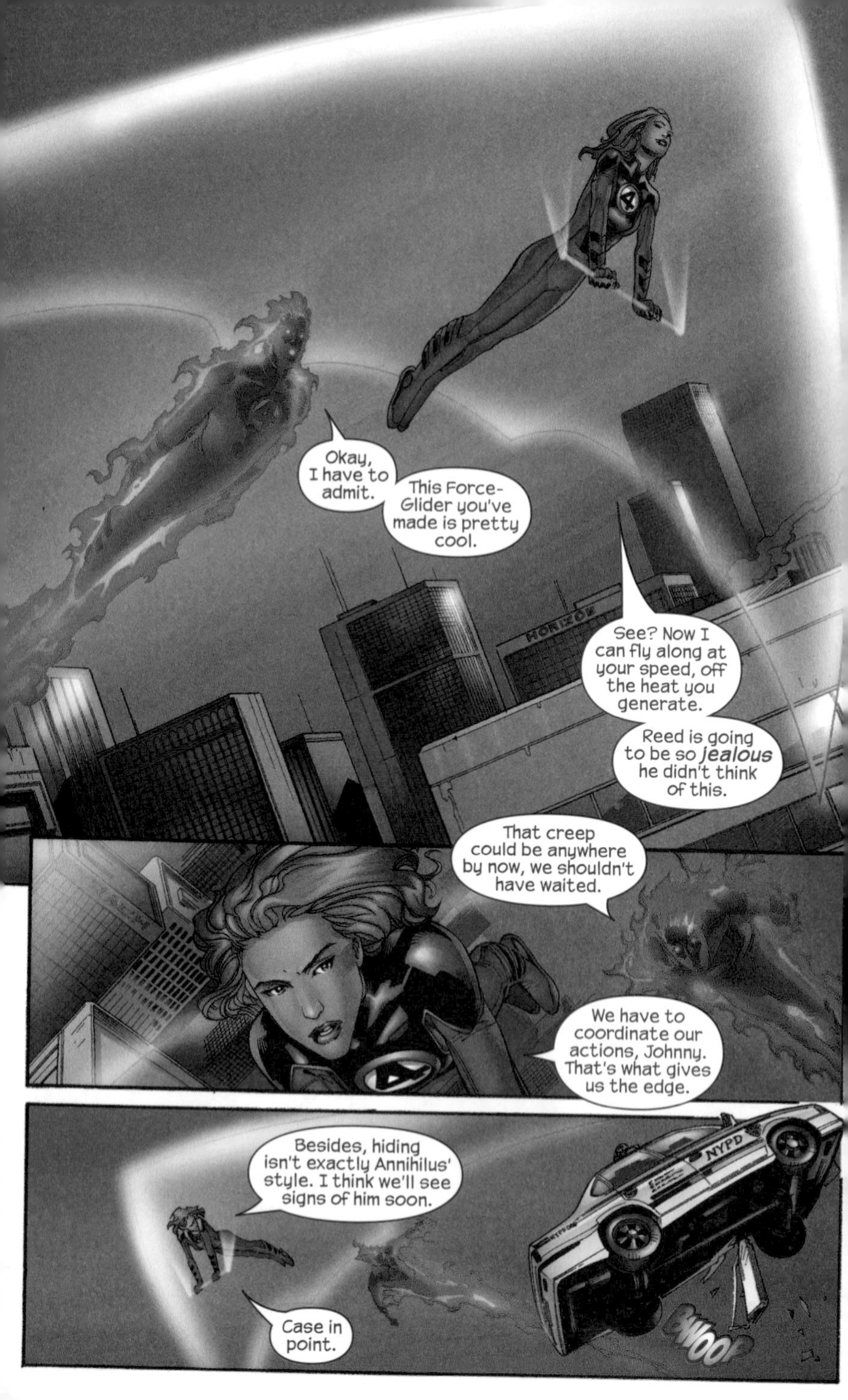
Okay, I have to admit.
This Force-Glider you've made is pretty cool.
See? Now I can fly along at your speed, off the heat you generate.
Reed is going to be so *jealous* he didn't think of this.
That creep could be anywhere by now, we shouldn't have waited.
We have to coordinate our actions, Johnny. That's what gives us the edge.
Besides, hiding isn't exactly Annihilus' style. I think we'll see signs of him soon.
NYPD
Case in point.

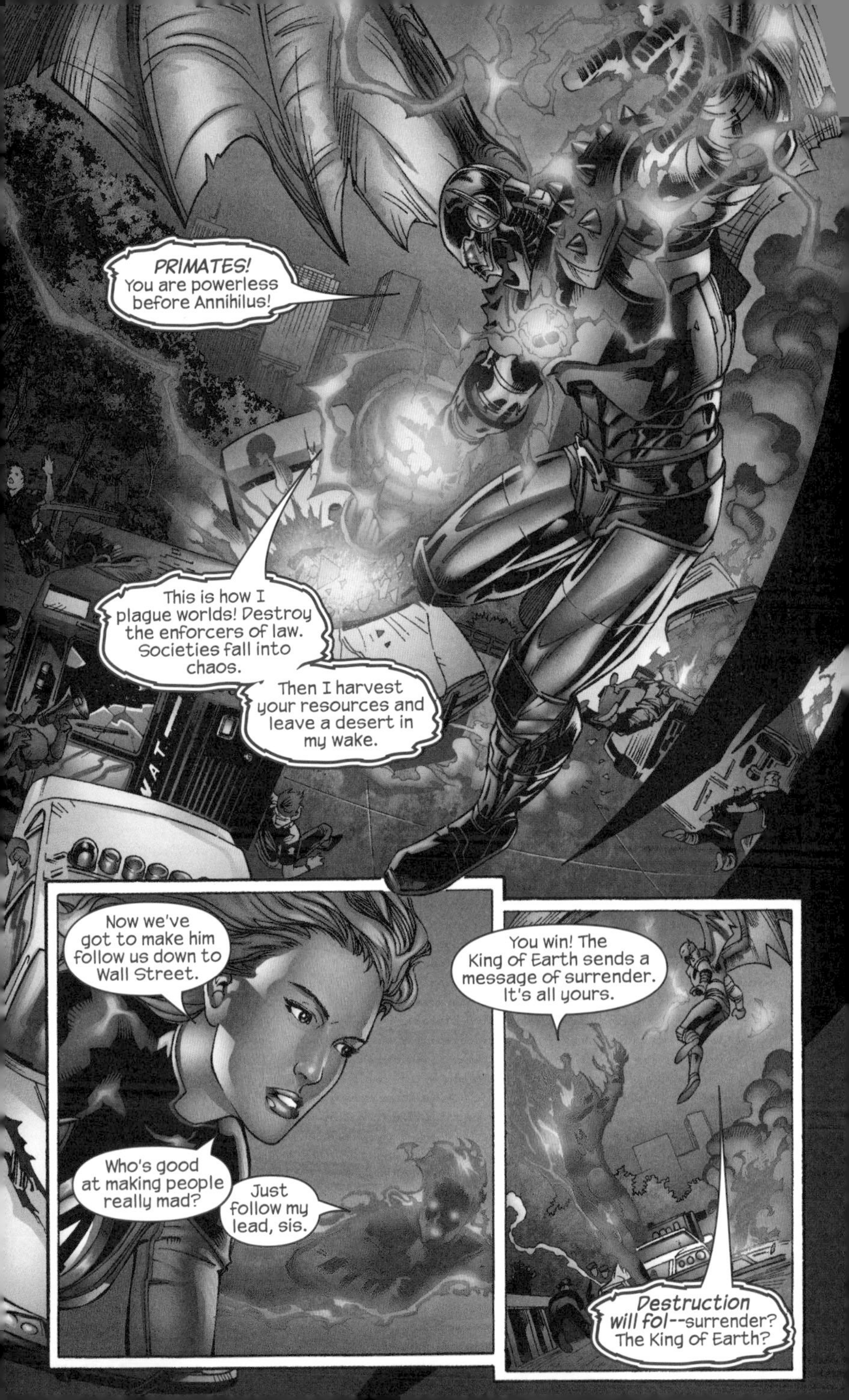
PRIMATES! You are powerless before Annihilus!
This is how I plague worlds! Destroy the enforcers of law. Societies fall into chaos.
Then I harvest your resources and leave a desert in my wake.
Now we've got to make him follow us down to Wall Street.
Who's good at making people really mad?
Just follow my lead, sis.
You win! The King of Earth sends a message of surrender. It's all yours.
Destruction will fol--surrender? The King of Earth?

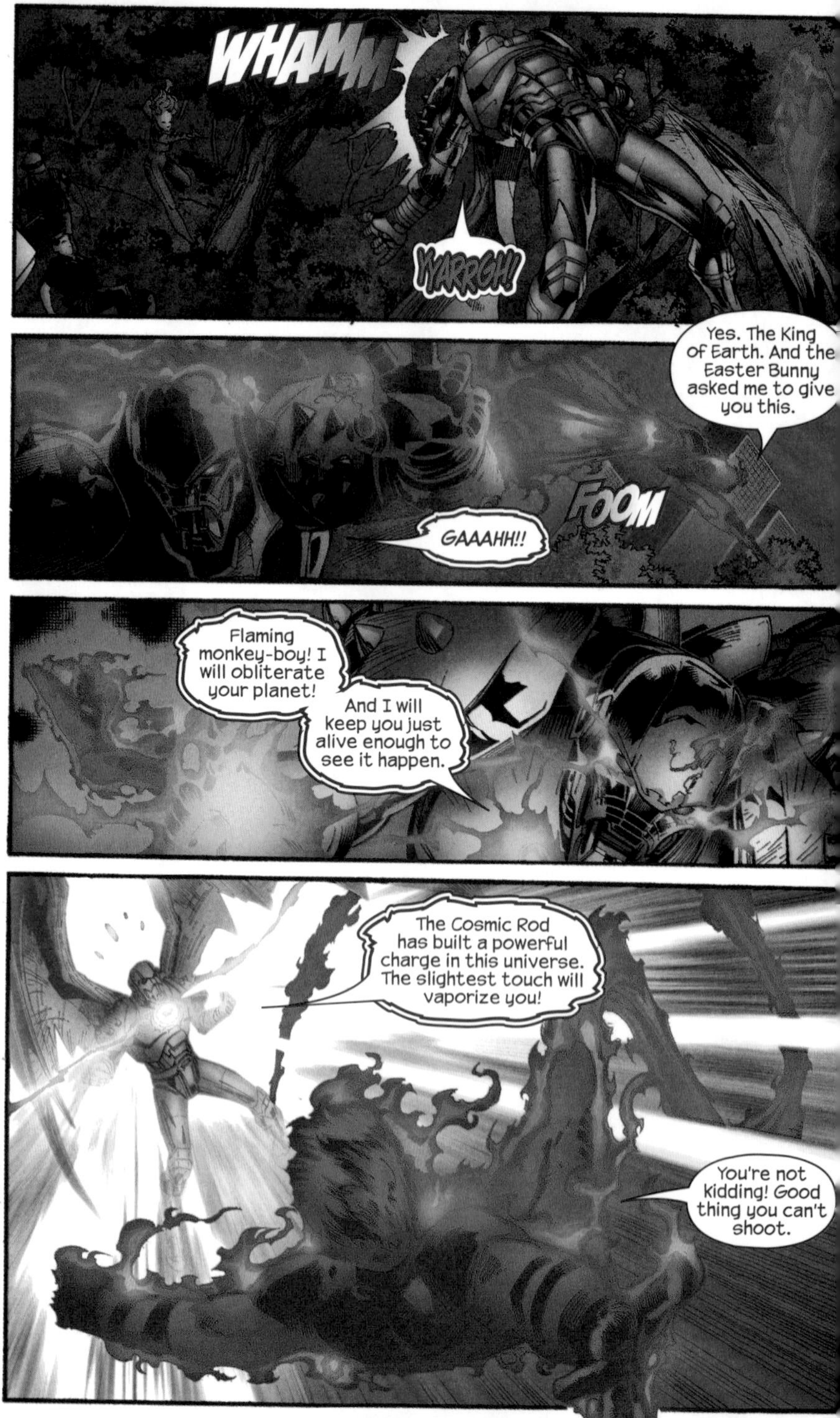
WHAMM
YYARRGH!
Yes. The King of Earth. And the Easter Bunny asked me to give you this.
FOOM
GAAAHH!!
Flaming monkey-boy! I will obliterate your planet!
And I will keep you just alive enough to see it happen.
The Cosmic Rod has built a powerful charge in this universe. The slightest touch will vaporize you!
You're not kidding! Good thing you can't shoot.

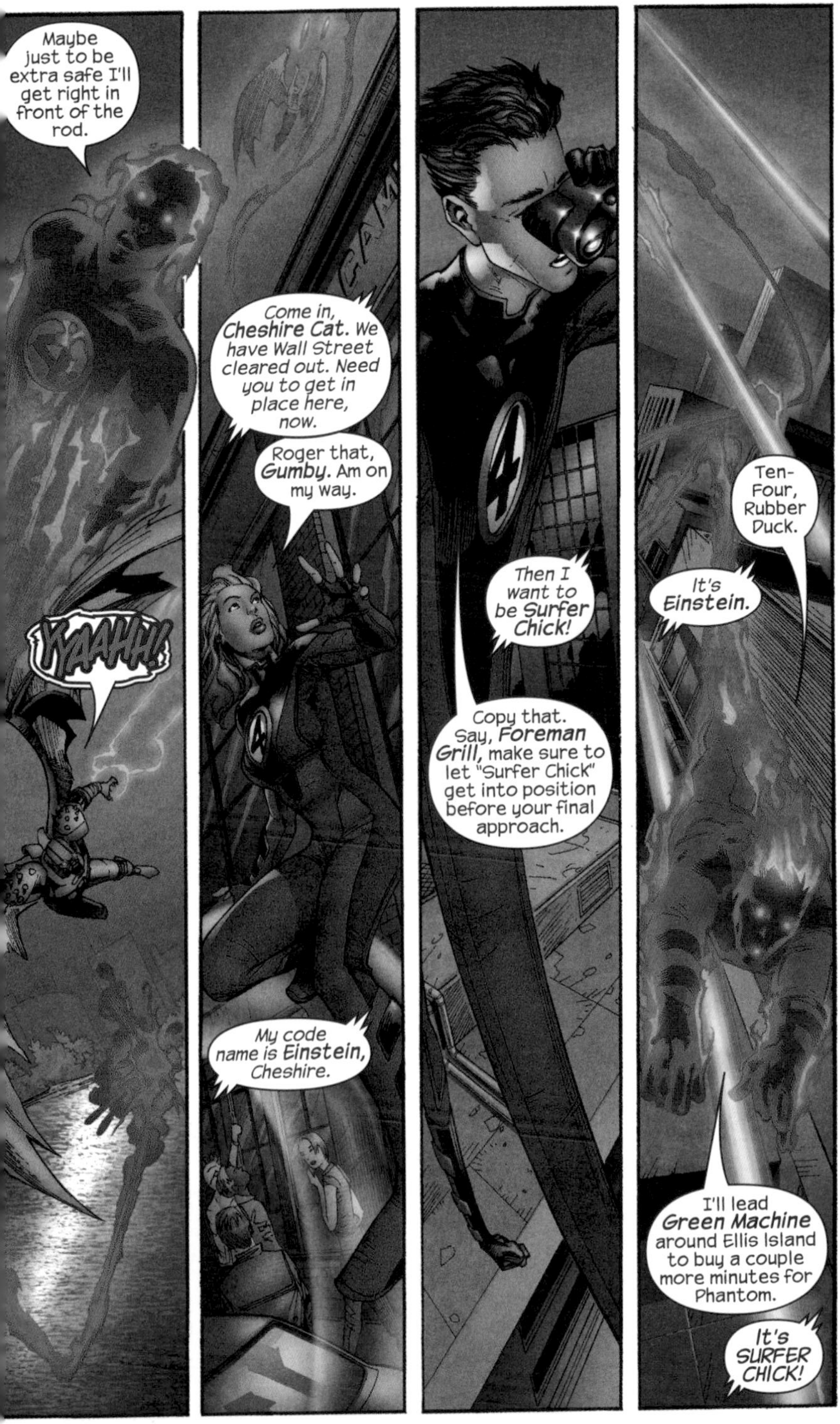
Maybe just to be extra safe I'll get right in front of the rod.
YAAHH!
Come in, Cheshire Cat. We have Wall Street cleared out. Need you to get in place here, now.
Roger that, Gumby. Am on my way.
My code name is Einstein, Cheshire.
Then I want to be Surfer Chick!
Copy that. Say, Foreman Grill, make sure to let "Surfer Chick" get into position before your final approach.
Ten-Four, Rubber Duck.
It's Einstein.
I'll lead Green Machine around Ellis Island to buy a couple more minutes for Phantom.
It's SURFER CHICK!

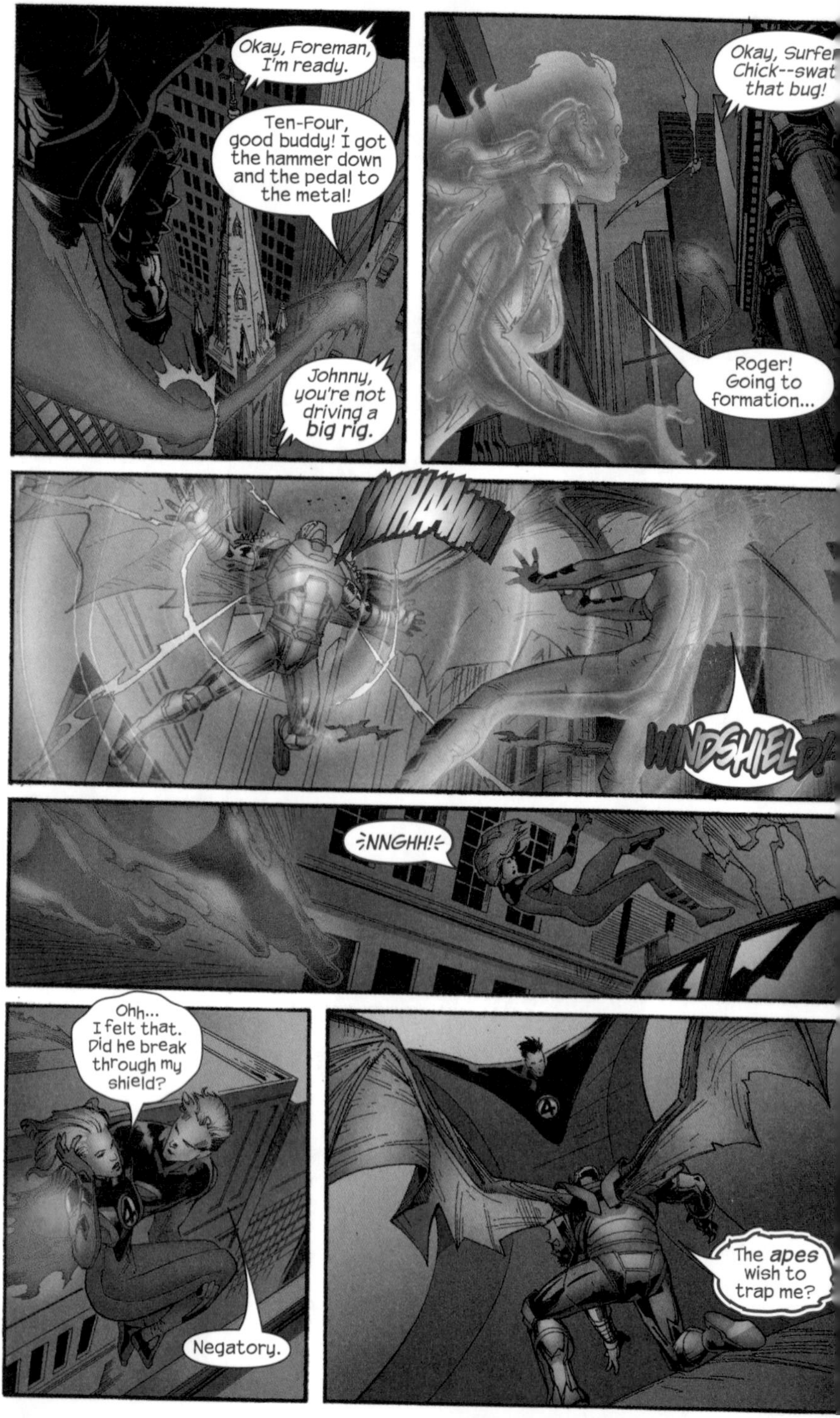
Okay, Foreman, I'm ready.
Ten-Four, good buddy! I got the hammer down and the pedal to the metal!
Johnny, you're not driving a big rig.
Okay, Surfe Chick--swat that bug!
Roger! Going to formation...
WHAAM
WINDSHIELD!
NNGHH!
Ohh... I felt that. Did he break through my shield?
Negatory.
The apes wish to trap me?

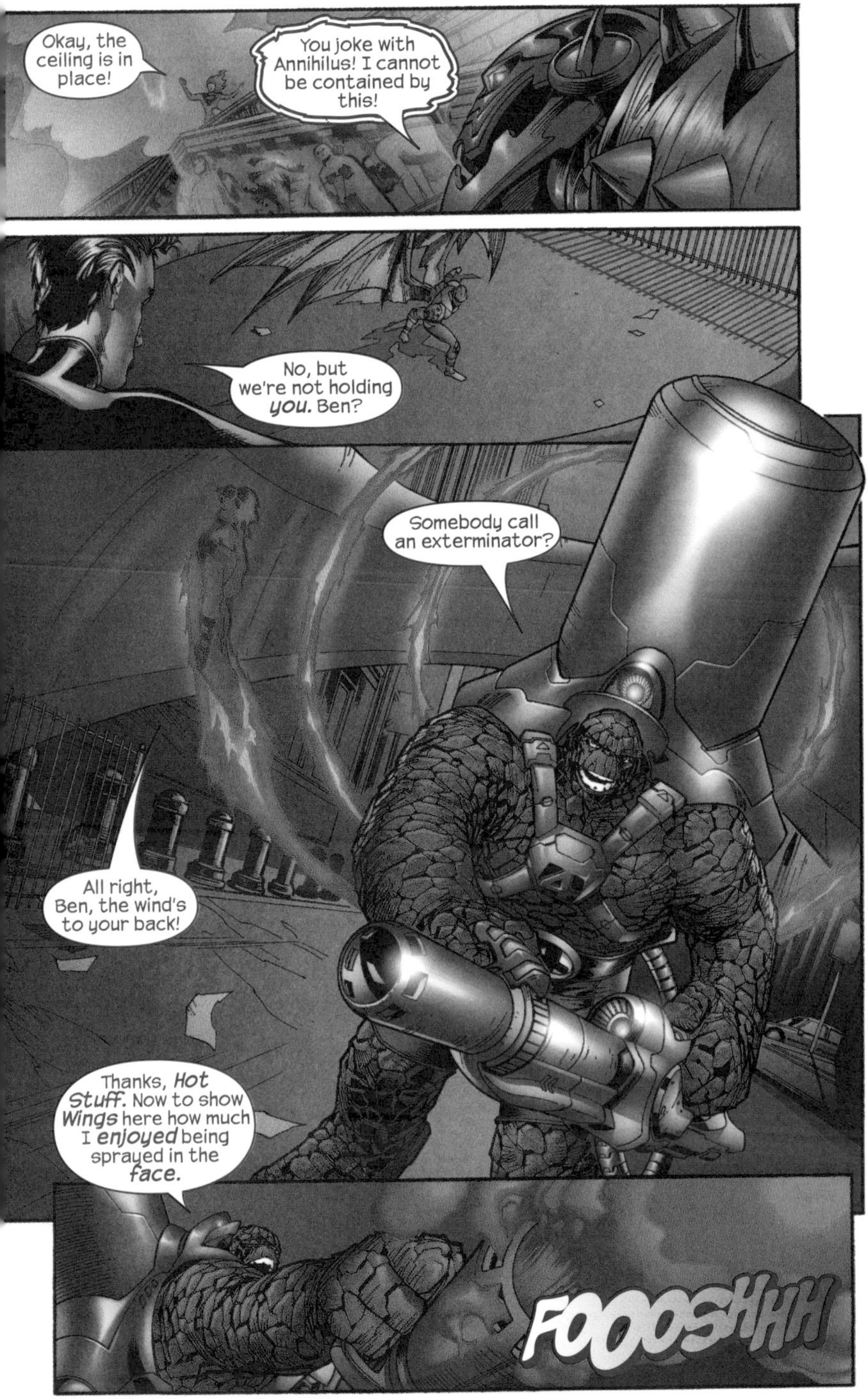
Okay, the ceiling is in place!
You joke with Annihilus! I cannot be contained by this!
No, but we're not holding *you.* Ben?
Somebody call an exterminator?
All right, Ben, the wind's to your back!
Thanks, *Hot Stuff.* Now to show *Wings* here how much I *enjoyed* being sprayed in the *face.*
FOOOSHHH

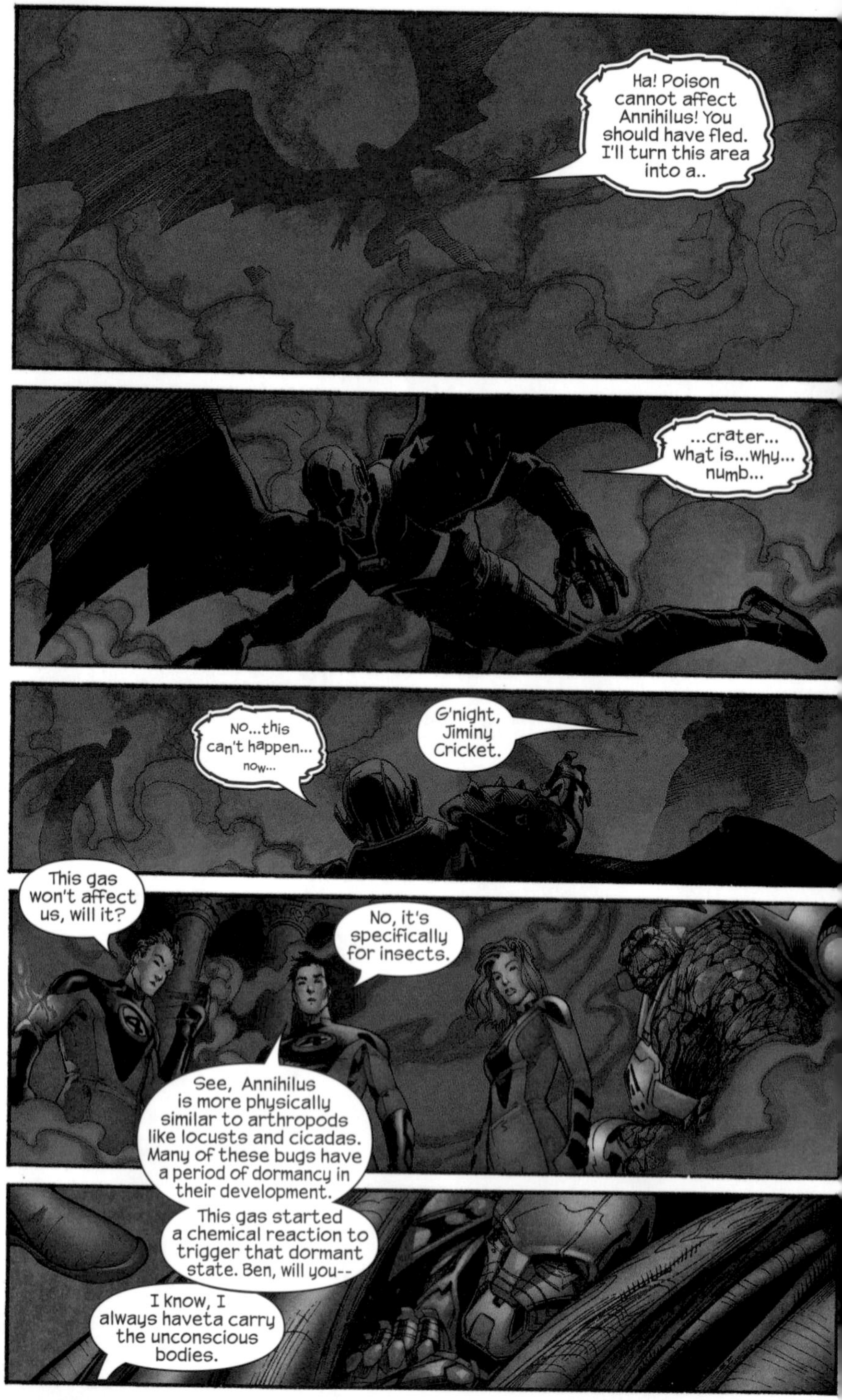
Ha! Poison cannot affect Annihilus! You should have fled. I'll turn this area into a..
...crater... what is...why... numb...
No...this can't happen... now...
G'night, Jiminy Cricket.
This gas won't affect us, will it?
No, it's specifically for insects.
See, Annihilus is more physically similar to arthropods like locusts and cicadas. Many of these bugs have a period of dormancy in their development.
This gas started a chemical reaction to trigger that dormant state. Ben, will you--
I know, I always haveta carry the unconscious bodies.

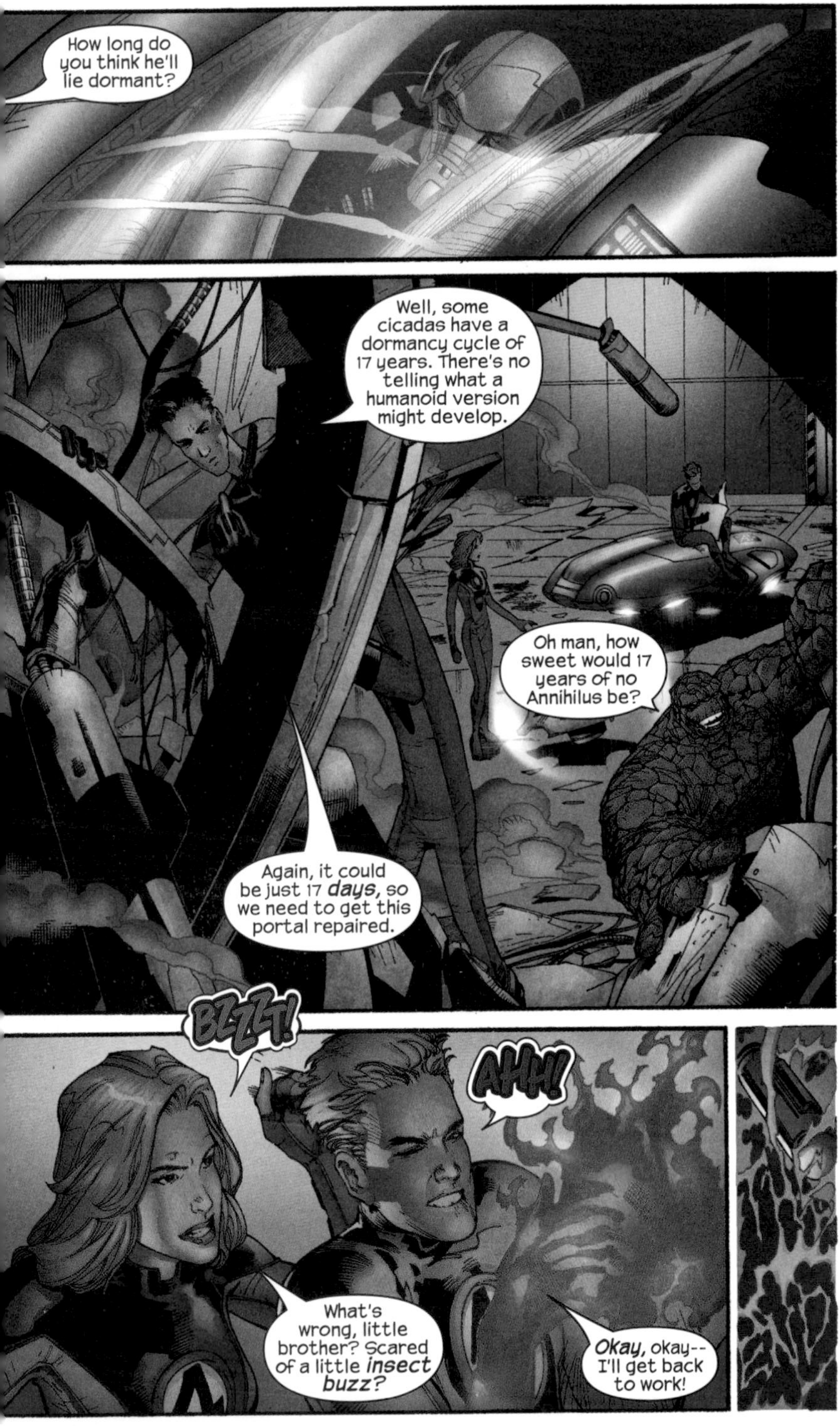
How long do you think he'll lie dormant?
Well, some cicadas have a dormancy cycle of 17 years. There's no telling what a humanoid version might develop.
Oh man, how sweet would 17 years of no Annihilus be?
Again, it could be just 17 *days,* so we need to get this portal repaired.
BZZZT!
AHH!
What's wrong, little brother? Scared of a little *insect buzz?*
Okay, okay-- I'll get back to work!

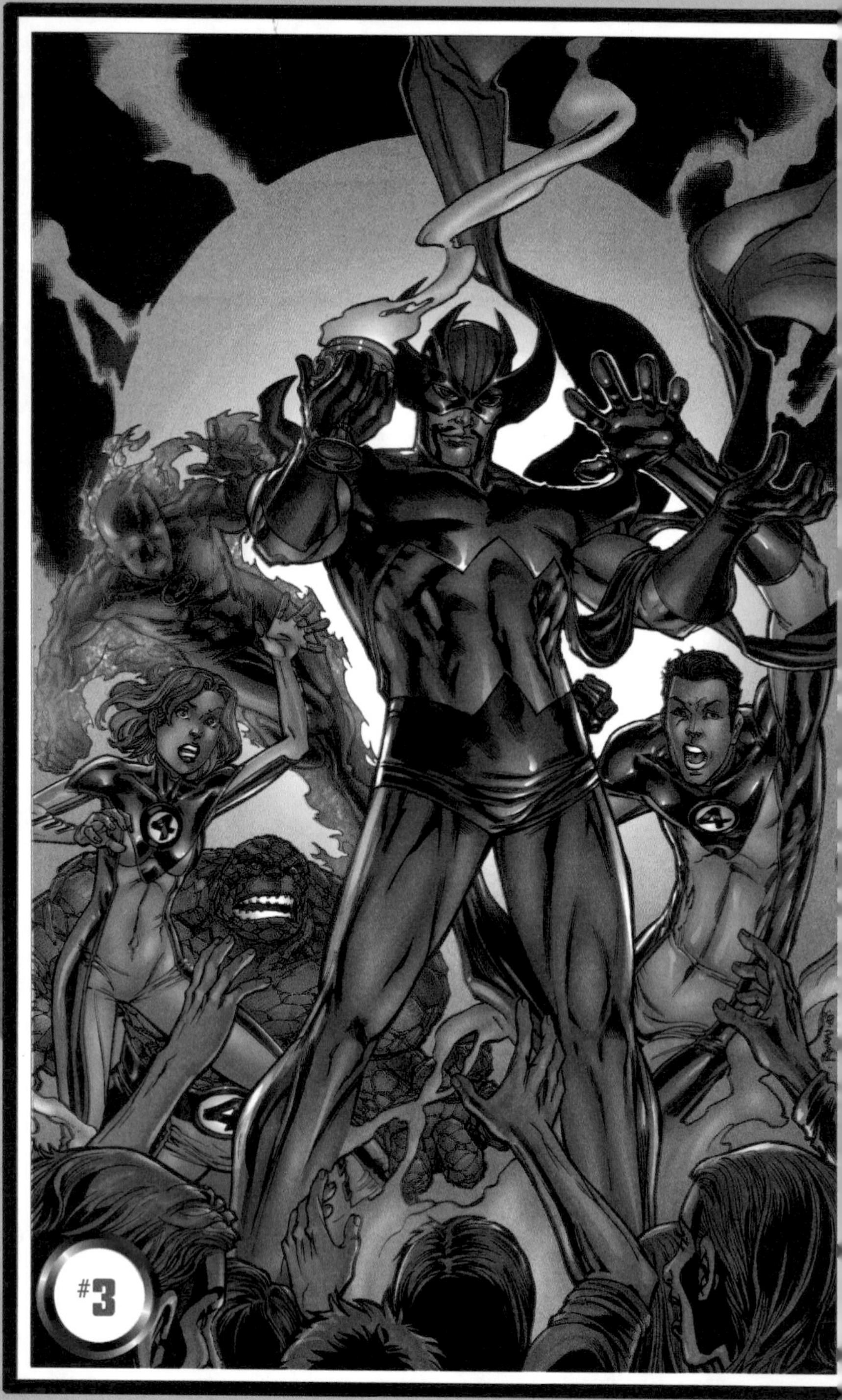
#3

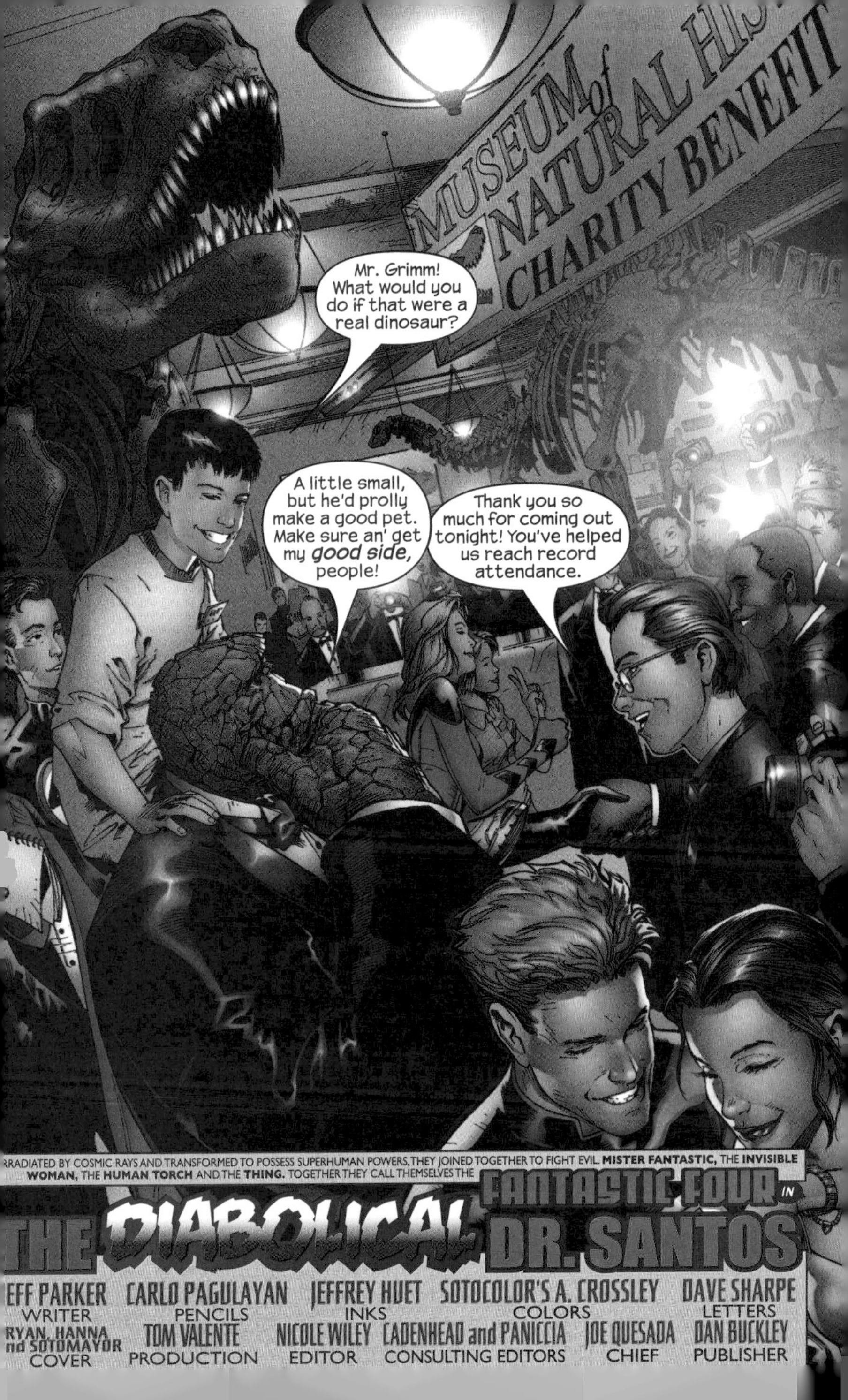
MUSEUM of NATURAL HIS
CHARITY BENEFIT
Mr. Grimm! What would you do if that were a real dinosaur?
A little small, but he'd prolly make a good pet. Make sure an' get my *good side,* people!
Thank you so much for coming out tonight! You've helped us reach record attendance.
RRADIATED BY COSMIC RAYS AND TRANSFORMED TO POSSESS SUPERHUMAN POWERS, THEY JOINED TOGETHER TO FIGHT EVIL. **MISTER FANTASTIC,** THE **INVISIBLE WOMAN,** THE **HUMAN TORCH** AND THE **THING.** TOGETHER THEY CALL THEMSELVES THE FANTASTIC FOUR IN
THE DIABOLICAL DR. SANTOS
EFF PARKER WRITER
CARLO PAGULAYAN PENCILS
JEFFREY HUET INKS
SOTOCOLOR'S A. CROSSLEY COLORS
DAVE SHARPE LETTERS
RYAN, HANNA nd SOTOMAYOR COVER
TOM VALENTE PRODUCTION
NICOLE WILEY EDITOR
CADENHEAD and PANICCIA CONSULTING EDITORS
JOE QUESADA CHIEF
DAN BUCKLEY PUBLISHER

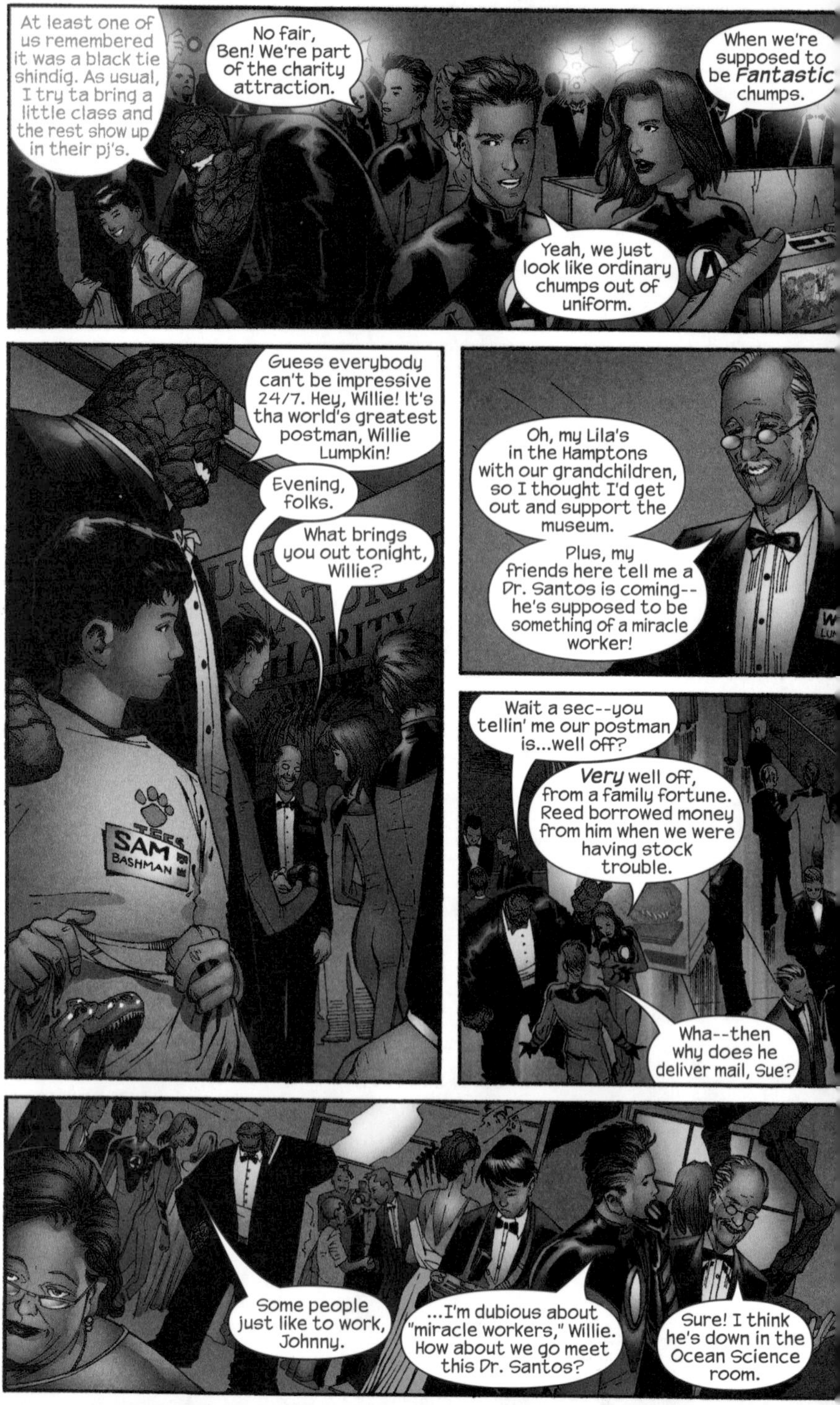
At least one of us remembered it was a black tie shindig. As usual, I try ta bring a little class and the rest show up in their pj's.
No fair, Ben! We're part of the charity attraction.
When we're supposed to be *Fantastic* chumps.
Yeah, we just look like ordinary chumps out of uniform.
Guess everybody can't be impressive 24/7. Hey, Willie! It's tha world's greatest postman, Willie Lumpkin!
Evening, folks.
What brings you out tonight, Willie?
SAM BASHMAN
Oh, my Lila's in the Hamptons with our grandchildren, so I thought I'd get out and support the museum.
Plus, my friends here tell me a Dr. Santos is coming--he's supposed to be something of a miracle worker!
Wait a sec--you tellin' me our postman is...well off?
Very well off, from a family fortune. Reed borrowed money from him when we were having stock trouble.
Wha--then why does he deliver mail, Sue?
Some people just like to work, Johnny.
...I'm dubious about "miracle workers," Willie. How about we go meet this Dr. Santos?
Sure! I think he's down in the Ocean Science room.

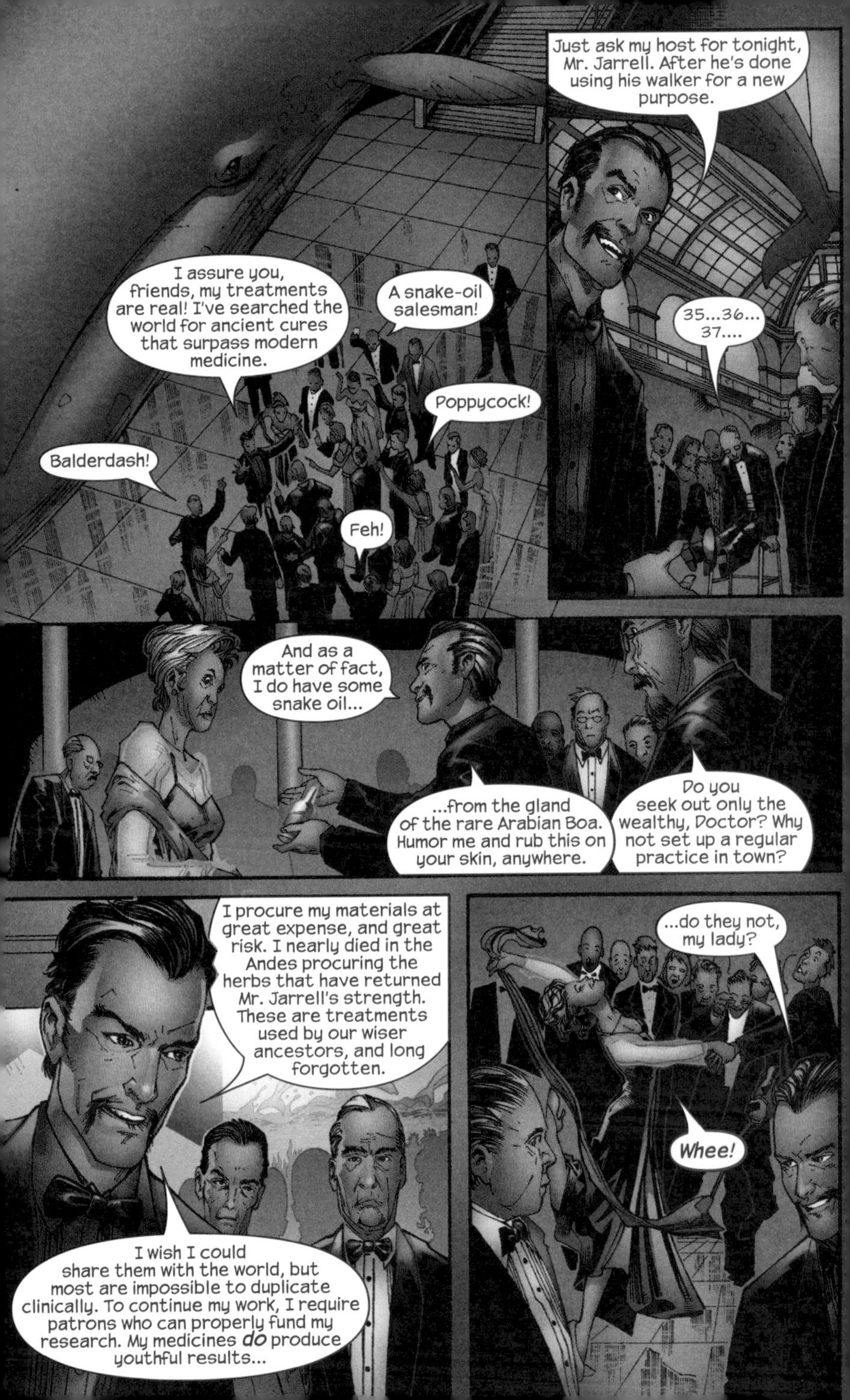
I assure you, friends, my treatments are real! I've searched the world for ancient cures that surpass modern medicine.
A snake-oil salesman!
Poppycock!
Balderdash!
Feh!
Just ask my host for tonight, Mr. Jarrell. After he's done using his walker for a new purpose.
35...36... 37....
And as a matter of fact, I do have some snake oil...
...from the gland of the rare Arabian Boa. Humor me and rub this on your skin, anywhere.
Do you seek out only the wealthy, Doctor? Why not set up a regular practice in town?
I procure my materials at great expense, and great risk. I nearly died in the Andes procuring the herbs that have returned Mr. Jarrell's strength. These are treatments used by our wiser ancestors, and long forgotten.
I wish I could share them with the world, but most are impossible to duplicate clinically. To continue my work, I require patrons who can properly fund my research. My medicines *do* produce youthful results...
...do they not, my lady?
Whee!

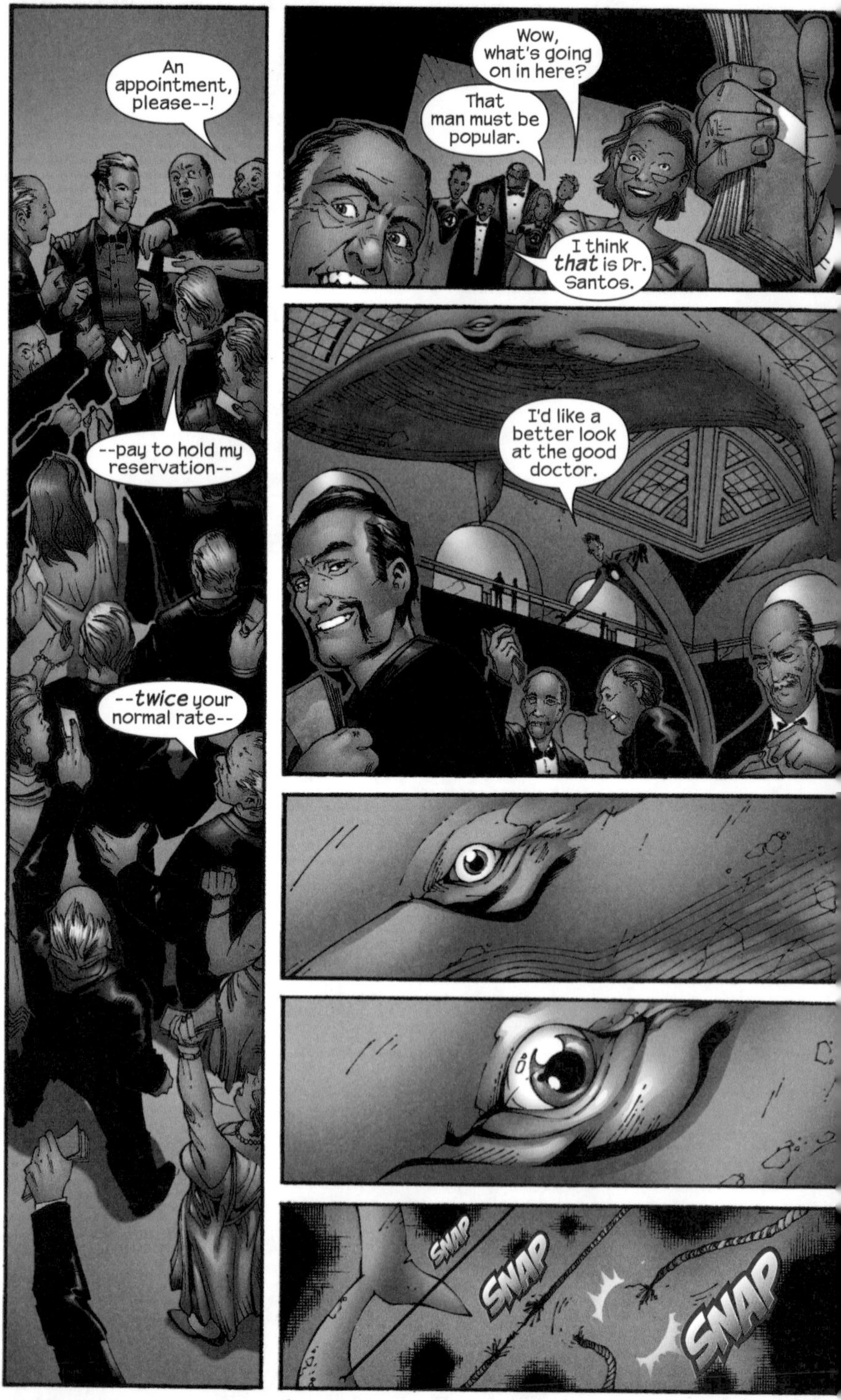
An appointment, please--!
--pay to hold my reservation--
--twice your normal rate--
Wow, what's going on in here?
That man must be popular.
I think that is Dr. Santos.
I'd like a better look at the good doctor.
SNAP
SNAP
SNAP

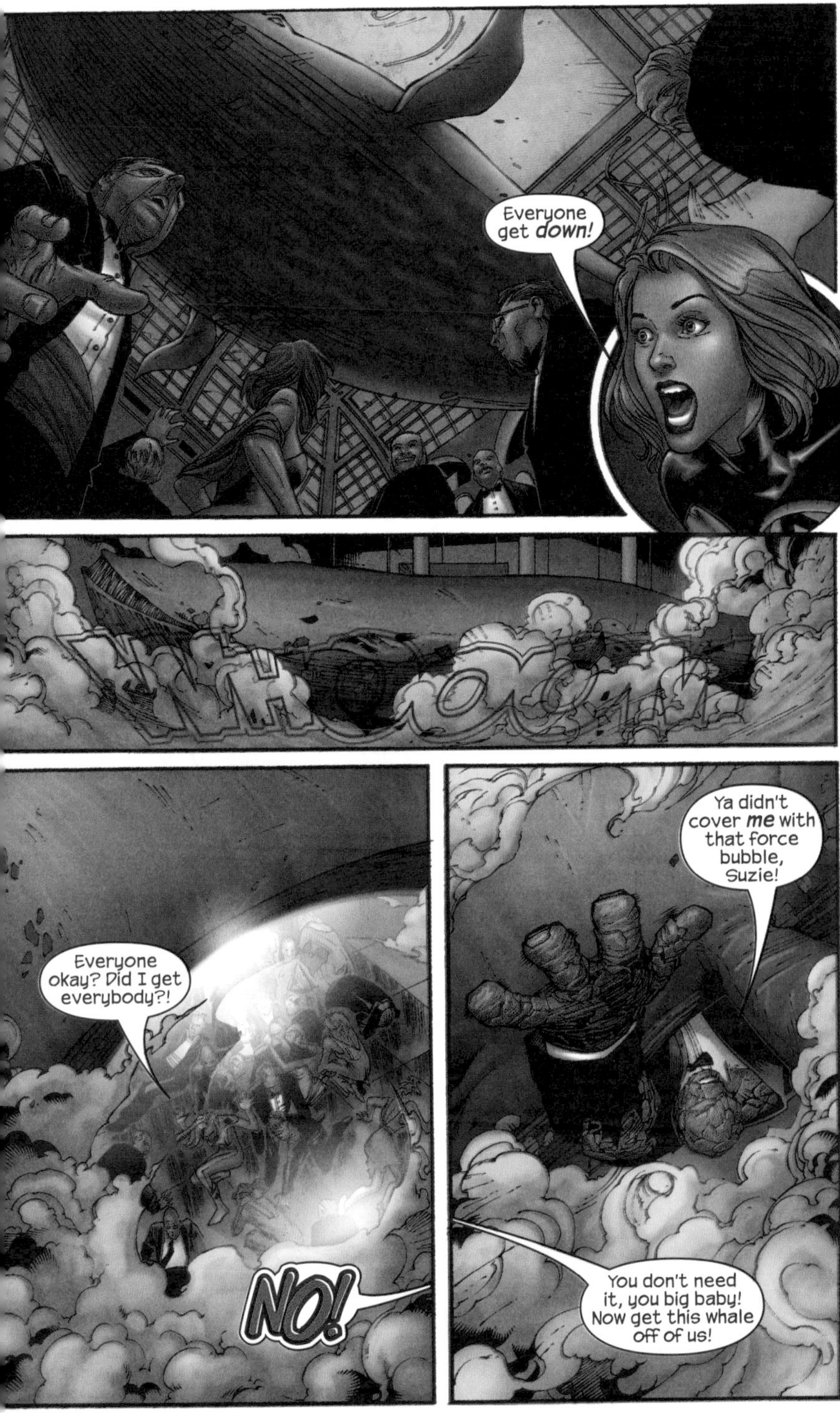

Everyone get *down!*
Everyone okay? Did I get everybody?!
NO!
Ya didn't cover *me* with that force bubble, Suzie!
You don't need it, you big baby! Now get this whale off of us!

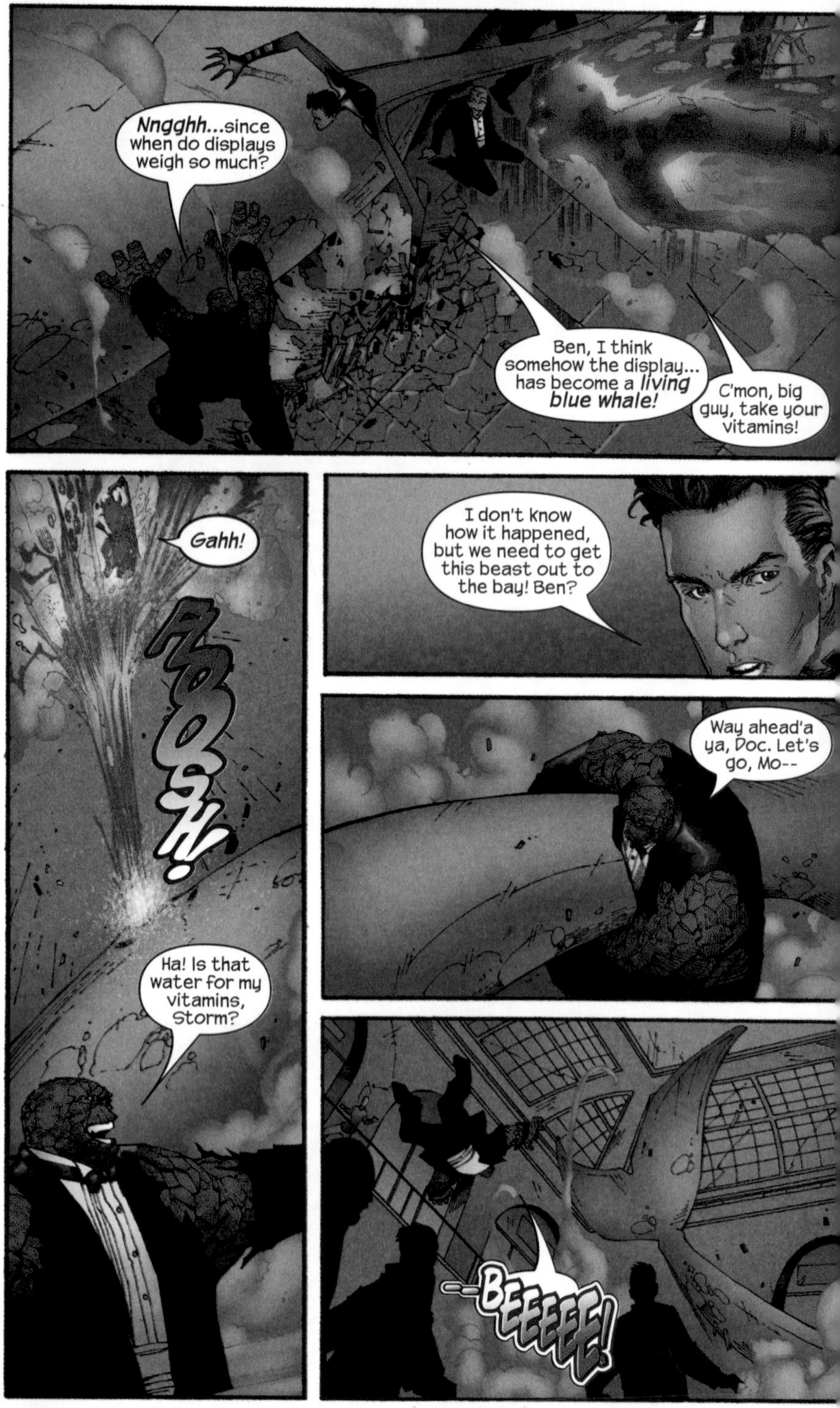
Nngghh...since when do displays weigh so much?
Ben, I think somehow the display... has become a living blue whale!
C'mon, big guy, take your vitamins!
Gahh!
FWOOSH!
Ha! Is that water for my vitamins, Storm?
I don't know how it happened, but we need to get this beast out to the bay! Ben?
Way ahead'a ya, Doc. Let's go, Mo--
--BEEEEEE!

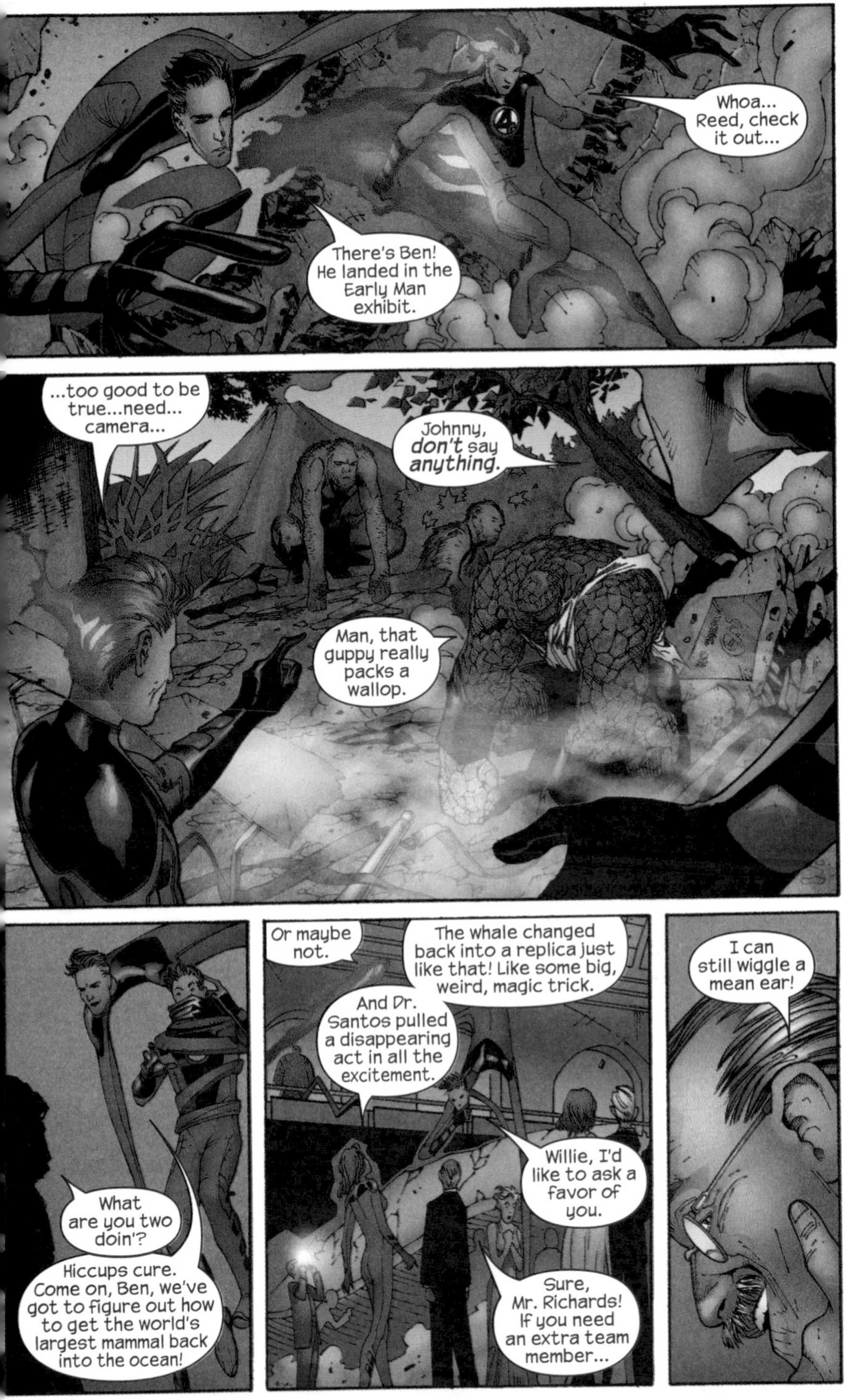
Whoa... Reed, check it out...
There's Ben! He landed in the Early Man exhibit.
...too good to be true...need... camera...
Johnny, *don't* say *anything*.
Man, that guppy really packs a wallop.
What are you two doin'?
Hiccups cure. Come on, Ben, we've got to figure out how to get the world's largest mammal back into the ocean!
Or maybe not.
The whale changed back into a replica just like that! Like some big, weird, magic trick.
And Dr. Santos pulled a disappearing act in all the excitement.
Willie, I'd like to ask a favor of you.
Sure, Mr. Richards! If you need an extra team member...
I can still wiggle a mean ear!

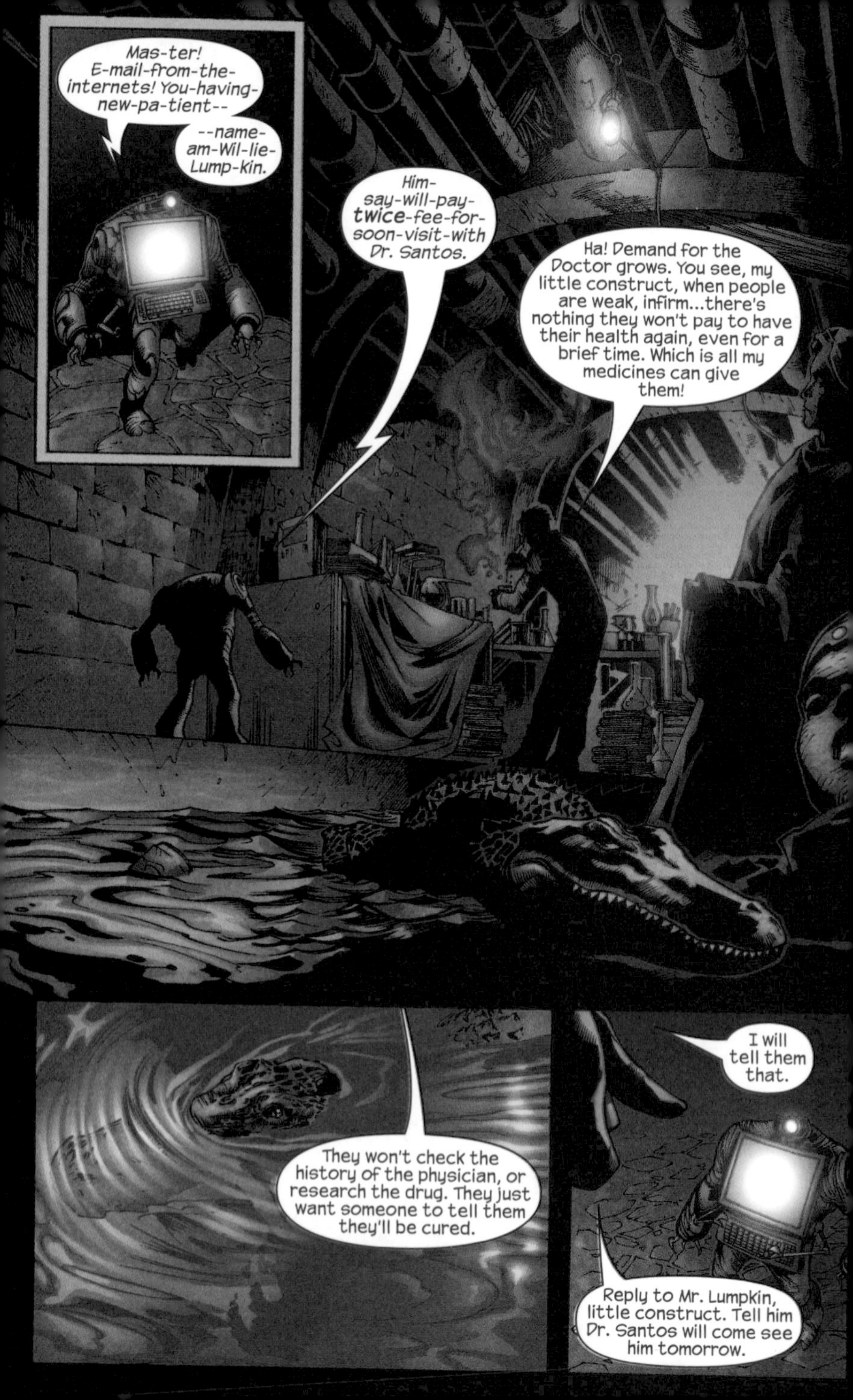
Mas-ter! E-mail-from-the-internets! You-having-new-pa-tient--
--name-am-Wil-lie-Lump-kin.
Him-say-will-pay-twice-fee-for-soon-visit-with Dr. Santos.
Ha! Demand for the Doctor grows. You see, my little construct, when people are weak, infirm...there's nothing they won't pay to have their health again, even for a brief time. Which is all my medicines can give them!
They won't check the history of the physician, or research the drug. They just want someone to tell them they'll be cured.
Reply to Mr. Lumpkin, little construct. Tell him Dr. Santos will come see him tomorrow.
I will tell them that.

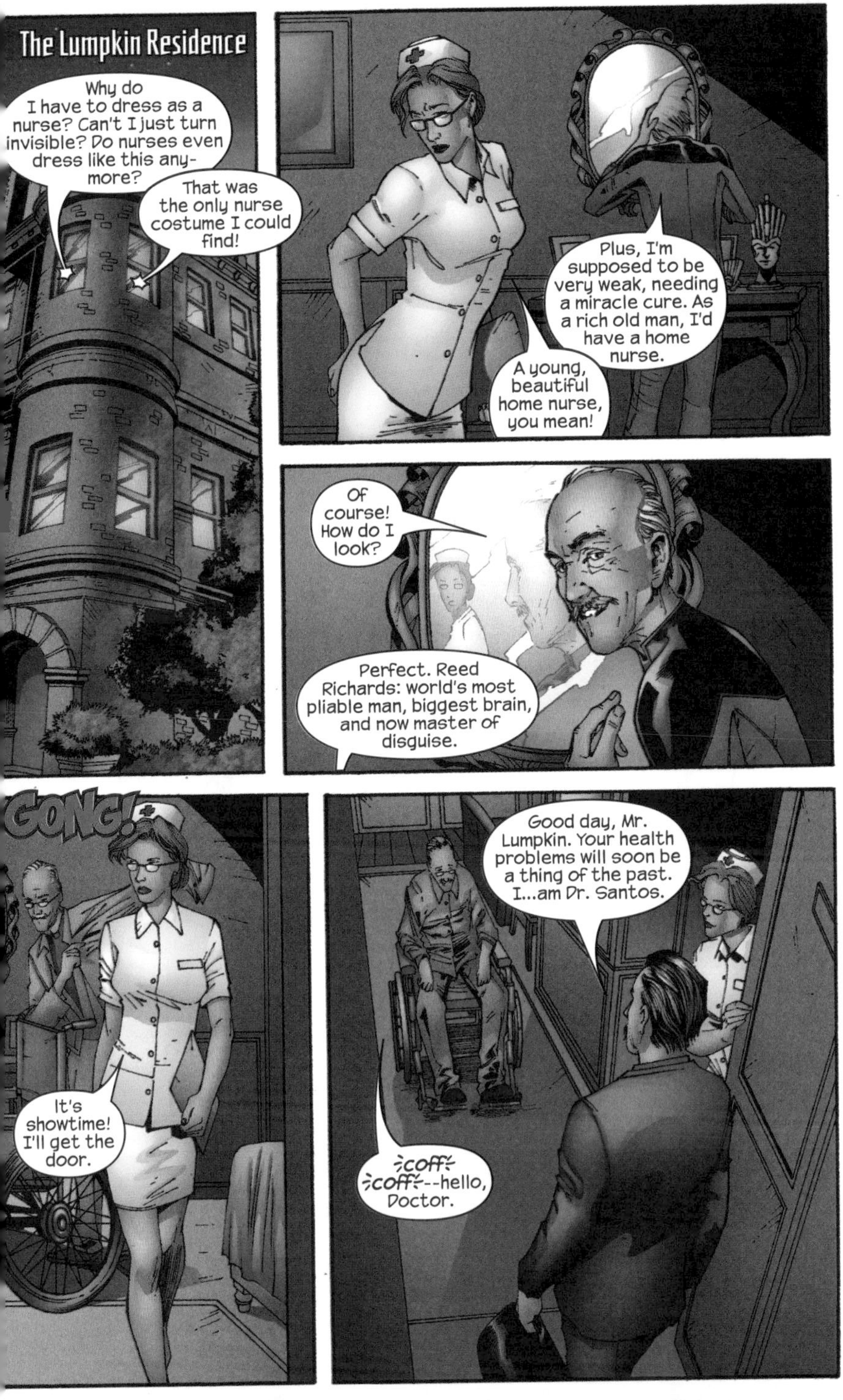
The Lumpkin Residence
Why do I have to dress as a nurse? Can't I just turn invisible? Do nurses even dress like this any-more?
That was the only nurse costume I could find!
Plus, I'm supposed to be very weak, needing a miracle cure. As a rich old man, I'd have a home nurse.
A young, beautiful home nurse, you mean!
Of course! How do I look?
Perfect. Reed Richards: world's most pliable man, biggest brain, and now master of disguise.
GONG!
It's showtime! I'll get the door.
Good day, Mr. Lumpkin. Your health problems will soon be a thing of the past. I...am Dr. Santos.
coff coff--hello, Doctor.

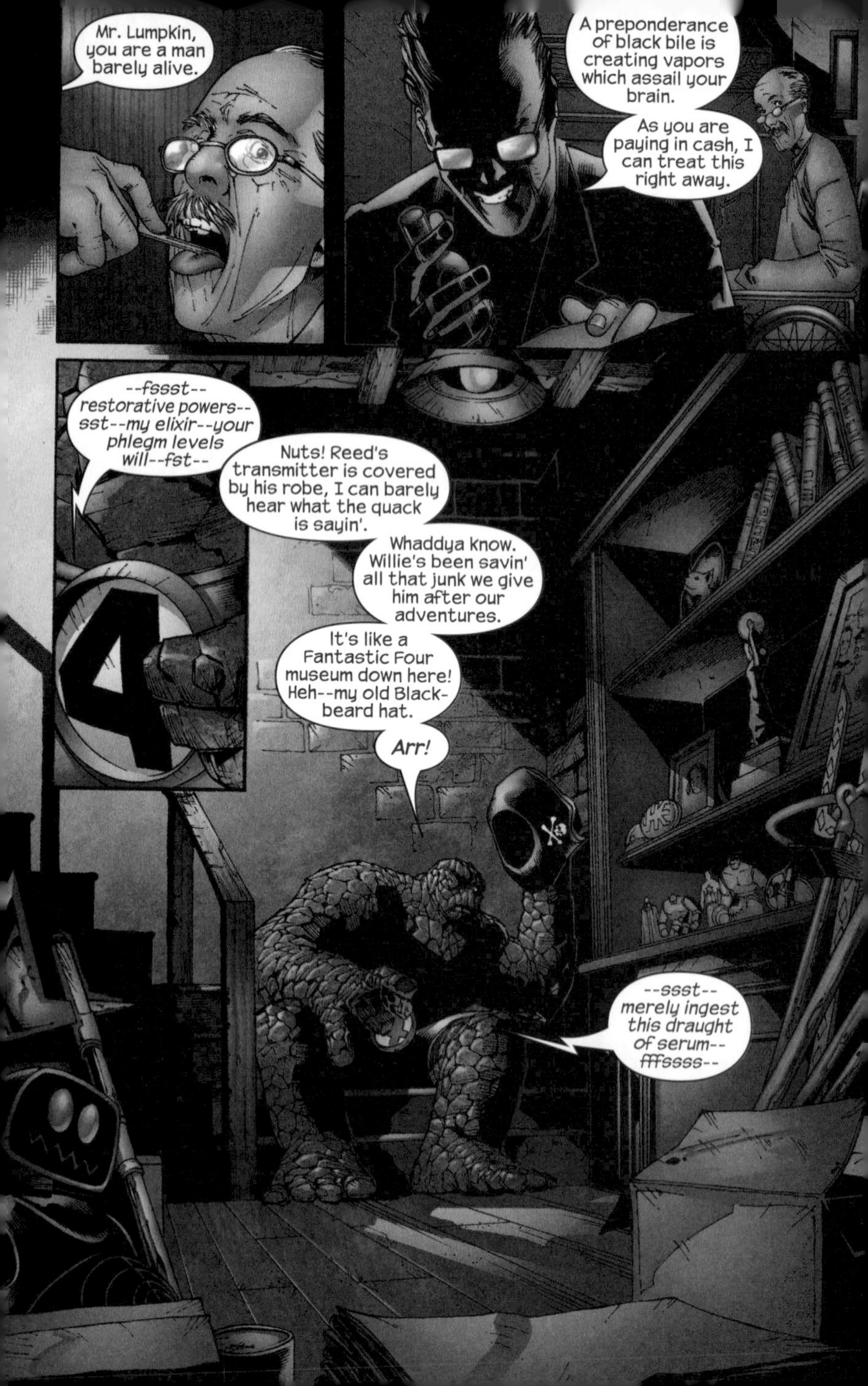
Mr. Lumpkin, you are a man barely alive.
A preponderance of black bile is creating vapors which assail your brain.
As you are paying in cash, I can treat this right away.
--fssst-- restorative powers--sst--my elixir--your phlegm levels will--fst--
Nuts! Reed's transmitter is covered by his robe, I can barely hear what the quack is sayin'.
Whaddya know. Willie's been savin' all that junk we give him after our adventures.
It's like a Fantastic Four museum down here! Heh--my old Black-beard hat.
Arr!
--ssst-- merely ingest this draught of serum--fffssss--

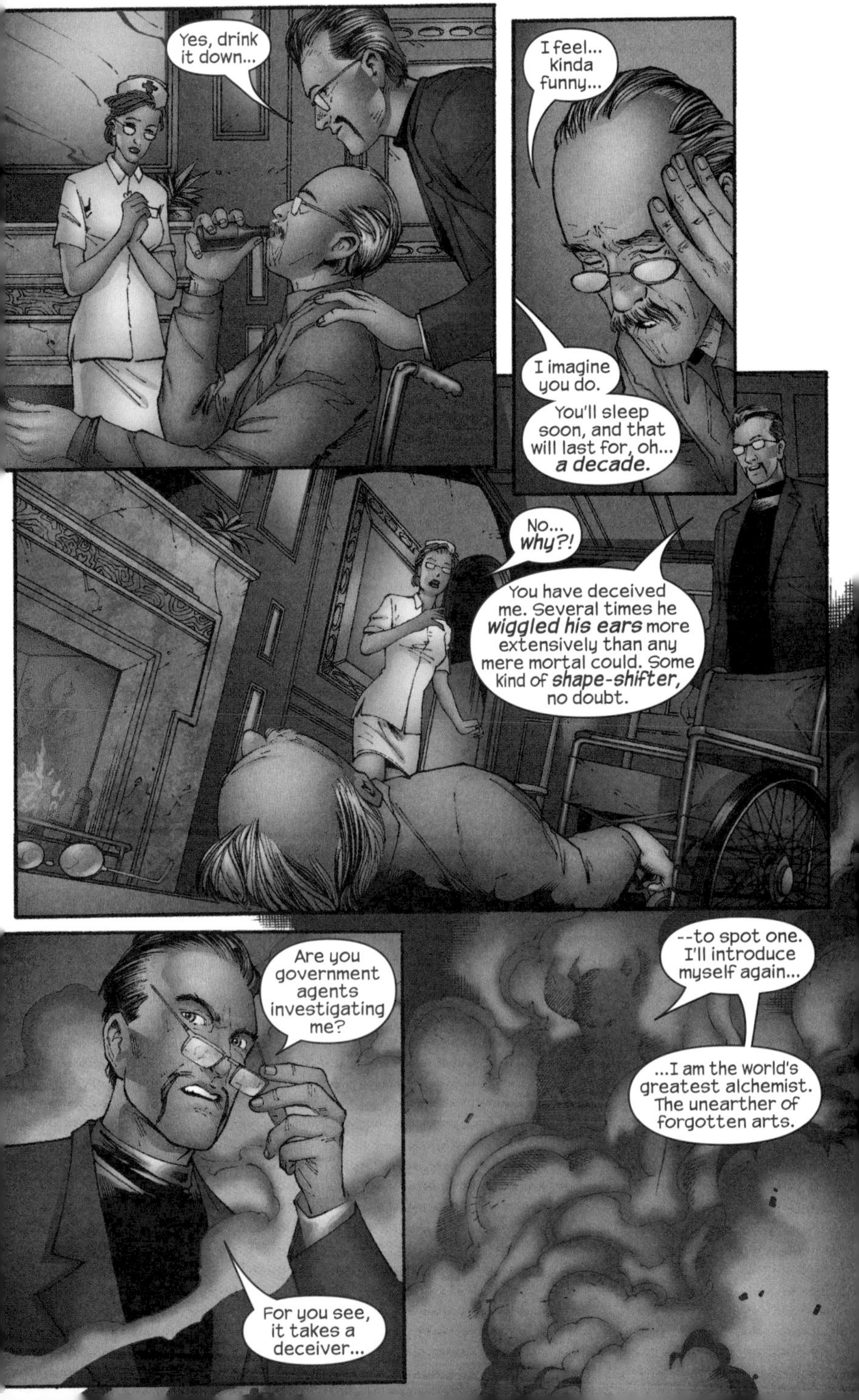
Yes, drink it down...
I feel... kinda funny...
I imagine you do.
You'll sleep soon, and that will last for, oh... *a decade.*
No... *why?!*
You have deceived me. Several times he *wiggled his ears* more extensively than any mere mortal could. Some kind of *shape-shifter,* no doubt.
Are you government agents investigating me?
For you see, it takes a deceiver...
--to spot one. I'll introduce myself again...
...I am the world's greatest alchemist. The unearther of forgotten arts.

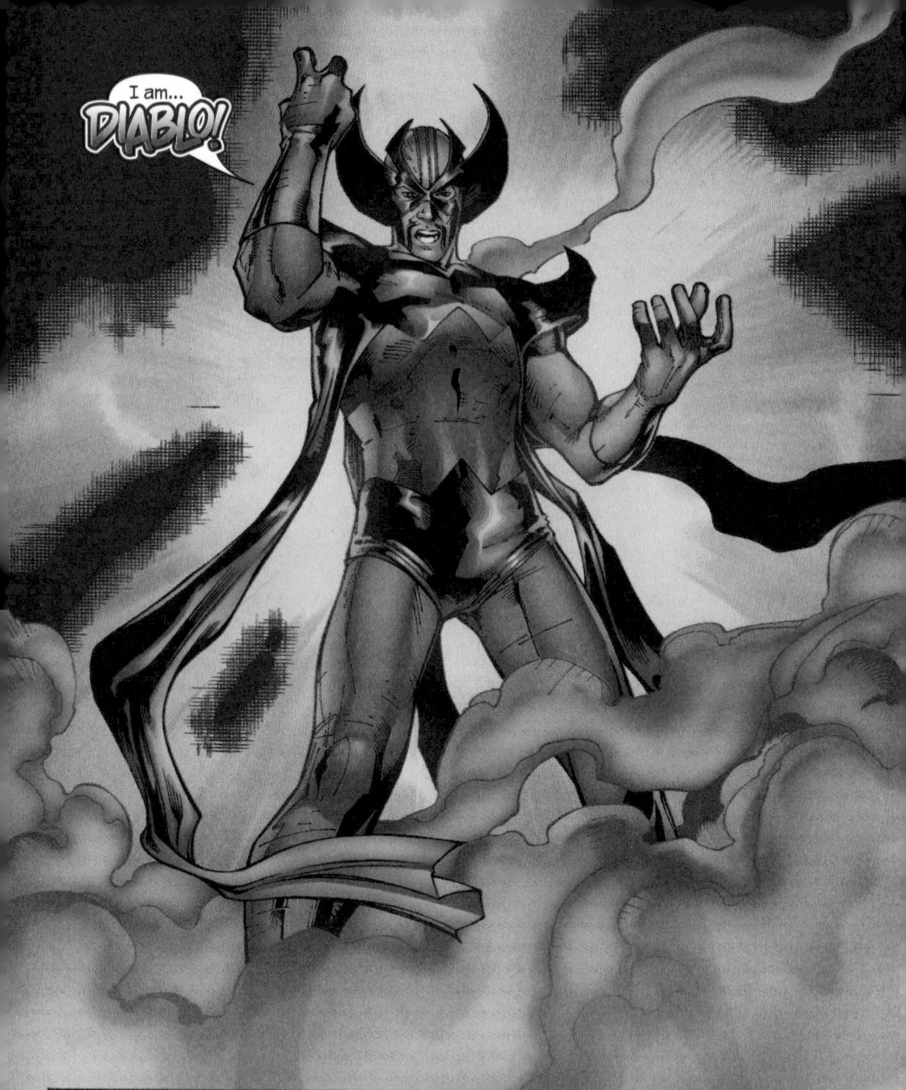
I am... DIABLO!

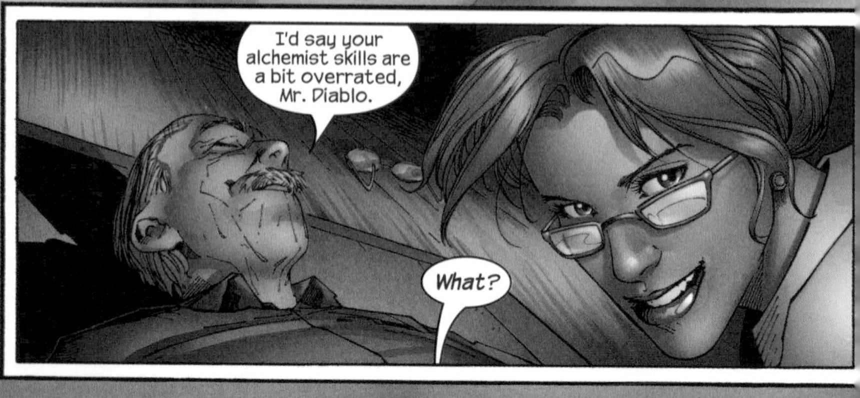
I'd say your alchemist skills are a bit overrated, Mr. Diablo.
What?

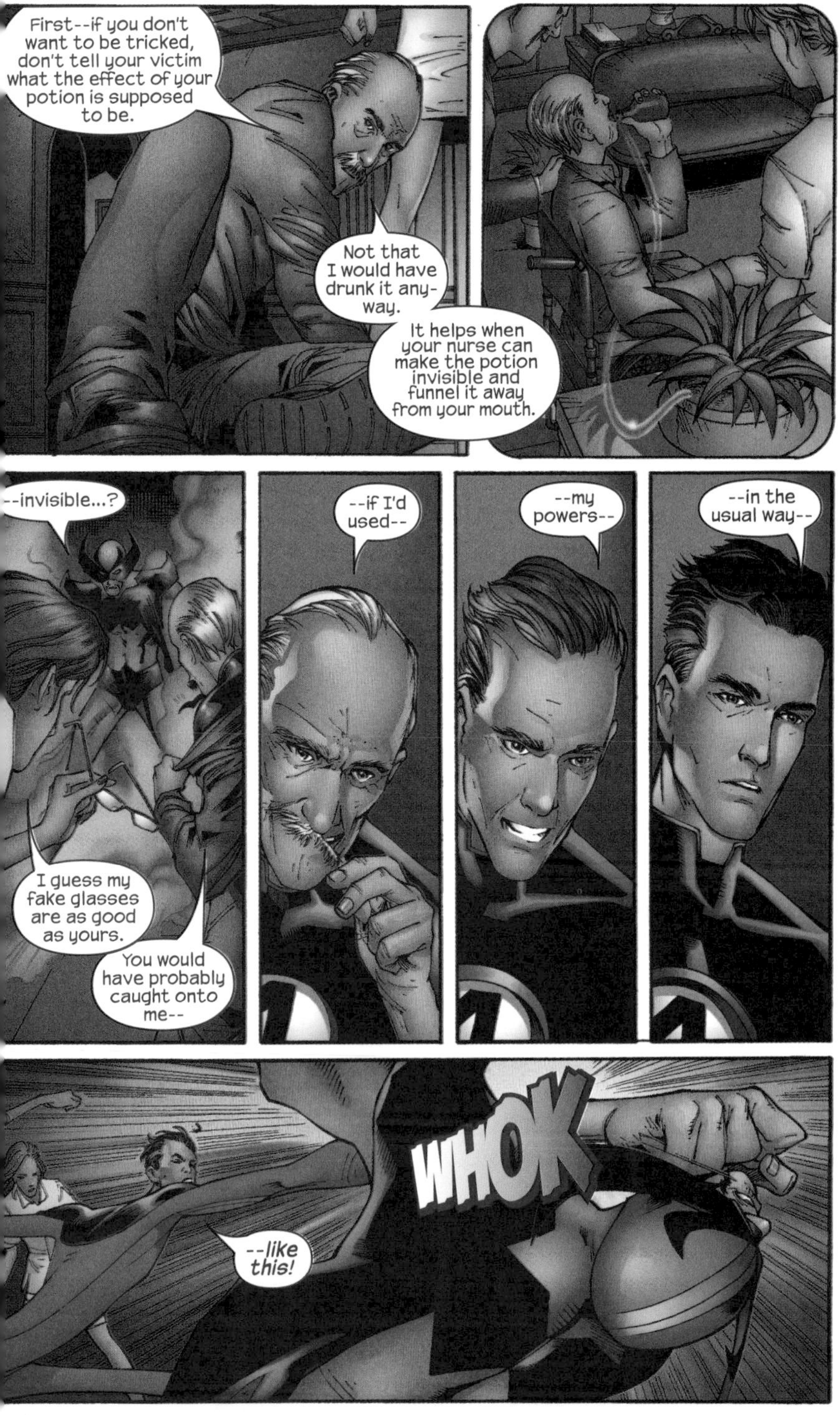
First--if you don't want to be tricked, don't tell your victim what the effect of your potion is supposed to be.
Not that I would have drunk it any-way.
It helps when your nurse can make the potion invisible and funnel it away from your mouth.
--invisible...?
I guess my fake glasses are as good as yours.
You would have probably caught onto me--
--if I'd used--
--my powers--
--in the usual way--
WHOK
--like this!

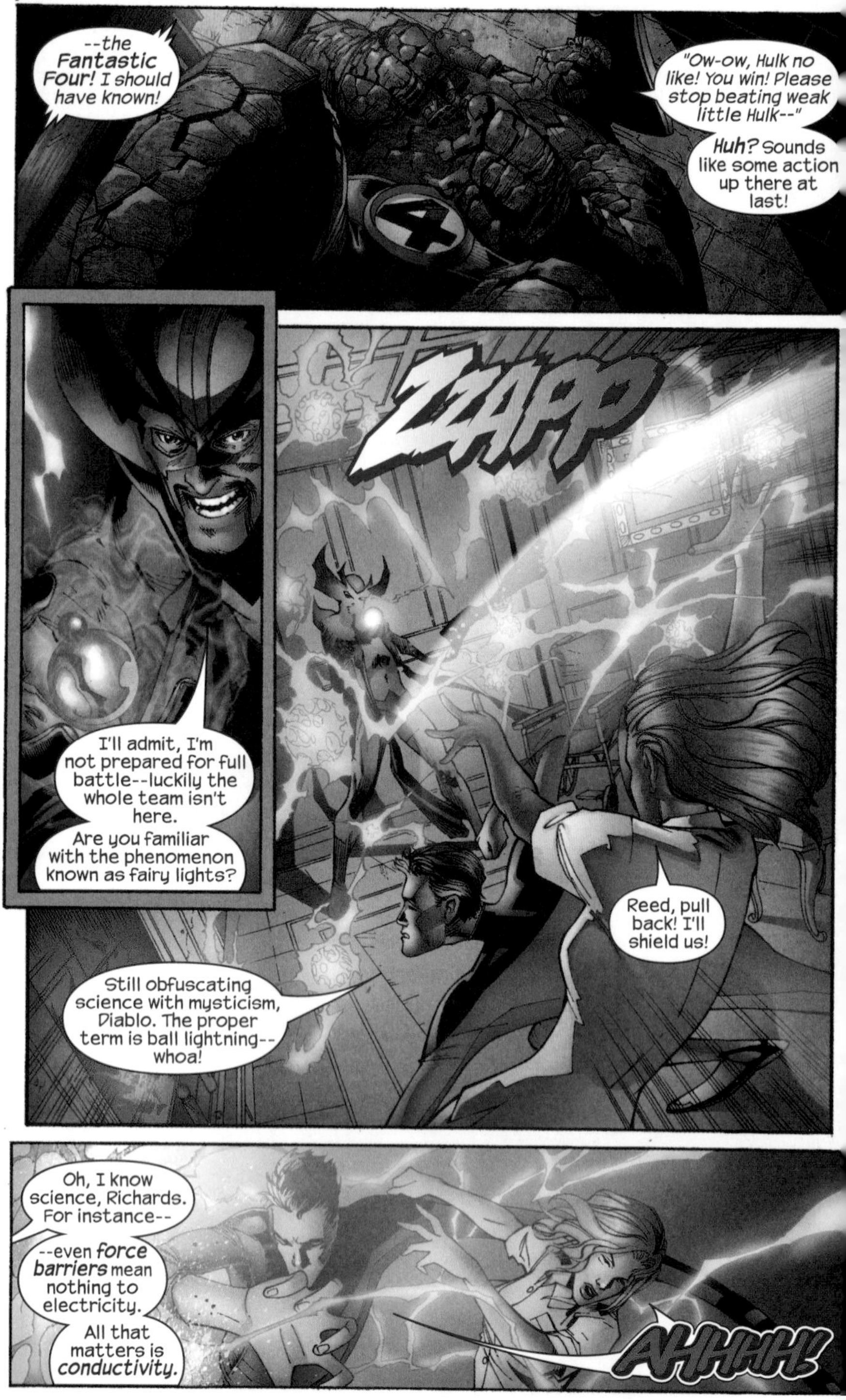
--the *Fantastic Four!* I should have known!
"Ow-ow, Hulk no like! You win! Please stop beating weak little Hulk--"
Huh? Sounds like some action up there at last!
ZZAPP
I'll admit, I'm not prepared for full battle--luckily the whole team isn't here.
Are you familiar with the phenomenon known as fairy lights?
Reed, pull back! I'll shield us!
Still obfuscating science with mysticism, Diablo. The proper term is ball lightning--whoa!
Oh, I know science, Richards. For instance--
--even ***force barriers*** mean nothing to electricity.
All that matters is ***conductivity.***
AHHHH!

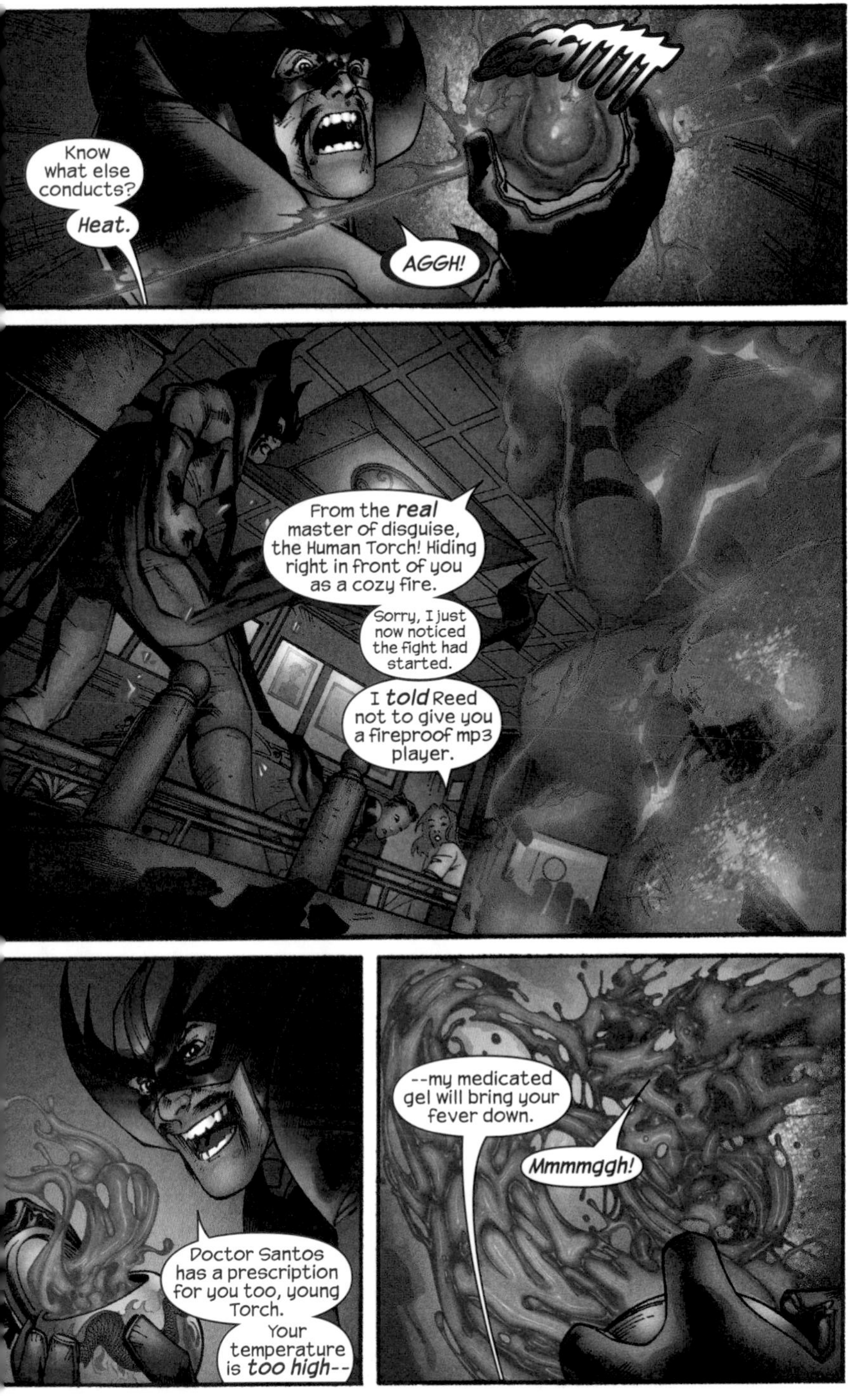
Know what else conducts?
Heat.
AGGH!
From the real master of disguise, the Human Torch! Hiding right in front of you as a cozy fire.
Sorry, I just now noticed the fight had started.
I told Reed not to give you a fireproof mp3 player.
Doctor Santos has a prescription for you too, young Torch.
Your temperature is too high--
--my medicated gel will bring your fever down.
Mmmmggh!

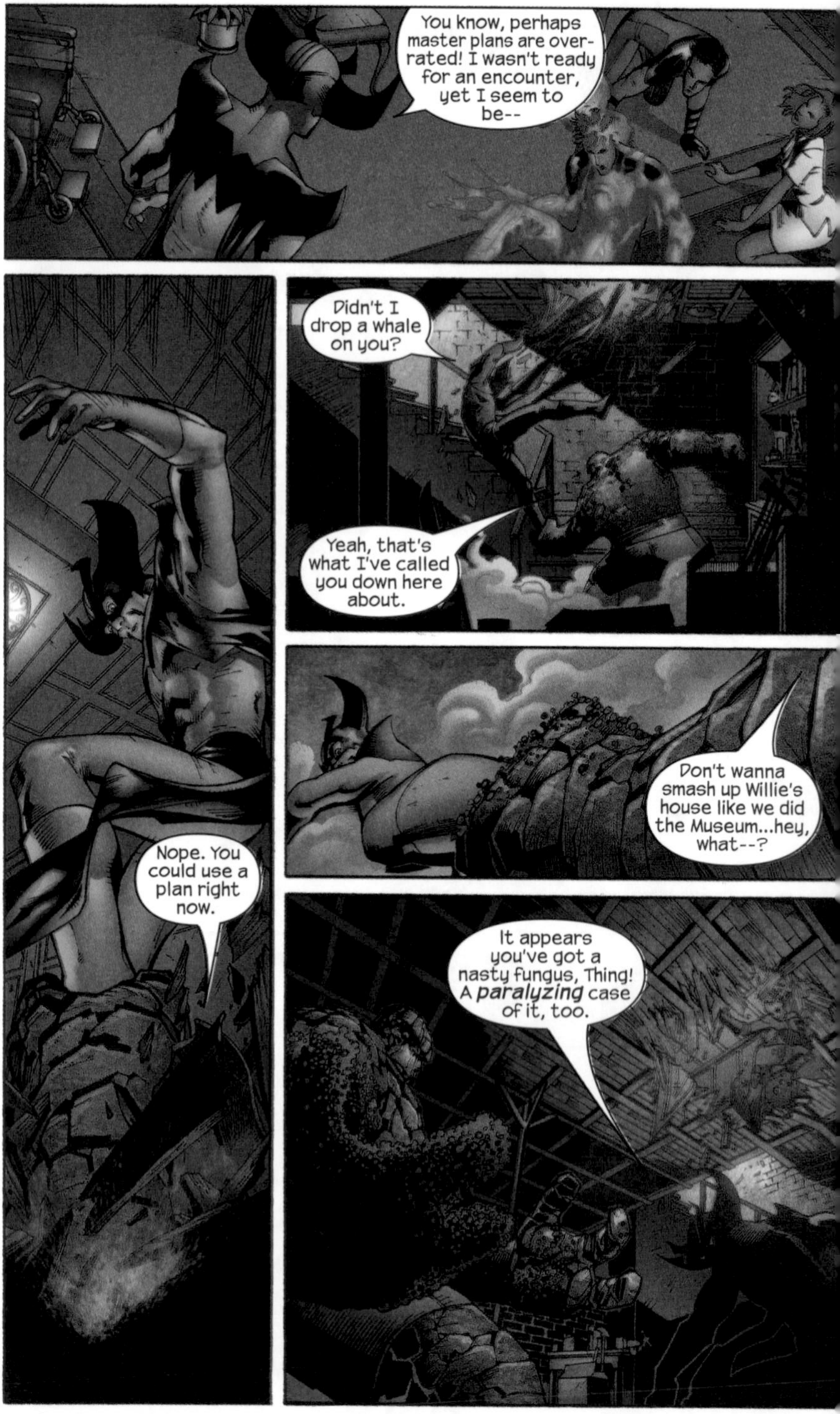
You know, perhaps master plans are over-rated! I wasn't ready for an encounter, yet I seem to be--
Didn't I drop a whale on you?
Yeah, that's what I've called you down here about.
Nope. You could use a plan right now.
Don't wanna smash up Willie's house like we did the Museum...hey, what--?
It appears you've got a nasty fungus, Thing! A *paralyzing* case of it, too.

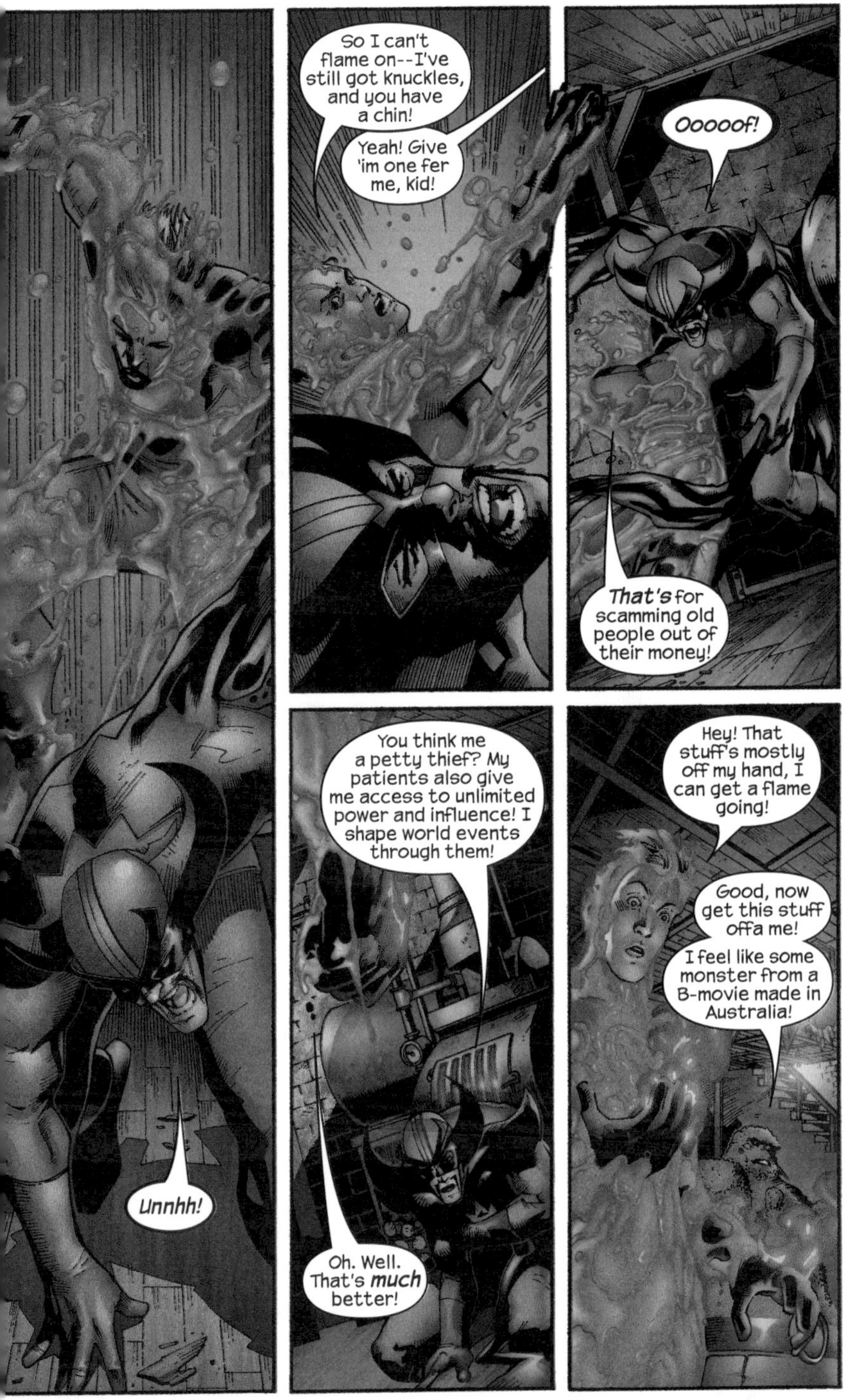
Unnhh!
So I can't flame on--I've still got knuckles, and you have a chin!
Yeah! Give 'im one fer me, kid!
Oooooof!
That's for scamming old people out of their money!
You think me a petty thief? My patients also give me access to unlimited power and influence! I shape world events through them!
Oh. Well. That's much better!
Hey! That stuff's mostly off my hand, I can get a flame going!
Good, now get this stuff offa me!
I feel like some monster from a B-movie made in Australia!

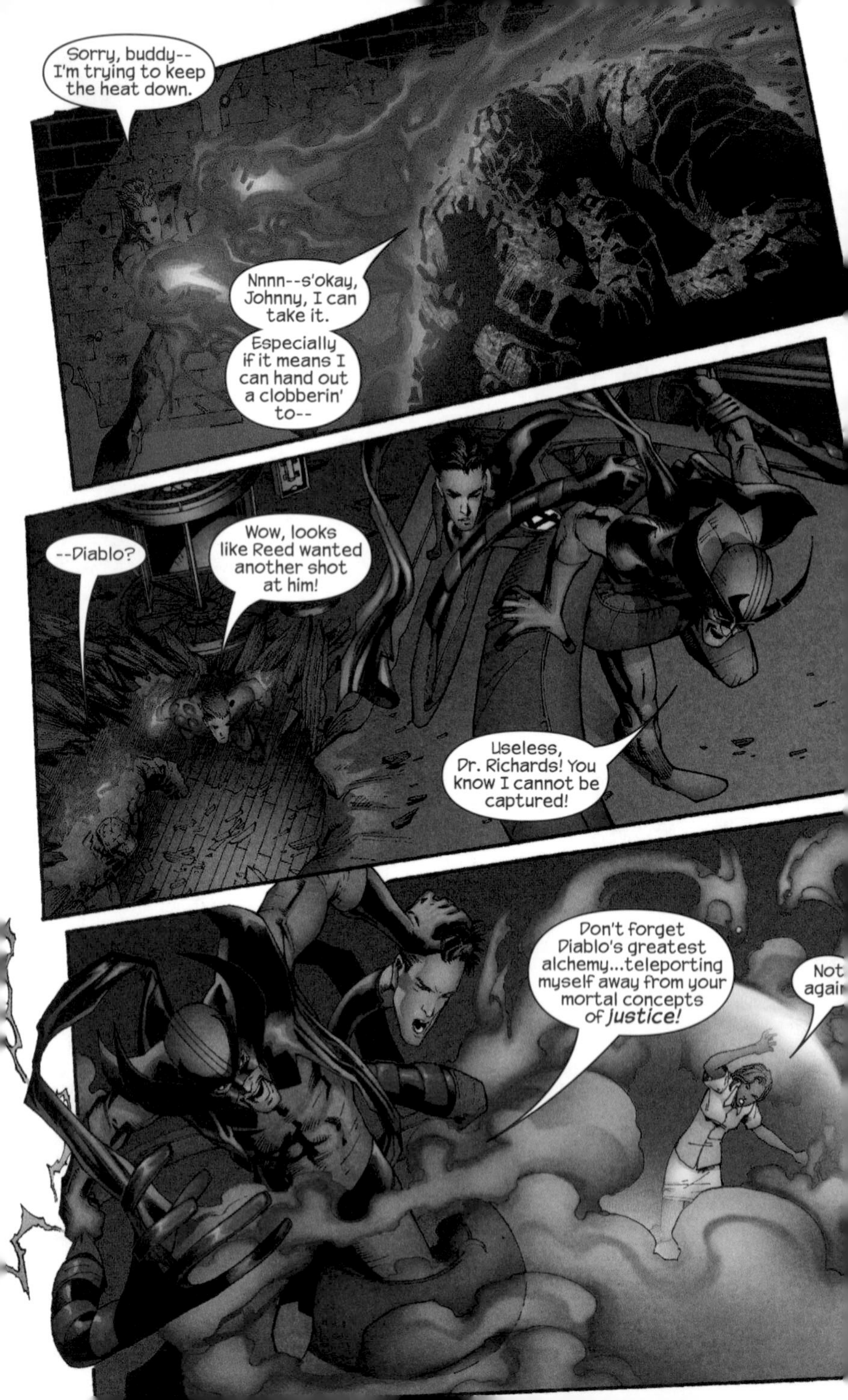
Sorry, buddy--
I'm trying to keep the heat down.
Nnnn--s'okay, Johnny, I can take it.
Especially if it means I can hand out a clobberin' to--
--Diablo?
Wow, looks like Reed wanted another shot at him!
Useless, Dr. Richards! You know I cannot be captured!
Don't forget Diablo's greatest alchemy...teleporting myself away from your mortal concepts of Justice!

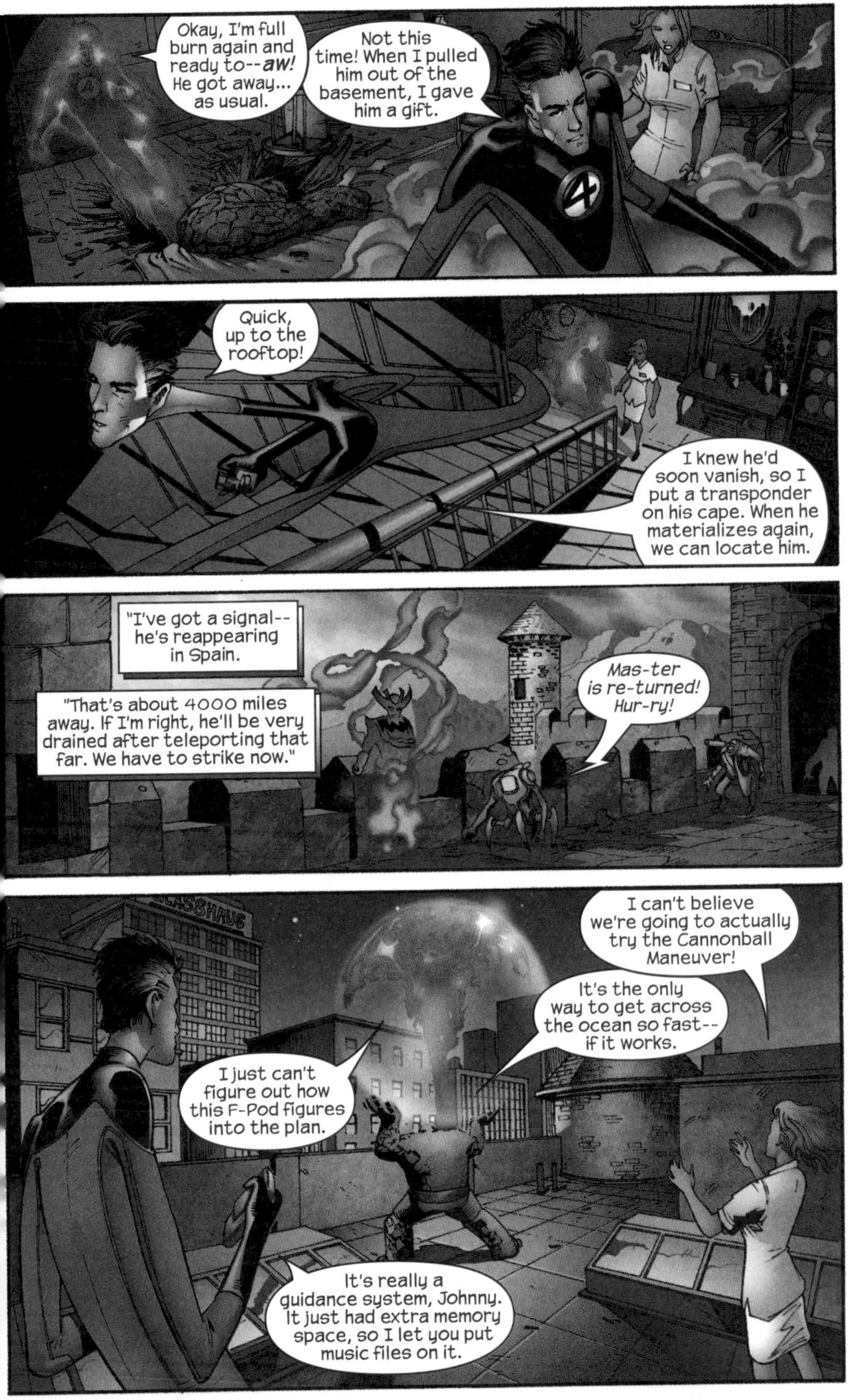
Okay, I'm full burn again and ready to--aw! He got away... as usual.
Not this time! When I pulled him out of the basement, I gave him a gift.
Quick, up to the rooftop!
I knew he'd soon vanish, so I put a transponder on his cape. When he materializes again, we can locate him.
"I've got a signal--he's reappearing in Spain.
"That's about 4000 miles away. If I'm right, he'll be very drained after teleporting that far. We have to strike now."
Mas-ter is re-turned! Hur-ry!
I can't believe we're going to actually try the Cannonball Maneuver!
It's the only way to get across the ocean so fast--if it works.
I just can't figure out how this F-Pod figures into the plan.
It's really a guidance system, Johnny. It just had extra memory space, so I let you put music files on it.

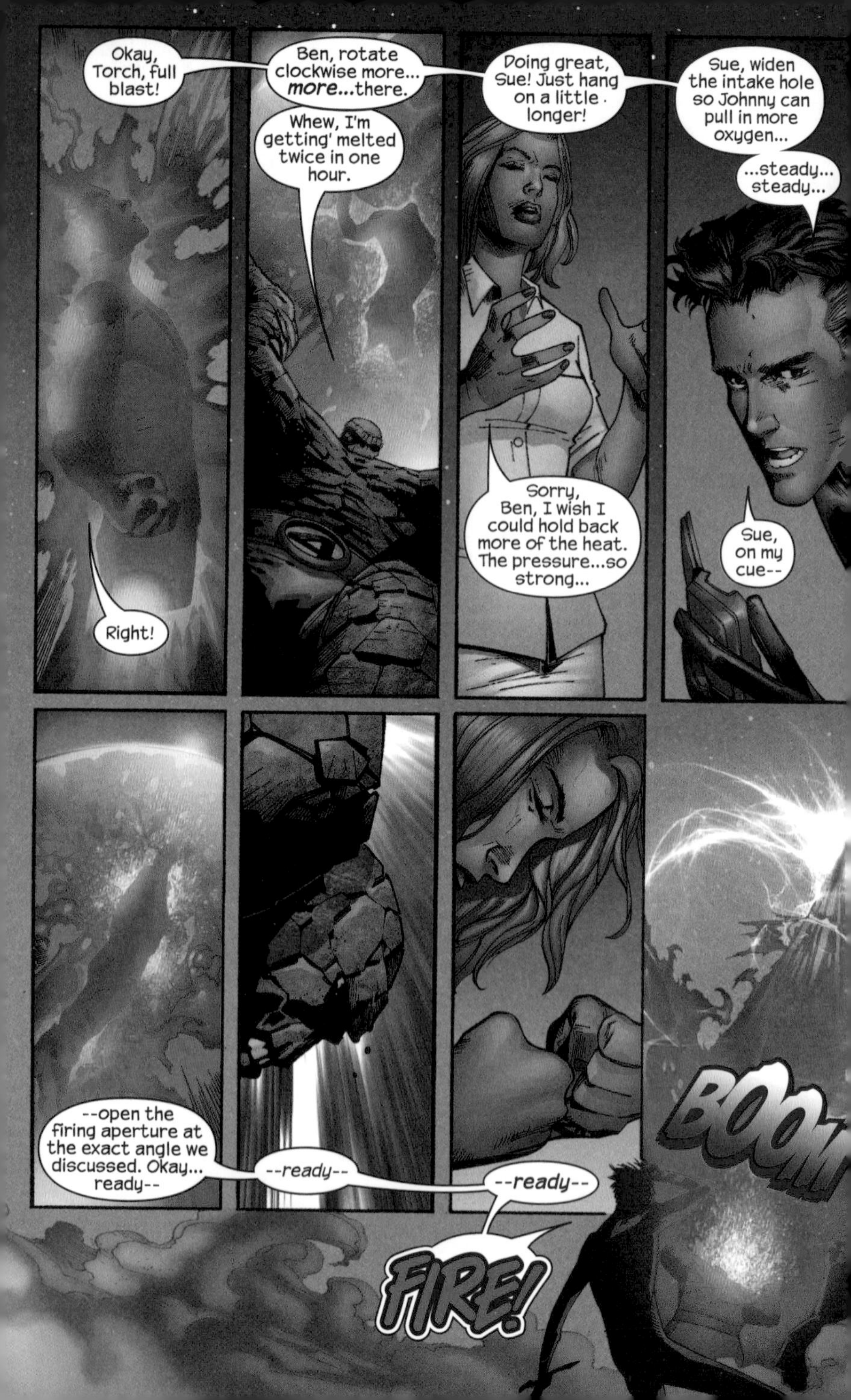
Okay, Torch, full blast!
Right!
Ben, rotate clockwise more... *more*...there.
Whew, I'm getting' melted twice in one hour.
Doing great, Sue! Just hang on a little longer!
Sorry, Ben, I wish I could hold back more of the heat. The pressure...so strong...
Sue, widen the intake hole so Johnny can pull in more oxygen...
...steady... steady...
Sue, on my cue--
--open the firing aperture at the exact angle we discussed. Okay... ready--
--ready--
--ready--
FIRE!
BOOM

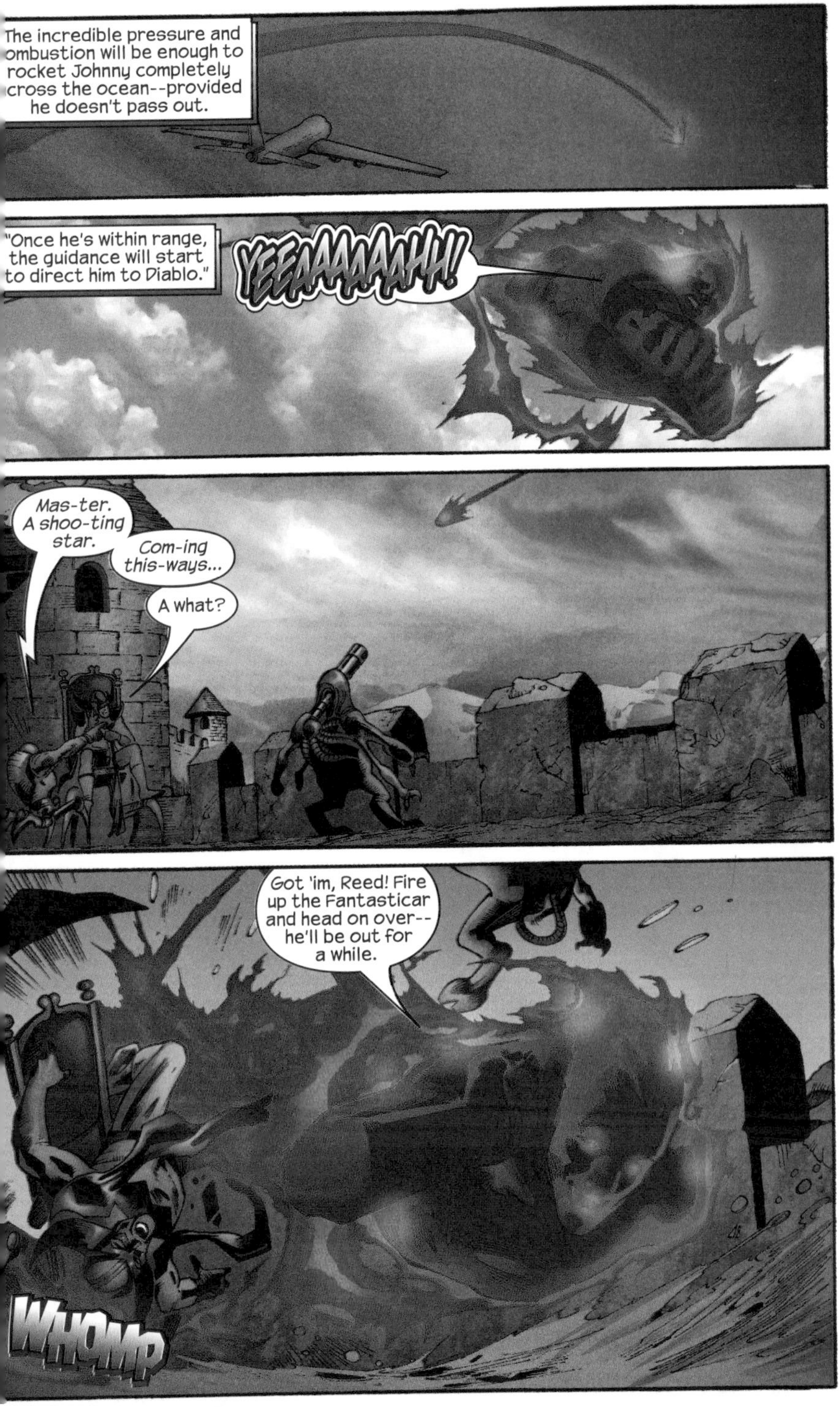
The incredible pressure and ombustion will be enough to rocket Johnny completely cross the ocean--provided he doesn't pass out.
"Once he's within range, the guidance will start to direct him to Diablo."
YEEAAAAAAHH!
Mas-ter. A shoo-ting star.
Com-ing this-ways...
A what?
Got 'im, Reed! Fire up the Fantasticar and head on over--he'll be out for a while.
WHOMP

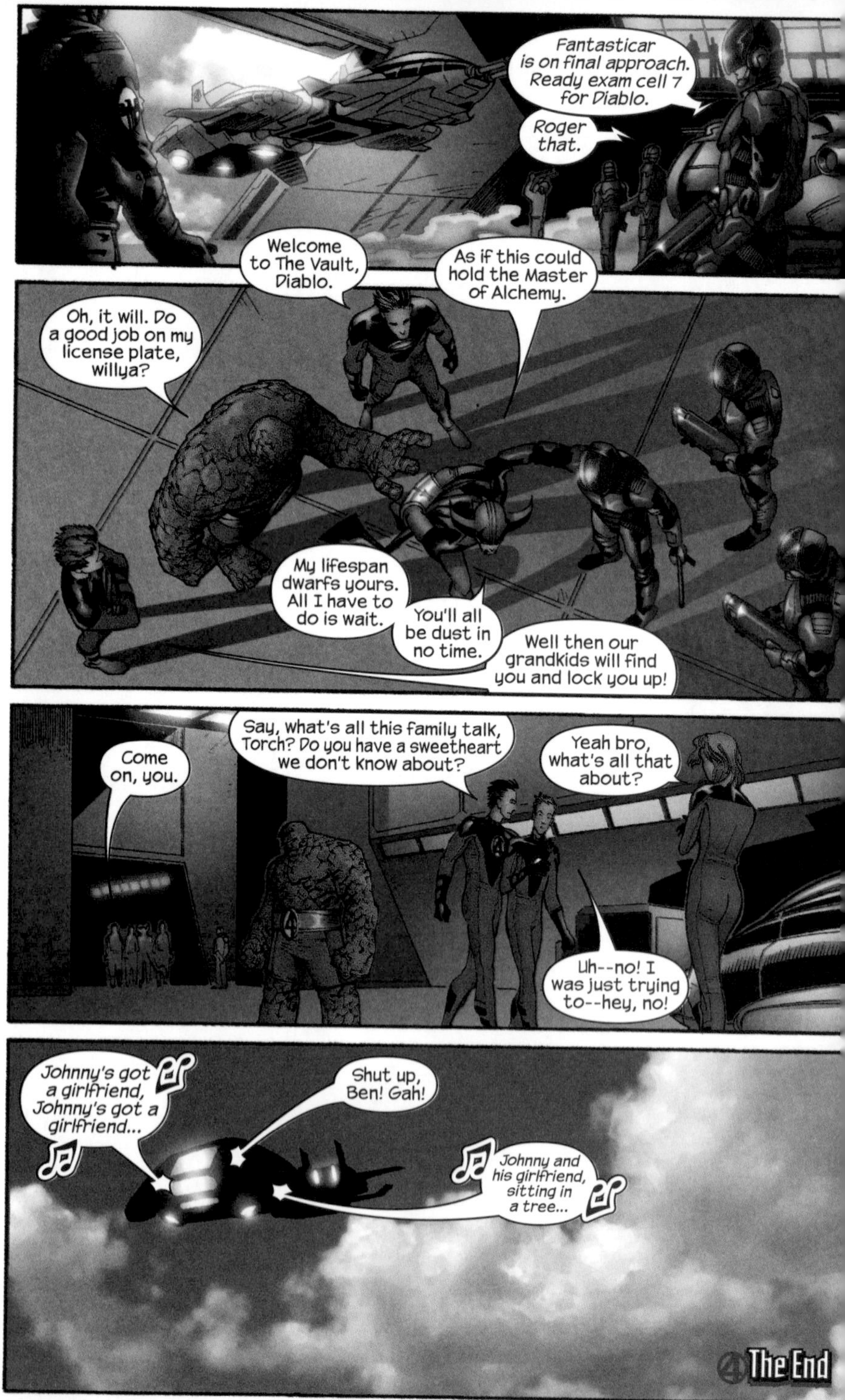
Fantasticar is on final approach. Ready exam cell 7 for Diablo.
Roger that.
Welcome to The Vault, Diablo.
As if this could hold the Master of Alchemy.
Oh, it will. Do a good job on my license plate, willya?
My lifespan dwarfs yours. All I have to do is wait.
You'll all be dust in no time.
Well then our grandkids will find you and lock you up!
Come on, you.
Say, what's all this family talk, Torch? Do you have a sweetheart we don't know about?
Yeah bro, what's all that about?
Uh--no! I was just trying to--hey, no!
Johnny's got a girlfriend, Johnny's got a girlfriend...
Shut up, Ben! Gah!
Johnny and his girlfriend, sitting in a tree...
The End

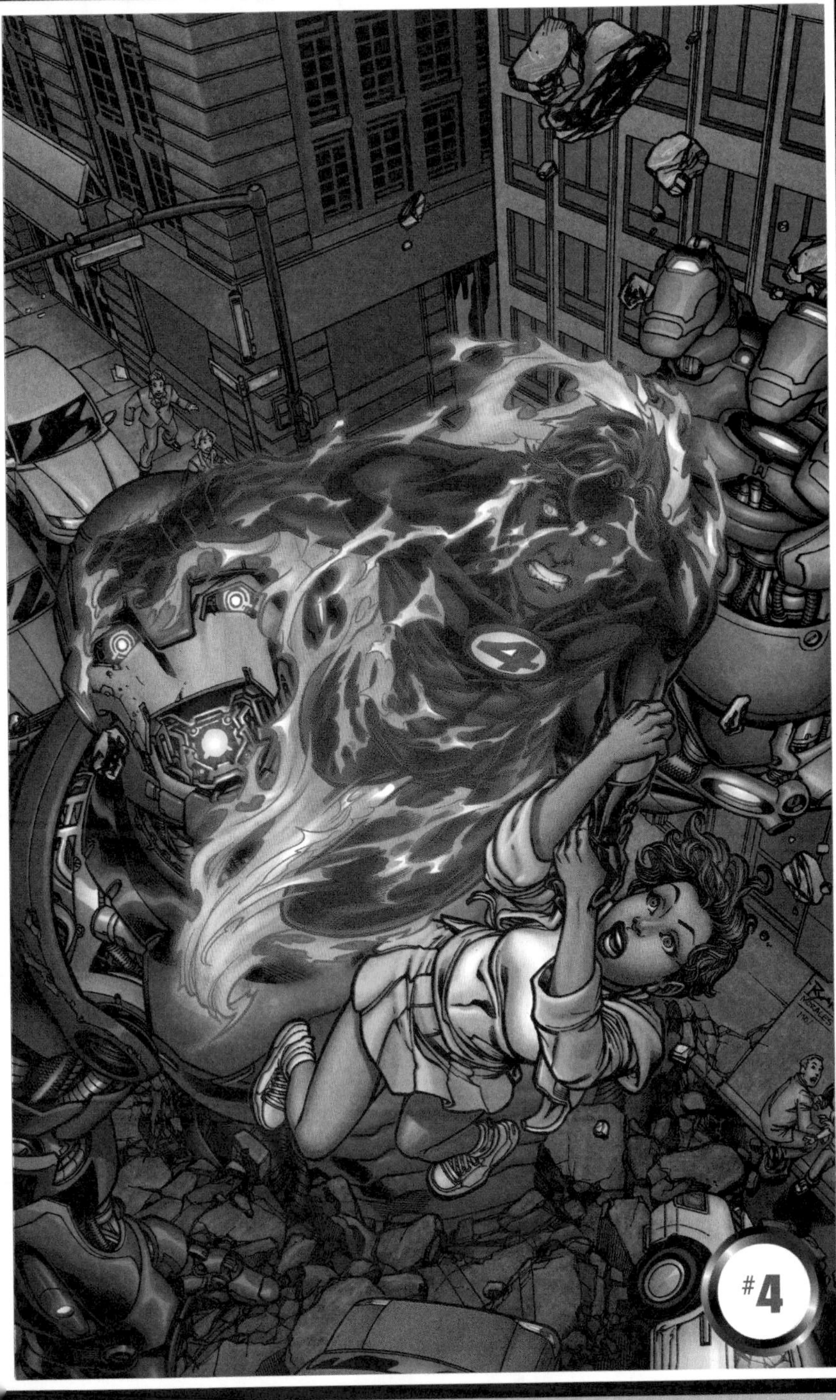
#4

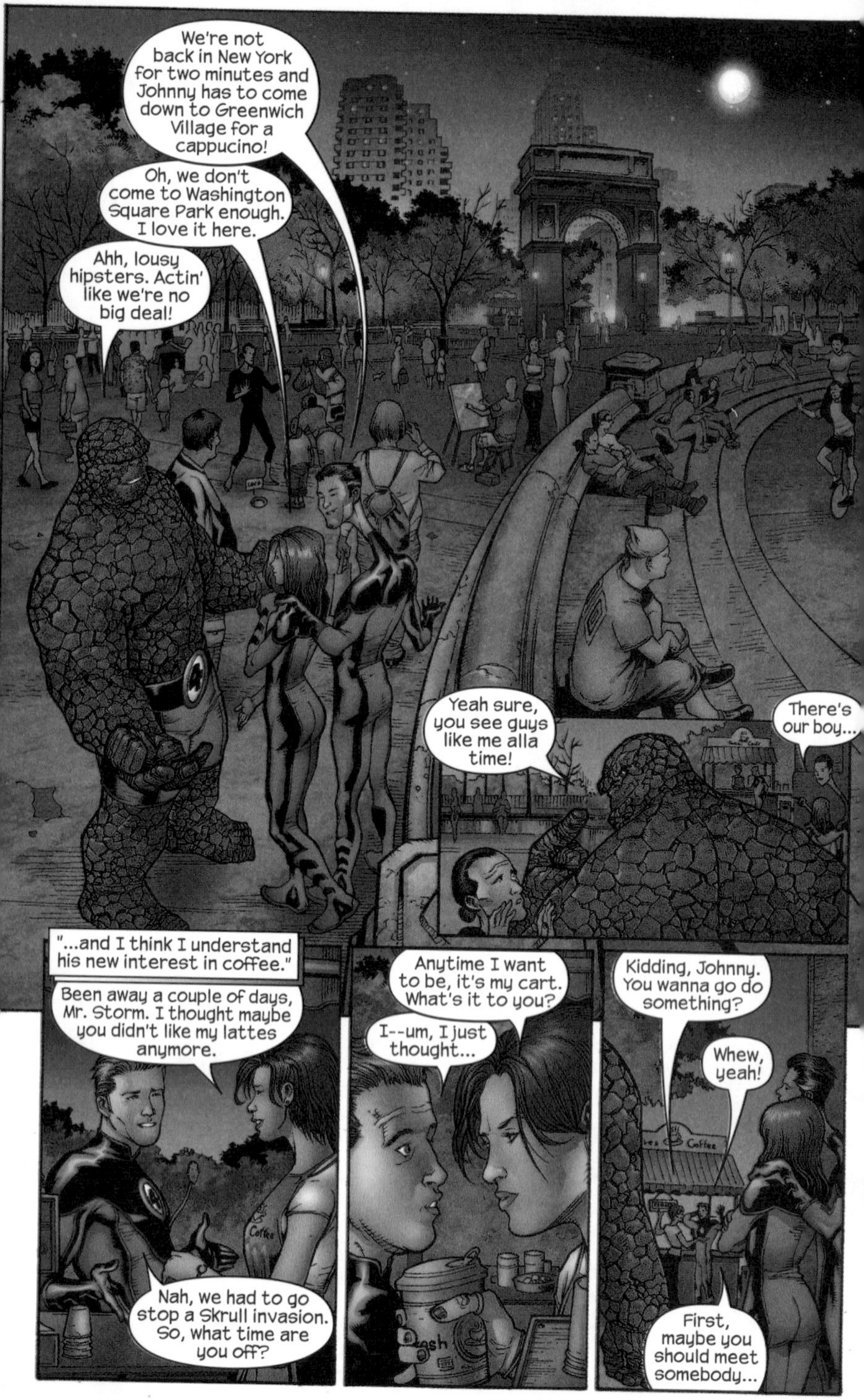
We're not back in New York for two minutes and Johnny has to come down to Greenwich Village for a cappucino!
Oh, we don't come to Washington Square Park enough. I love it here.
Ahh, lousy hipsters. Actin' like we're no big deal!
Yeah sure, you see guys like me alla time!
There's our boy...
"...and I think I understand his new interest in coffee."
Been away a couple of days, Mr. Storm. I thought maybe you didn't like my lattes anymore.
Nah, we had to go stop a Skrull invasion. So, what time are you off?
Anytime I want to be, it's my cart. What's it to you?
I--um, I just thought...
Kidding, Johnny. You wanna go do something?
Whew, yeah!
First, maybe you should meet somebody...

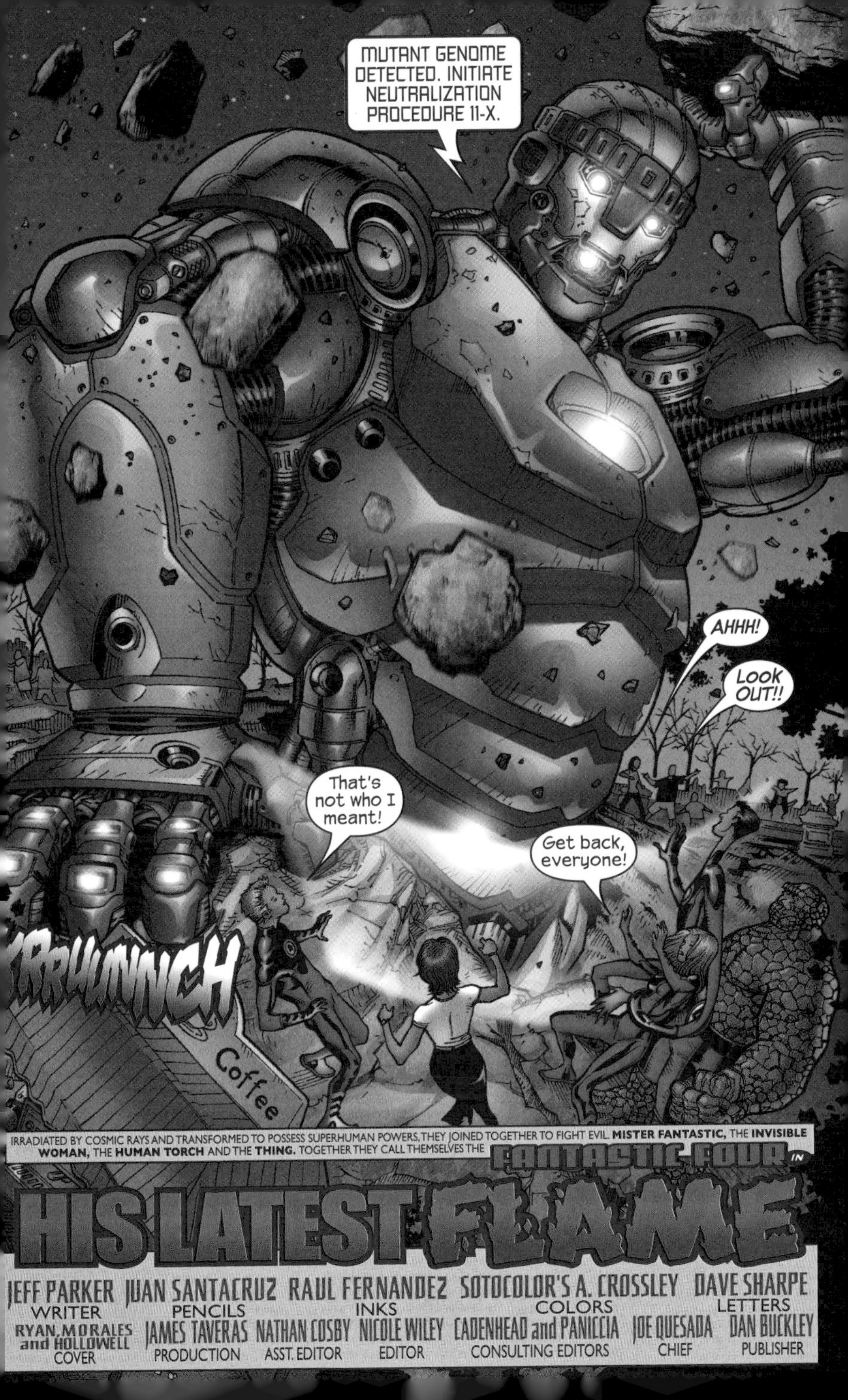
MUTANT GENOME DETECTED. INITIATE NEUTRALIZATION PROCEDURE 11-X.
AHHH!
LOOK OUT!!
That's not who I meant!
Get back, everyone!
RRUNNCH
Coffee
IRRADIATED BY COSMIC RAYS AND TRANSFORMED TO POSSESS SUPERHUMAN POWERS, THEY JOINED TOGETHER TO FIGHT EVIL. MISTER FANTASTIC, THE INVISIBLE WOMAN, THE HUMAN TORCH AND THE THING. TOGETHER THEY CALL THEMSELVES THE FANTASTIC FOUR IN
HIS LATEST FLAME
JEFF PARKER WRITER
JUAN SANTACRUZ PENCILS
RAUL FERNANDEZ INKS
SOTOCOLOR'S A. CROSSLEY COLORS
DAVE SHARPE LETTERS
RYAN, MORALES and HOLLOWELL COVER
JAMES TAVERAS PRODUCTION
NATHAN COSBY ASST. EDITOR
NICOLE WILEY EDITOR
CADENHEAD and PANICCIA CONSULTING EDITORS
JOE QUESADA CHIEF
DAN BUCKLEY PUBLISHER

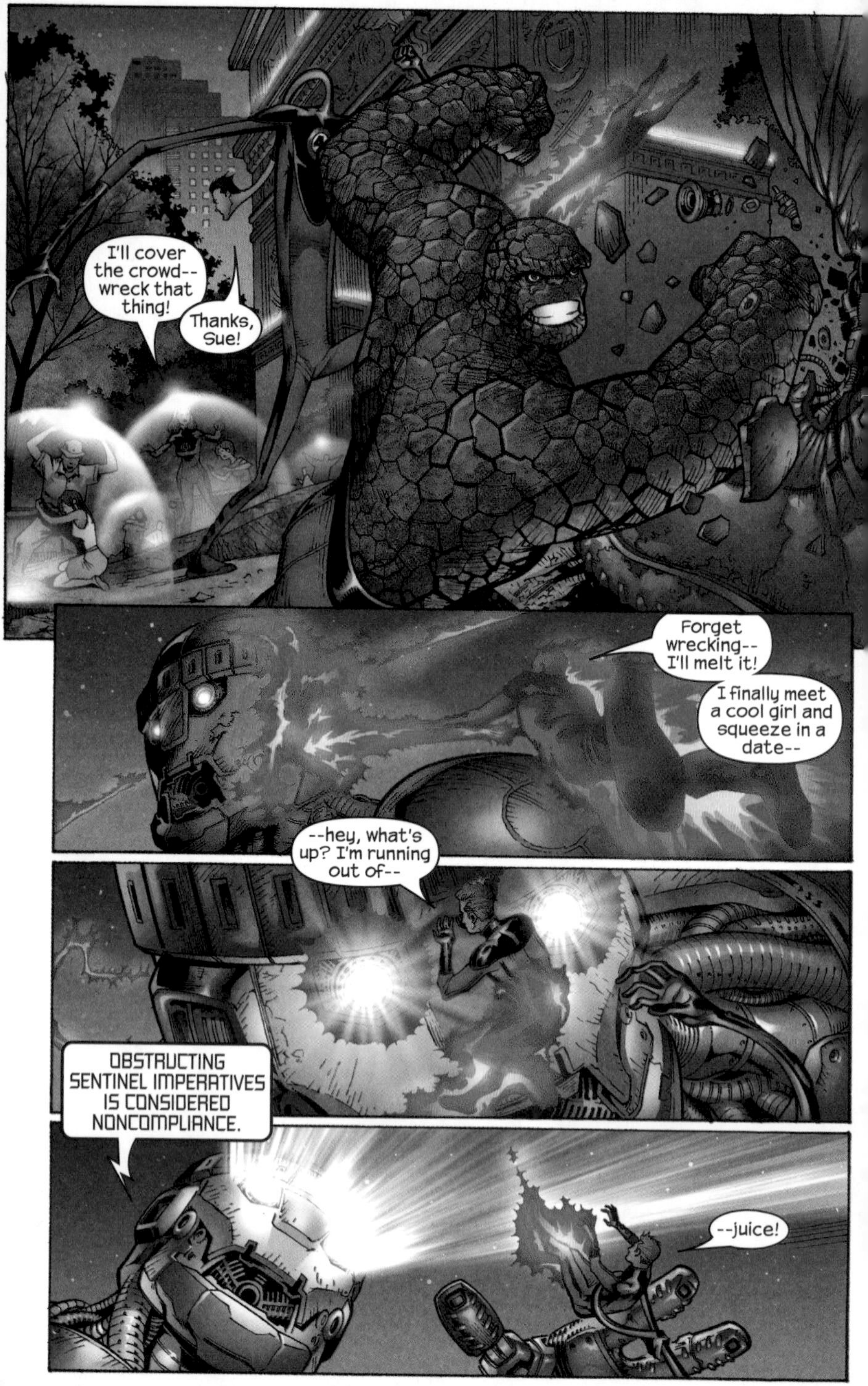
I'll cover the crowd--wreck that thing!
Thanks, Sue!
Forget wrecking--I'll melt it!
I finally meet a cool girl and squeeze in a date--
--hey, what's up? I'm running out of--
OBSTRUCTING SENTINEL IMPERATIVES IS CONSIDERED NONCOMPLIANCE.
--juice!

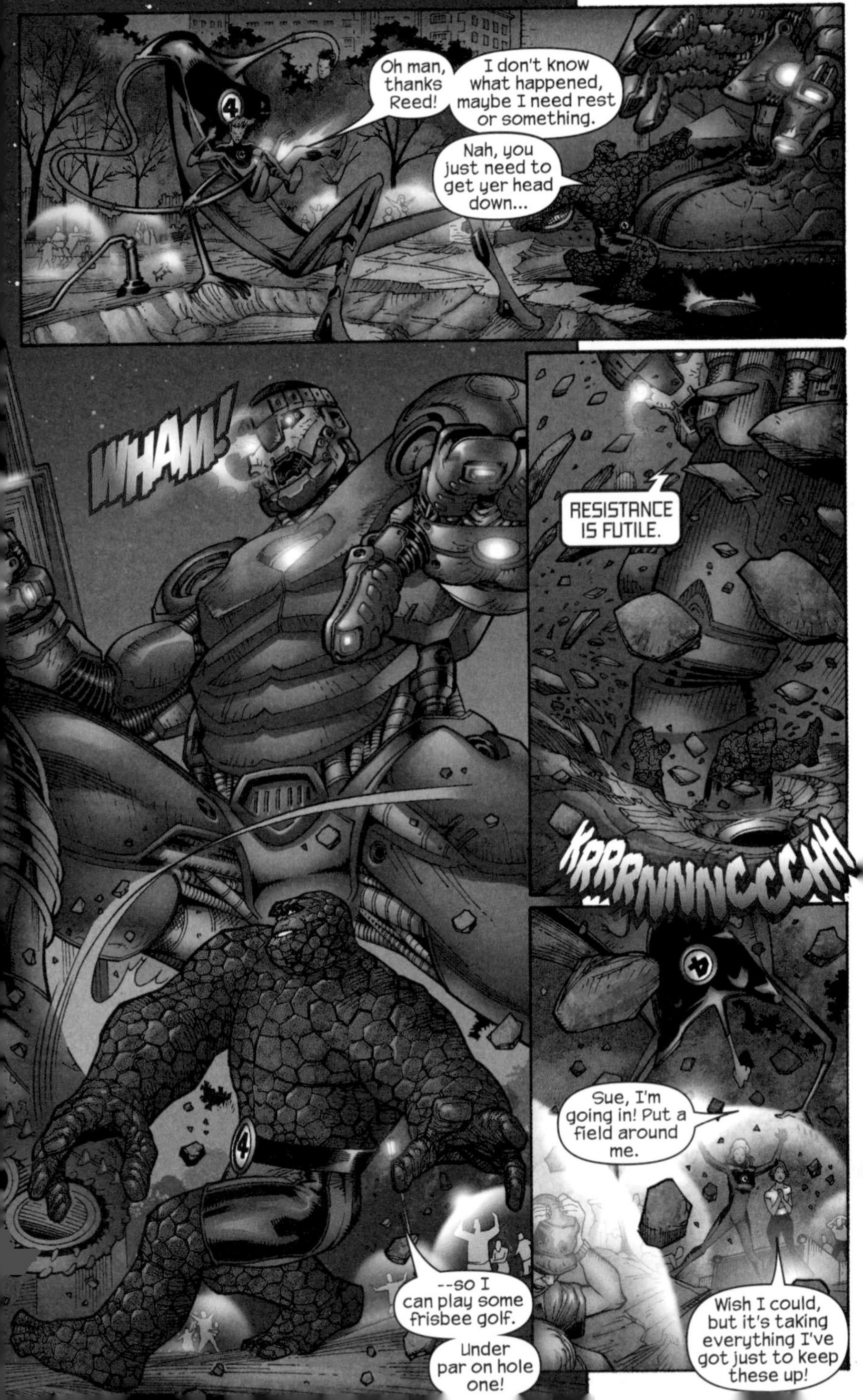
Oh man, thanks Reed!
I don't know what happened, maybe I need rest or something.
Nah, you just need to get yer head down...
WHAM!
RESISTANCE IS FUTILE.
KRRRNNNNCCCHH
--so I can play some frisbee golf.
Under par on hole one!
Sue, I'm going in! Put a field around me.
Wish I could, but it's taking everything I've got just to keep these up!

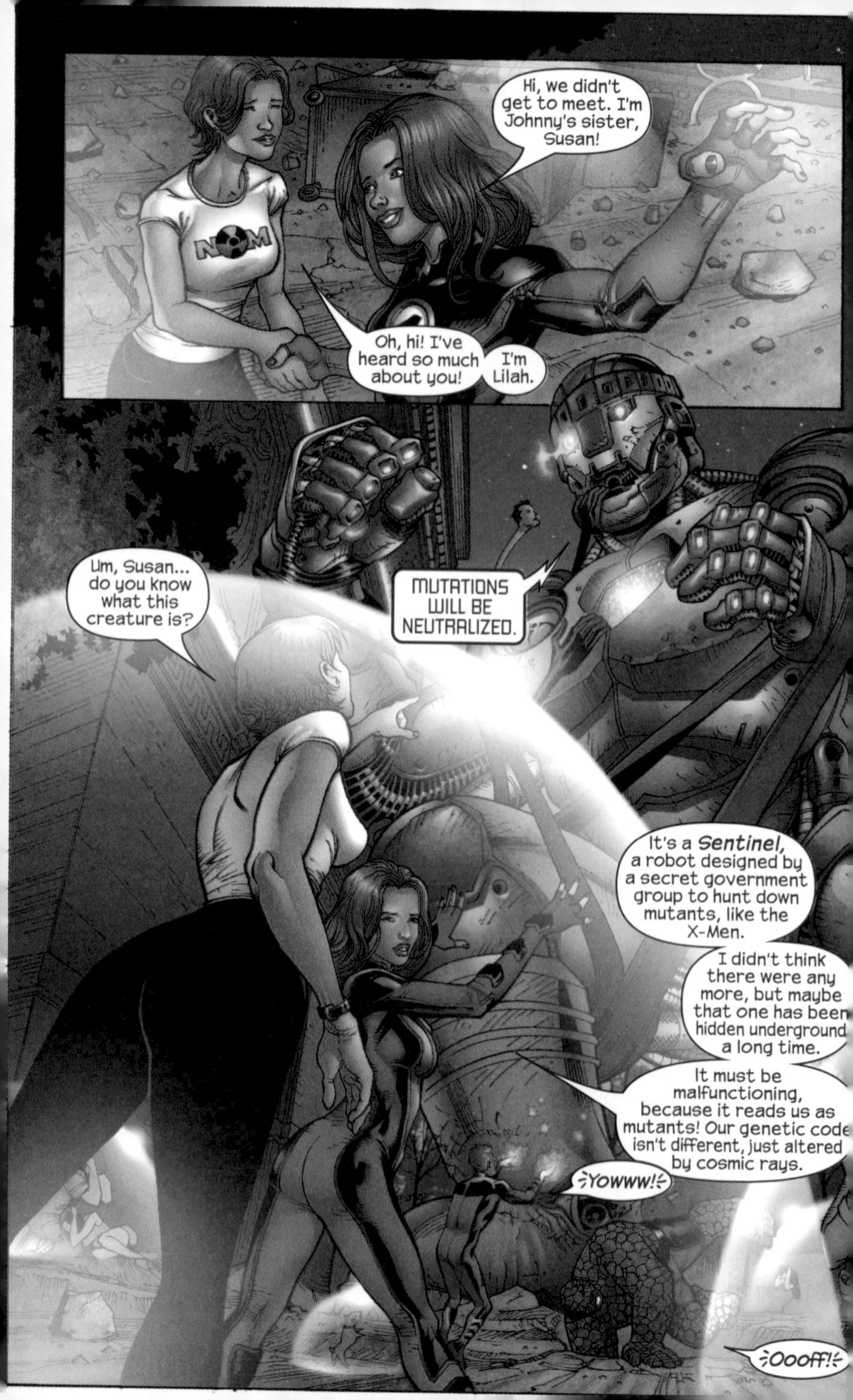
Hi, we didn't get to meet. I'm Johnny's sister, Susan!
Oh, hi! I've heard so much about you!
I'm Lilah.
Um, Susan... do you know what this creature is?
MUTATIONS WILL BE NEUTRALIZED.
It's a *Sentinel,* a robot designed by a secret government group to hunt down mutants, like the X-Men.
I didn't think there were any more, but maybe that one has been hidden underground a long time.
It must be malfunctioning, because it reads us as mutants! Our genetic code isn't different, just altered by cosmic rays.
YOWWW!
Oooff!

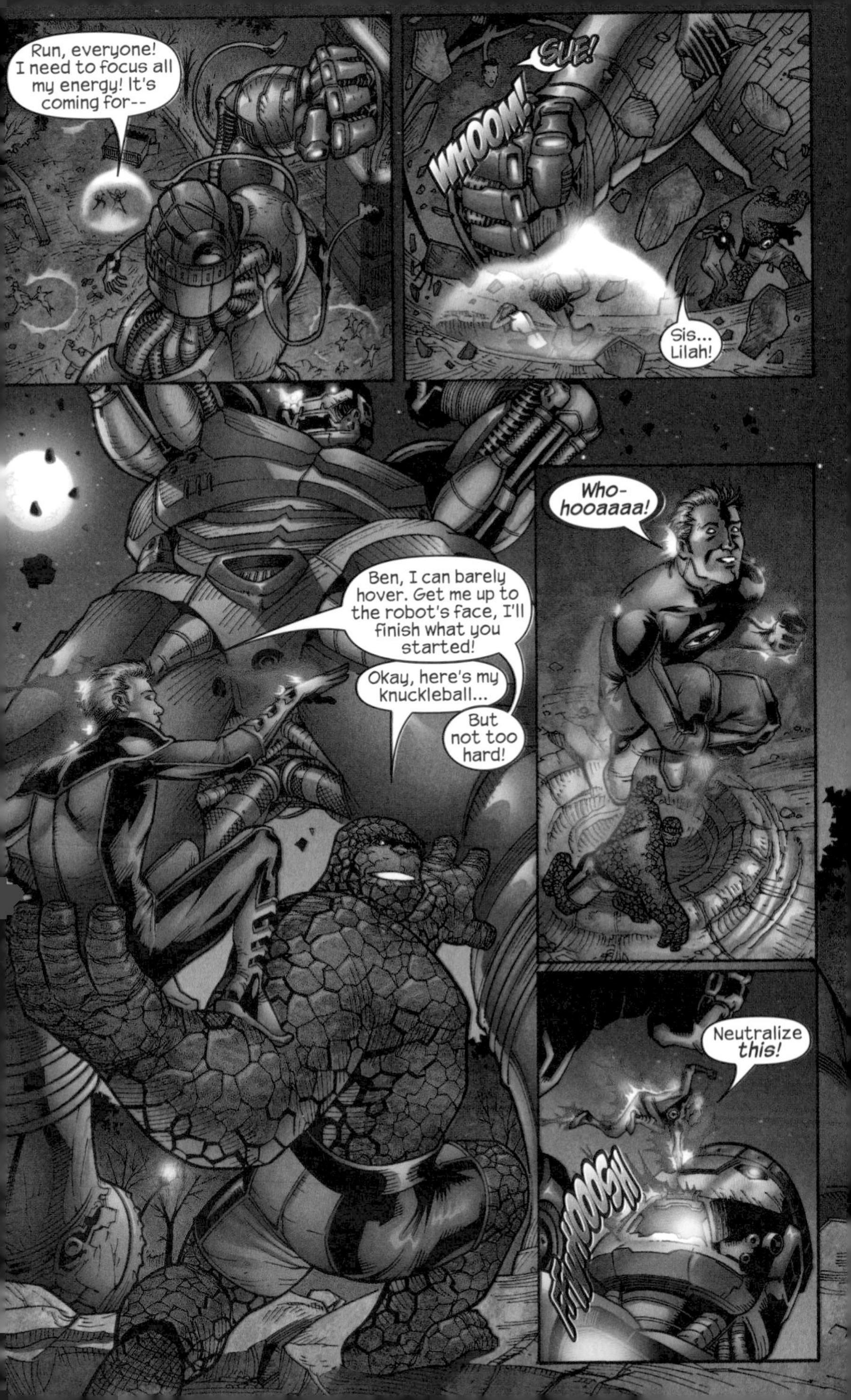
Run, everyone! I need to focus all my energy! It's coming for--
SUE!
WHOOM!
Sis... Lilah!
Ben, I can barely hover. Get me up to the robot's face, I'll finish what you started!
Okay, here's my knuckleball...
But not too hard!
Who-hooaaaa!
Neutralize this!
FWOOOSH!

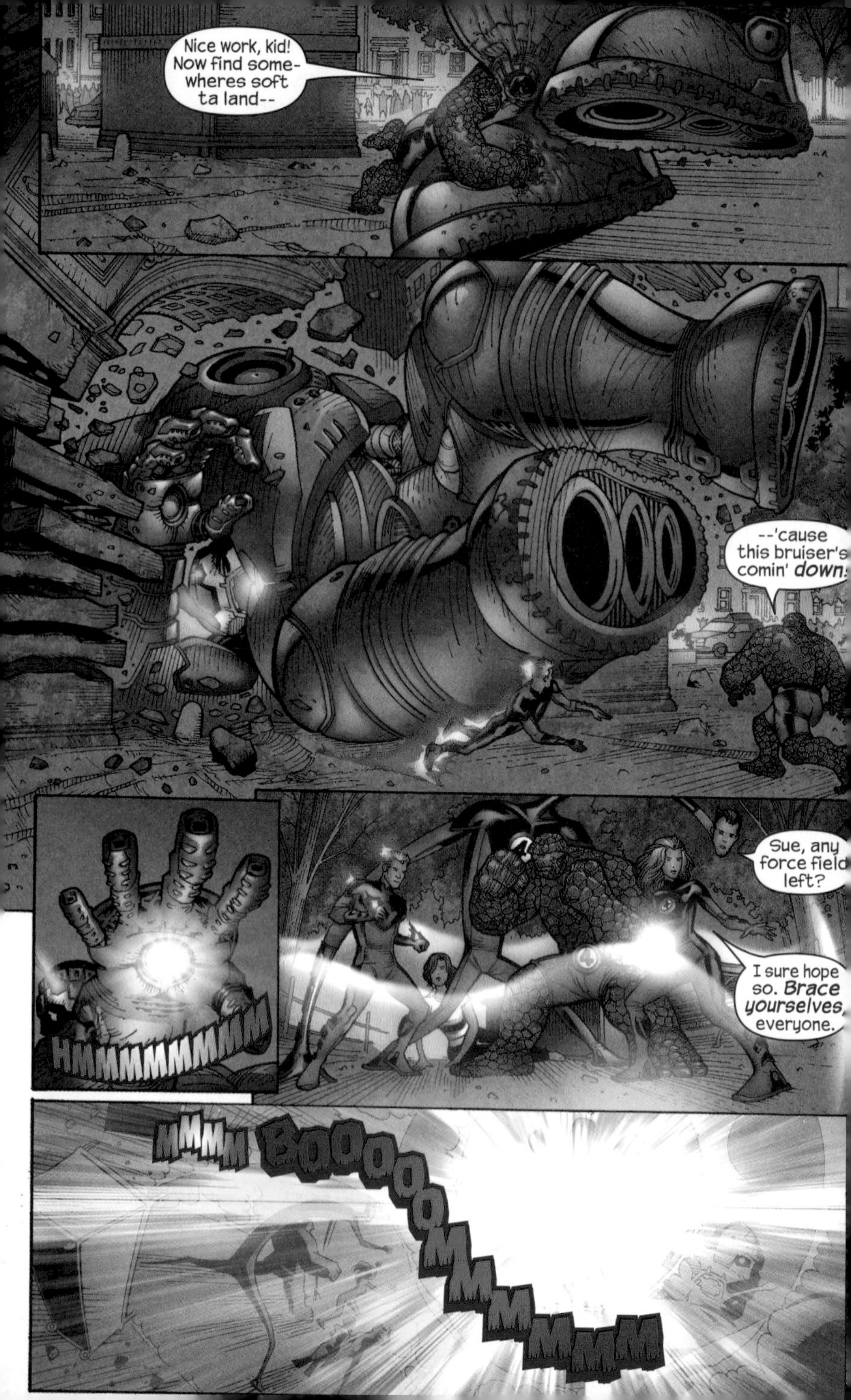
Nice work, kid! Now find some-wheres soft ta land--
--'cause this bruiser's comin' *down*!
HMMMMMMMMM
Sue, any force field left?
I sure hope so. *Brace yourselves,* everyone.
MMMM BOOOOOOMMMMMMMMM

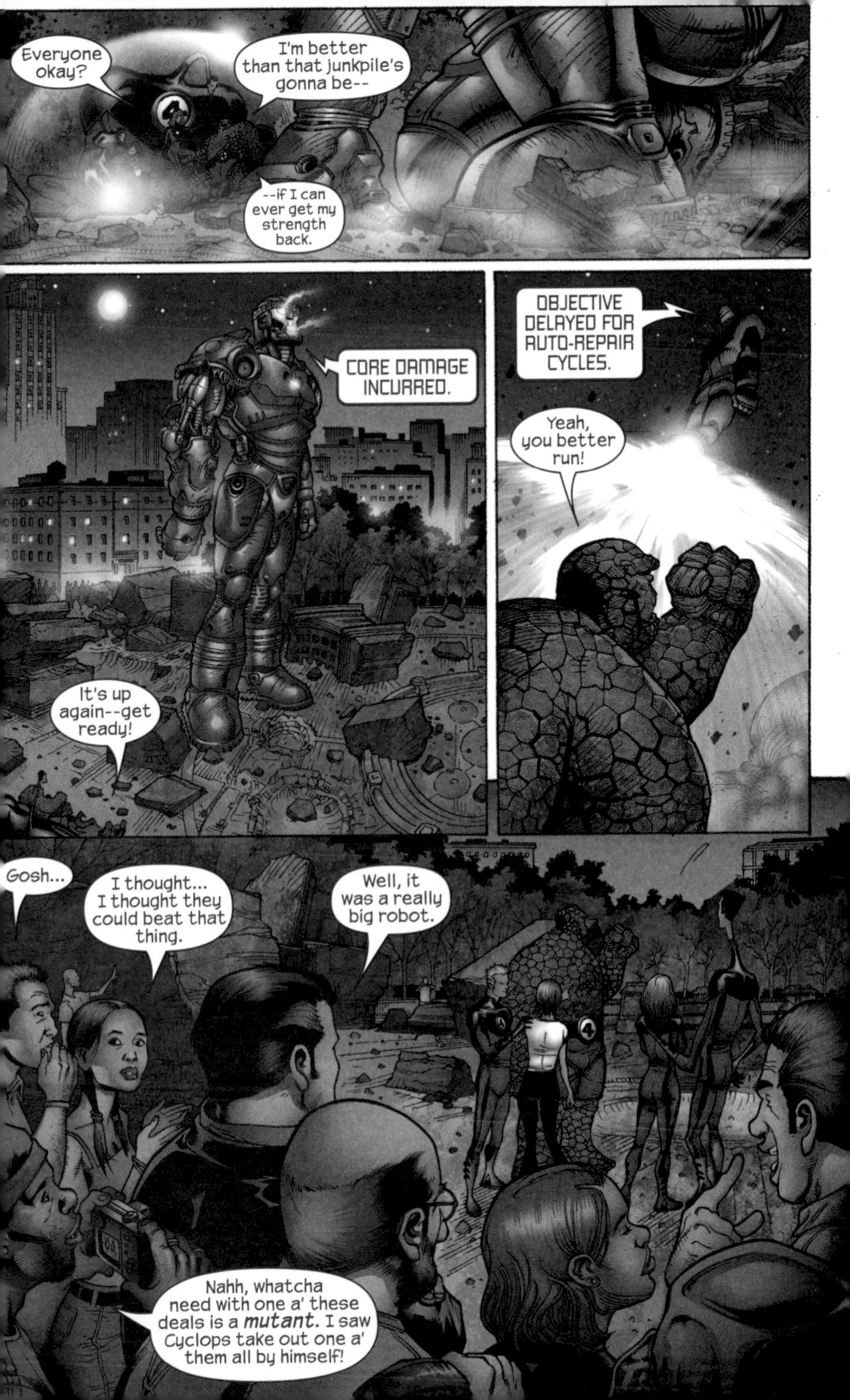
Everyone okay?
I'm better than that junkpile's gonna be--
--if I can ever get my strength back.
CORE DAMAGE INCURRED.
It's up again--get ready!
OBJECTIVE DELAYED FOR AUTO-REPAIR CYCLES.
Yeah, you better run!
Gosh...
I thought... I thought they could beat that thing.
Well, it was a really big robot.
Nahh, whatcha need with one a' these deals is a *mutant*. I saw Cyclops take out one a' them all by himself!

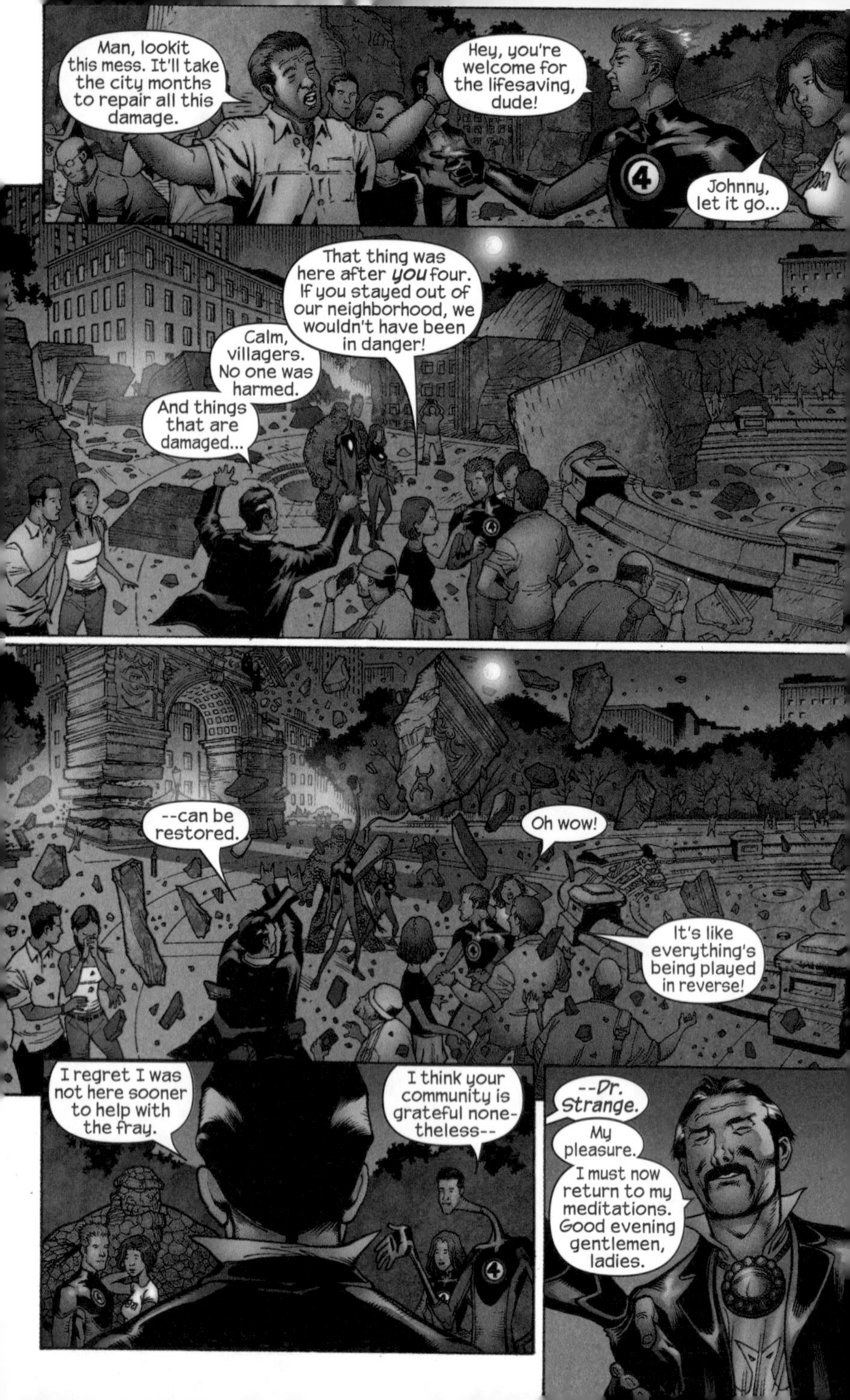
Man, lookit this mess. It'll take the city months to repair all this damage.
Hey, you're welcome for the lifesaving, dude!
Johnny, let it go...
That thing was here after *YOU* four. If you stayed out of our neighborhood, we wouldn't have been in danger!
Calm, villagers. No one was harmed.
And things that are damaged...
--can be restored.
Oh wow!
It's like everything's being played in reverse!
I regret I was not here sooner to help with the fray.
I think your community is grateful none-theless--
--Dr. Strange.
My pleasure.
I must now return to my meditations. Good evening gentlemen, ladies.

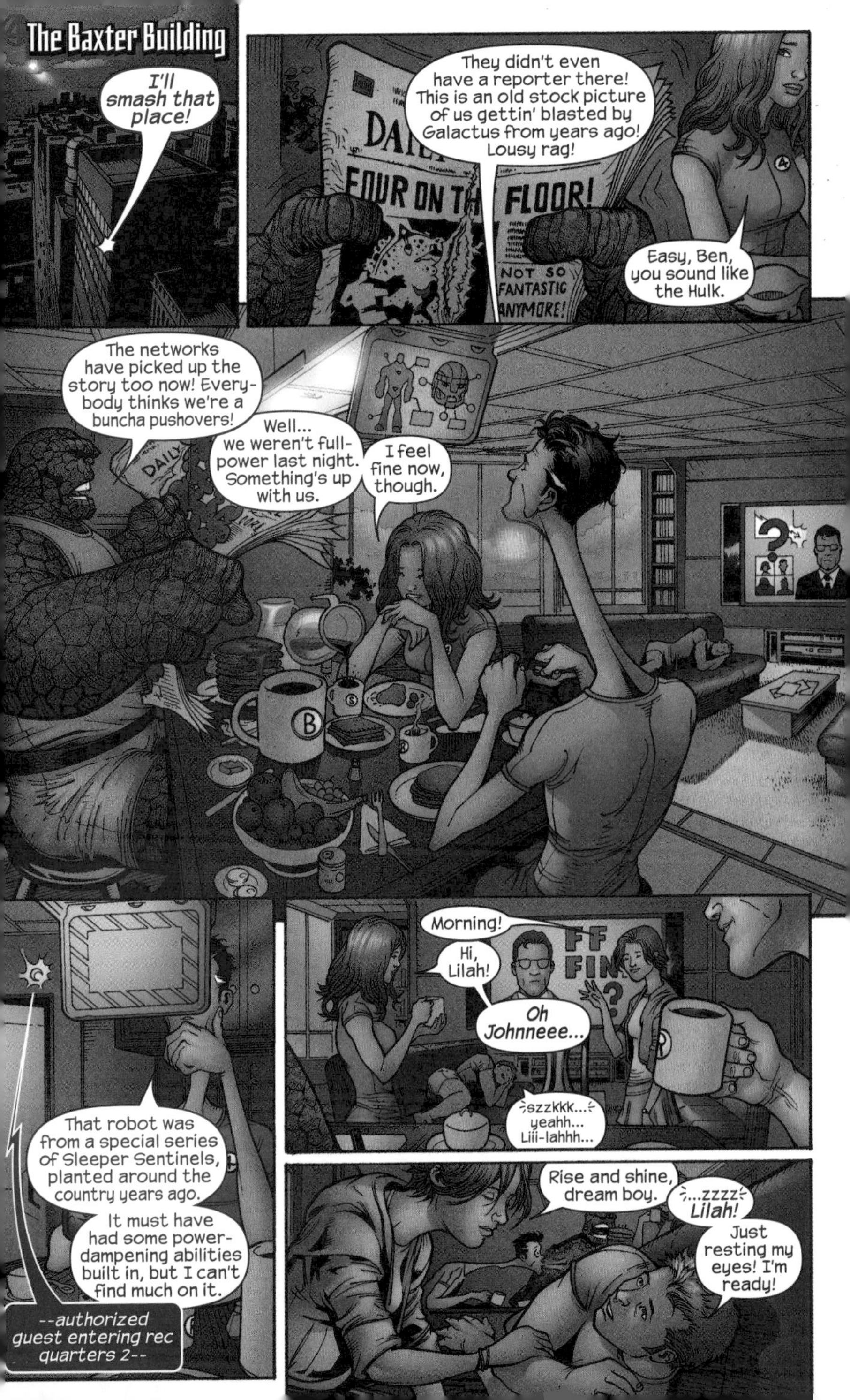

The Baxter Building
I'll smash that place!
They didn't even have a reporter there! This is an old stock picture of us gettin' blasted by Galactus from years ago! Lousy rag!
DAILY
FOUR ON THE FLOOR!
NOT SO FANTASTIC ANYMORE!
Easy, Ben, you sound like the Hulk.
The networks have picked up the story too now! Everybody thinks we're a buncha pushovers!
Well... we weren't full-power last night. Something's up with us.
I feel fine now, though.
That robot was from a special series of Sleeper Sentinels, planted around the country years ago.
It must have had some power-dampening abilities built in, but I can't find much on it.
--authorized guest entering rec quarters 2--
Morning!
Hi, Lilah!
Oh Johnneee...
...szzkkk... yeahh... Liii-lahhh...
Rise and shine, dream boy.
...zzzz Lilah!
Just resting my eyes! I'm ready!

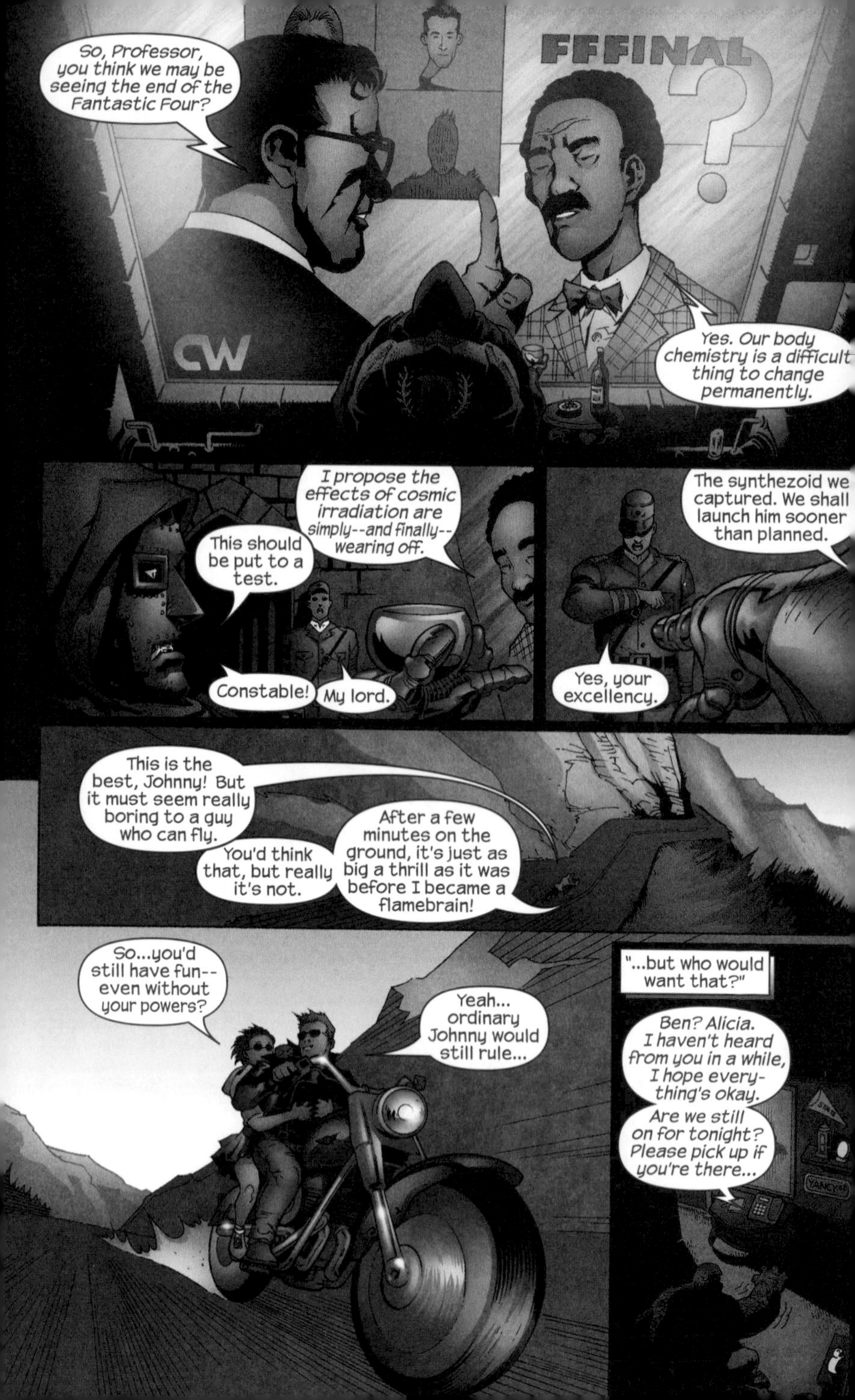

FFFINAL ?
So, Professor, you think we may be seeing the end of the Fantastic Four?
Yes. Our body chemistry is a difficult thing to change permanently.
CW
I propose the effects of cosmic irradiation are simply--and finally--wearing off.
This should be put to a test.
Constable!
My lord.
The synthezoid we captured. We shall launch him sooner than planned.
Yes, your excellency.
This is the best, Johnny! But it must seem really boring to a guy who can fly.
You'd think that, but really it's not.
After a few minutes on the ground, it's just as big a thrill as it was before I became a flamebrain!
So...you'd still have fun--even without your powers?
Yeah... ordinary Johnny would still rule...
"...but who would want that?"
Ben? Alicia. I haven't heard from you in a while, I hope every-thing's okay.
Are we still on for tonight? Please pick up if you're there...

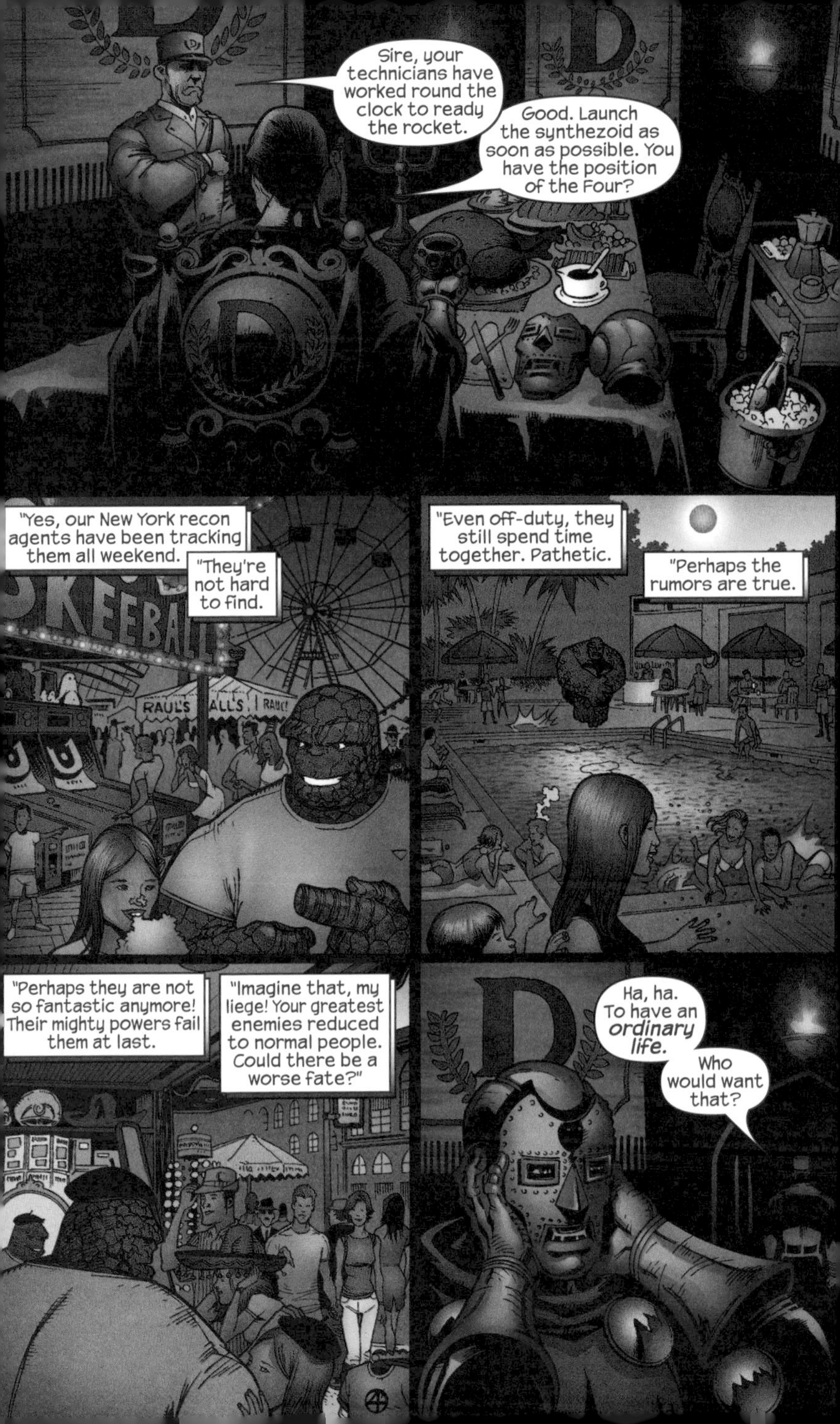
Sire, your technicians have worked round the clock to ready the rocket.
Good. Launch the synthezoid as soon as possible. You have the position of the Four?
"Yes, our New York recon agents have been tracking them all weekend.
"They're not hard to find.
SKEEBALL
RAUL'S
"Even off-duty, they still spend time together. Pathetic.
"Perhaps the rumors are true.
"Perhaps they are not so fantastic anymore! Their mighty powers fail them at last.
"Imagine that, my liege! Your greatest enemies reduced to normal people. Could there be a worse fate?"
Ha, ha. To have an *ordinary life.*
Who would want that?

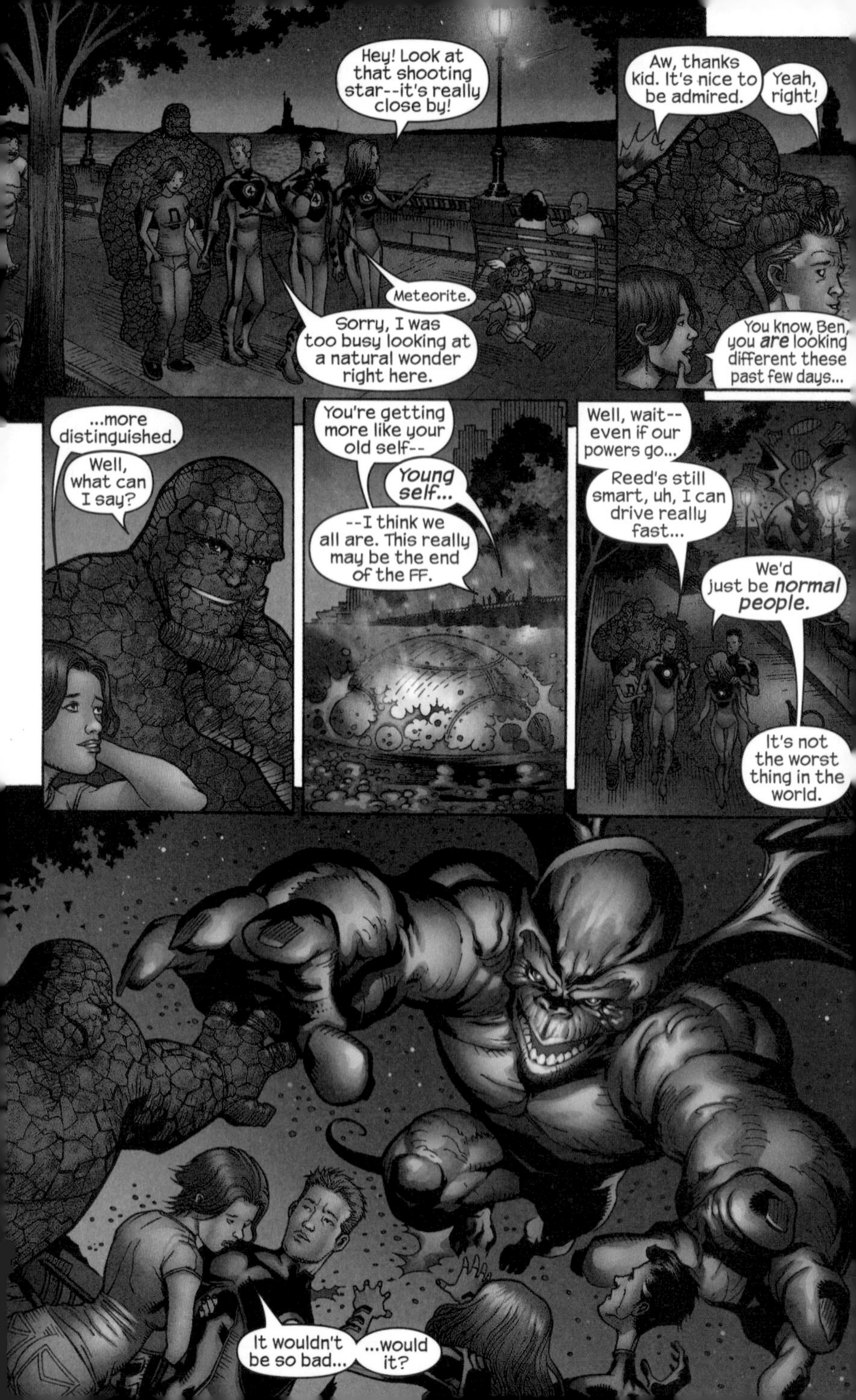
Hey! Look at that shooting star--it's really close by!
Meteorite.
Sorry, I was too busy looking at a natural wonder right here.
Aw, thanks kid. It's nice to be admired.
Yeah, right!
You know, Ben, you *are* looking different these past few days...
...more distinguished.
Well, what can I say?
You're getting more like your old self--
Young self...
--I think we all are. This really may be the end of the FF.
Well, wait--even if our powers go...
Reed's still smart, uh, I can drive really fast...
We'd just be ***normal people.***
It's not the worst thing in the world.
It wouldn't be so bad...
...would it?

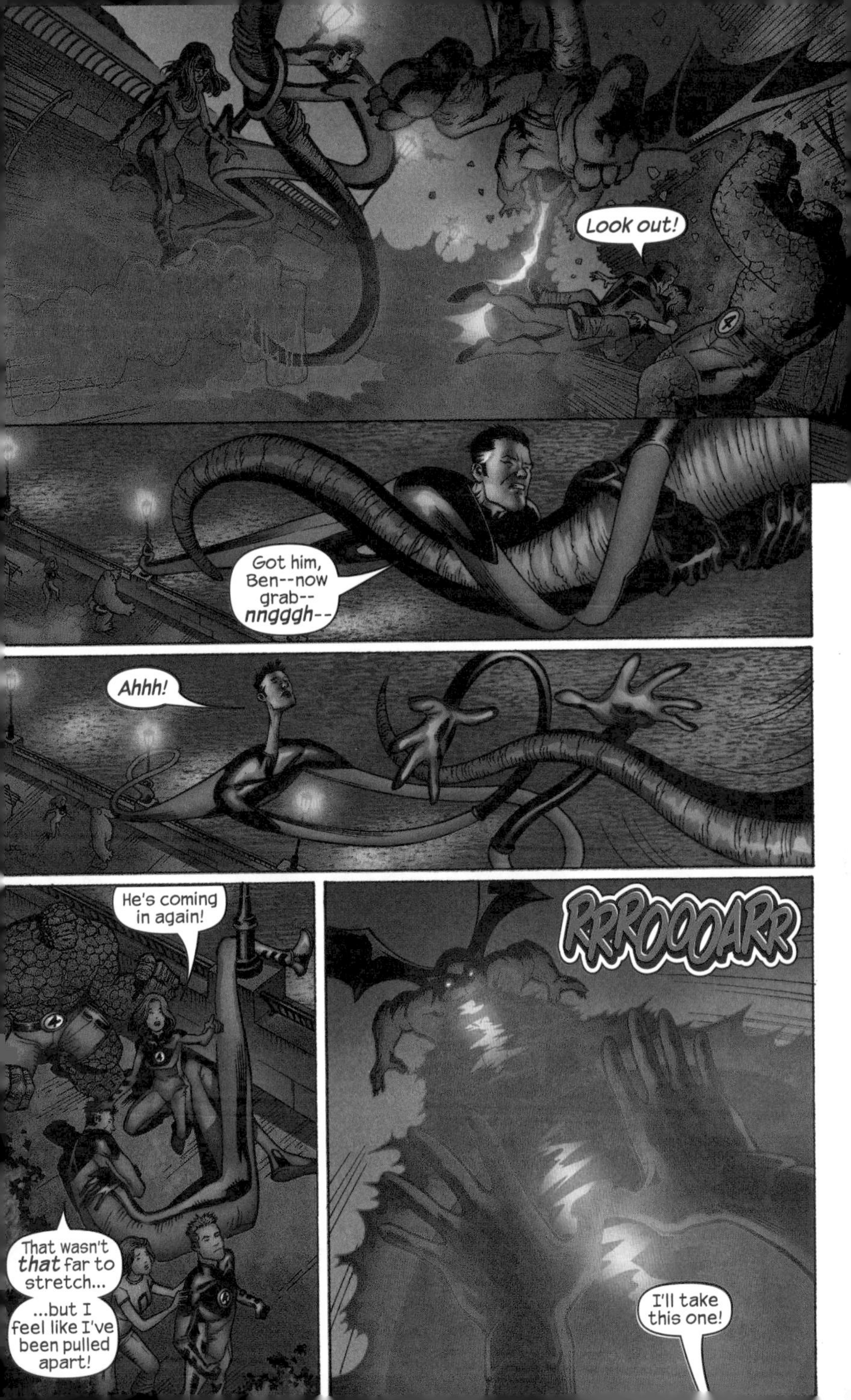
Look out!
Got him, Ben--now grab--*nngggh*--
Ahhh!
He's coming in again!
That wasn't *that* far to stretch...
...but I feel like I've been pulled apart!
RRROOOARR
I'll take this one!

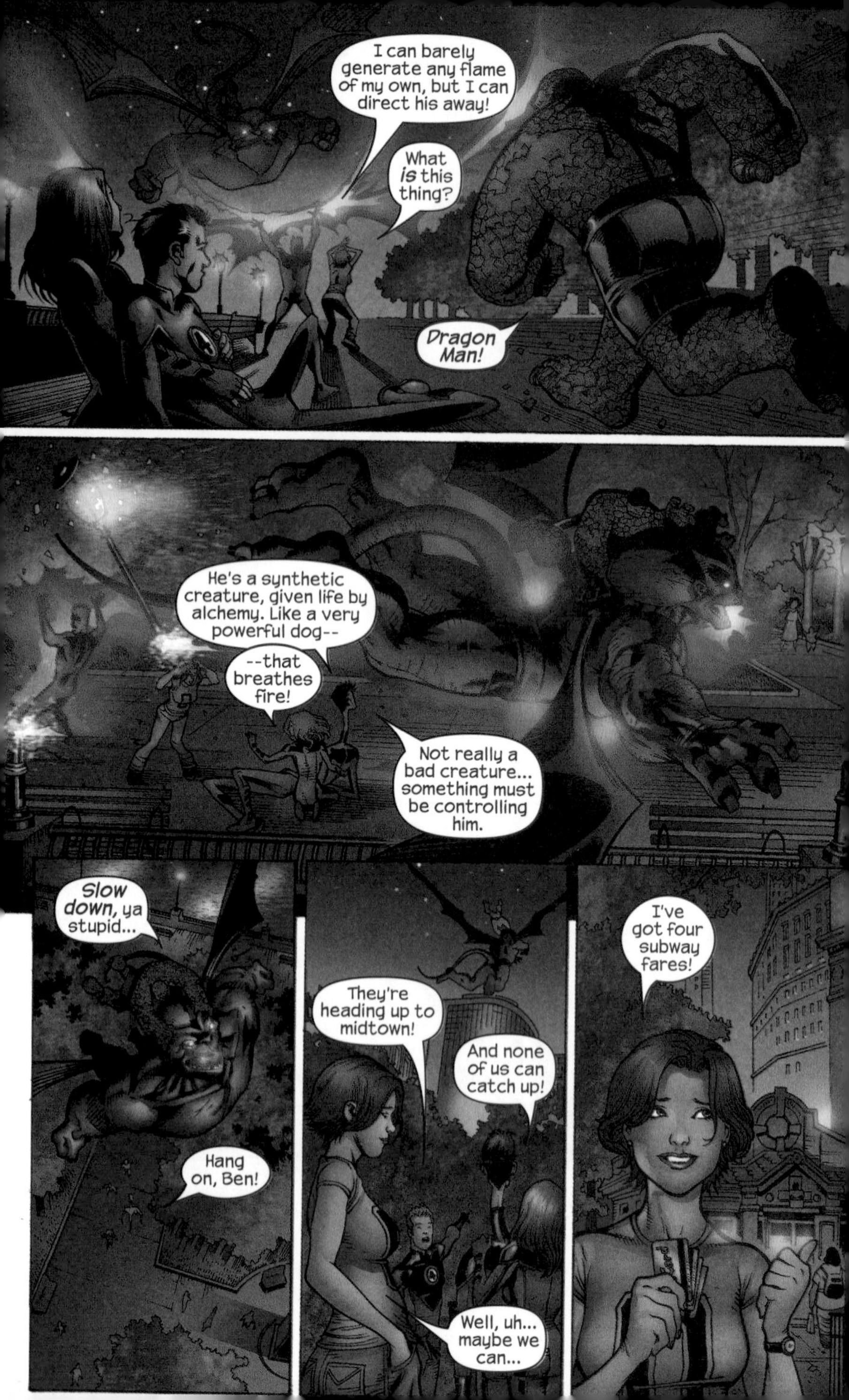
I can barely generate any flame of my own, but I can direct his away!
What *is* this thing?
Dragon Man!
He's a synthetic creature, given life by alchemy. Like a very powerful dog--
--that breathes fire!
Not really a bad creature... something must be controlling him.
Slow down, ya stupid...
Hang on, Ben!
They're heading up to midtown!
And none of us can catch up!
Well, uh... maybe we can...
I've got four subway fares!

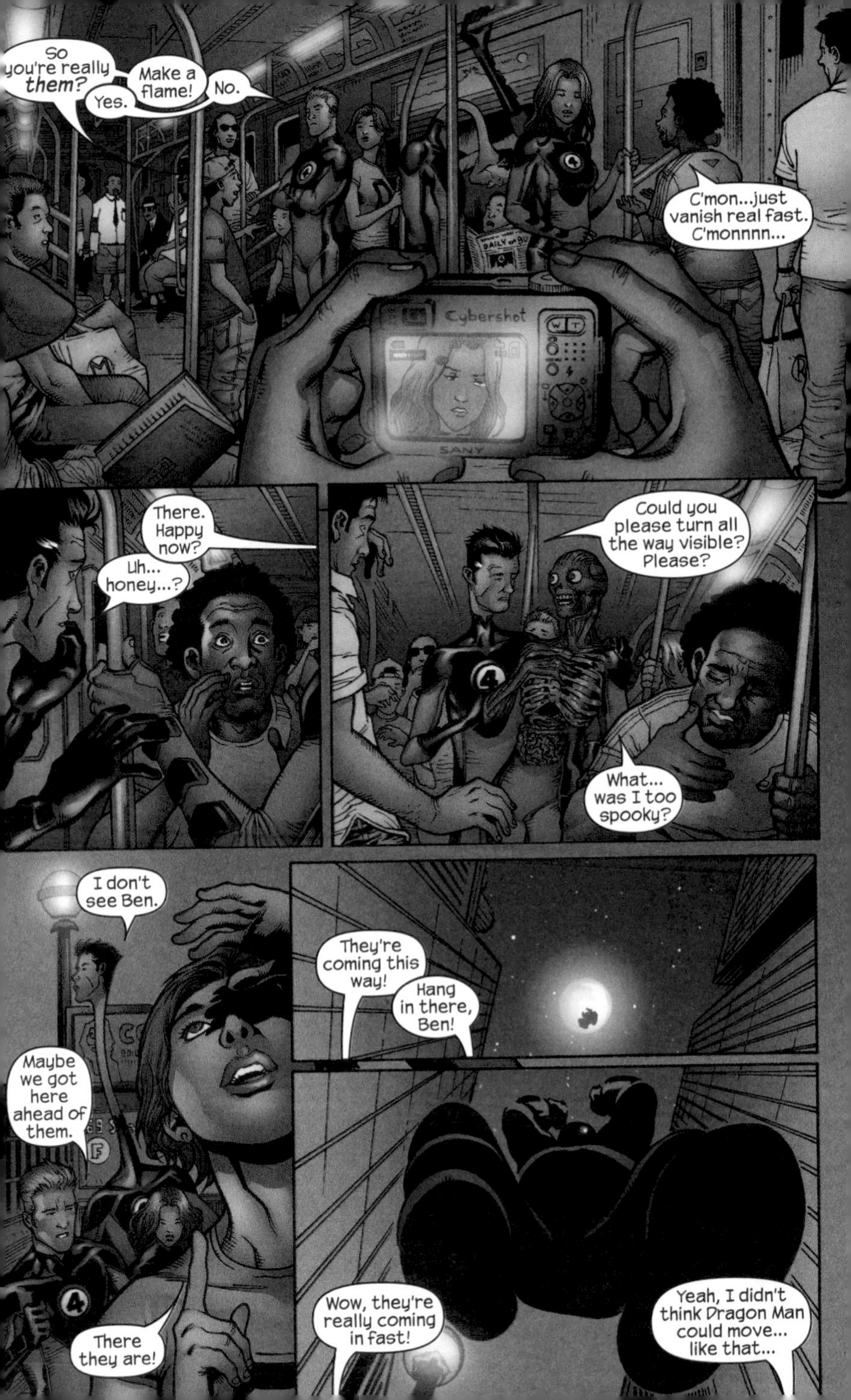

So you're really *them*?
Yes.
Make a flame!
No.
C'mon...just vanish real fast. C'monnnn...
Cybershot
SANY
There. Happy now?
Uh... honey...?
Could you please turn all the way visible? Please?
What... was I too spooky?
I don't see Ben.
Maybe we got here ahead of them.
There they are!
They're coming this way!
Hang in there, Ben!
Wow, they're really coming in fast!
Yeah, I didn't think Dragon Man could move... like that...

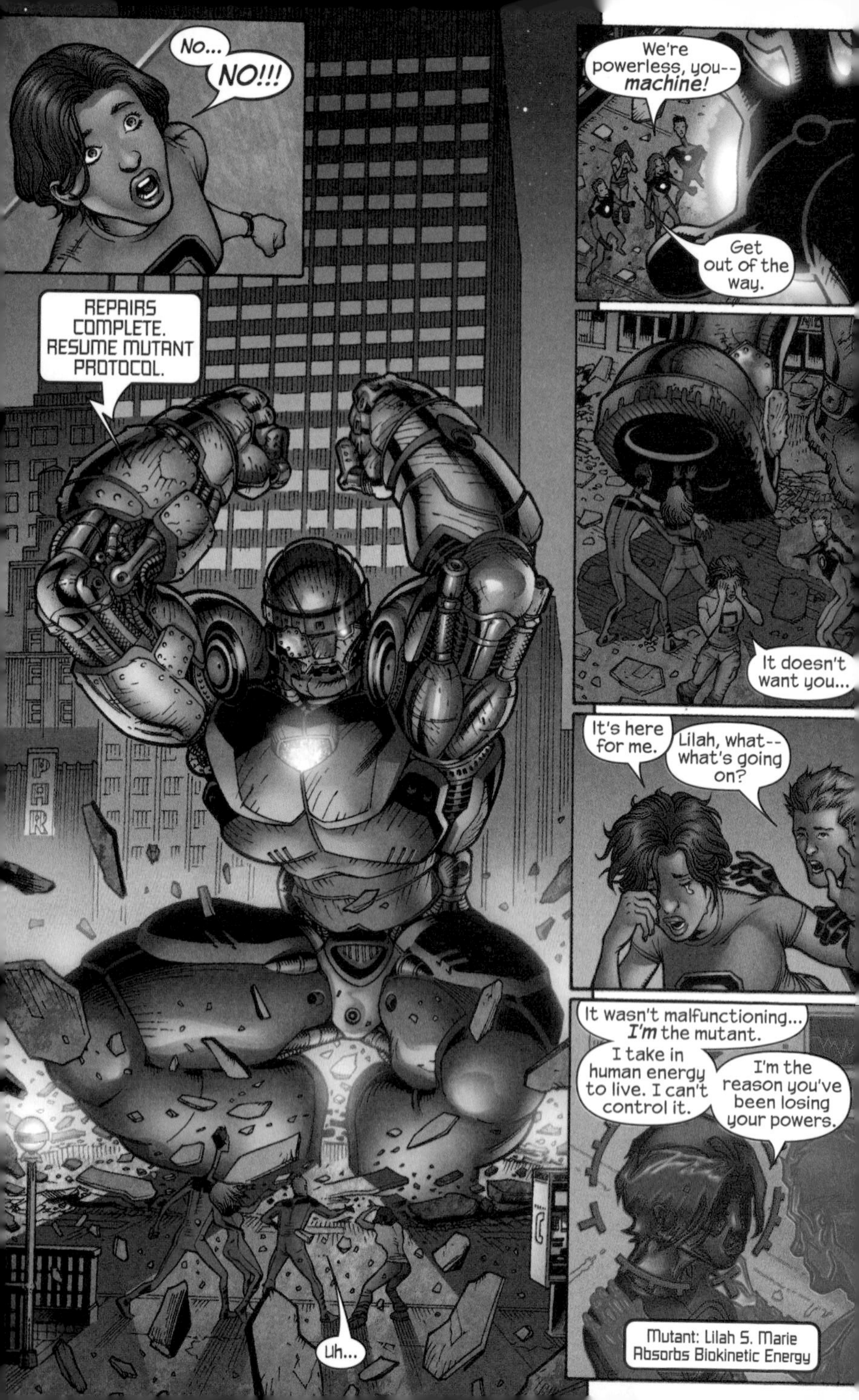
No...
NO!!!
REPAIRS COMPLETE. RESUME MUTANT PROTOCOL.
Uh...
We're powerless, you-- *machine!*
Get out of the way.
It doesn't want you...
It's here for me.
Lilah, what-- what's going on?
It wasn't malfunctioning... *I'm* the mutant.
I take in human energy to live. I can't control it.
I'm the reason you've been losing your powers.
Mutant: Lilah S. Marie
Absorbs Biokinetic Energy

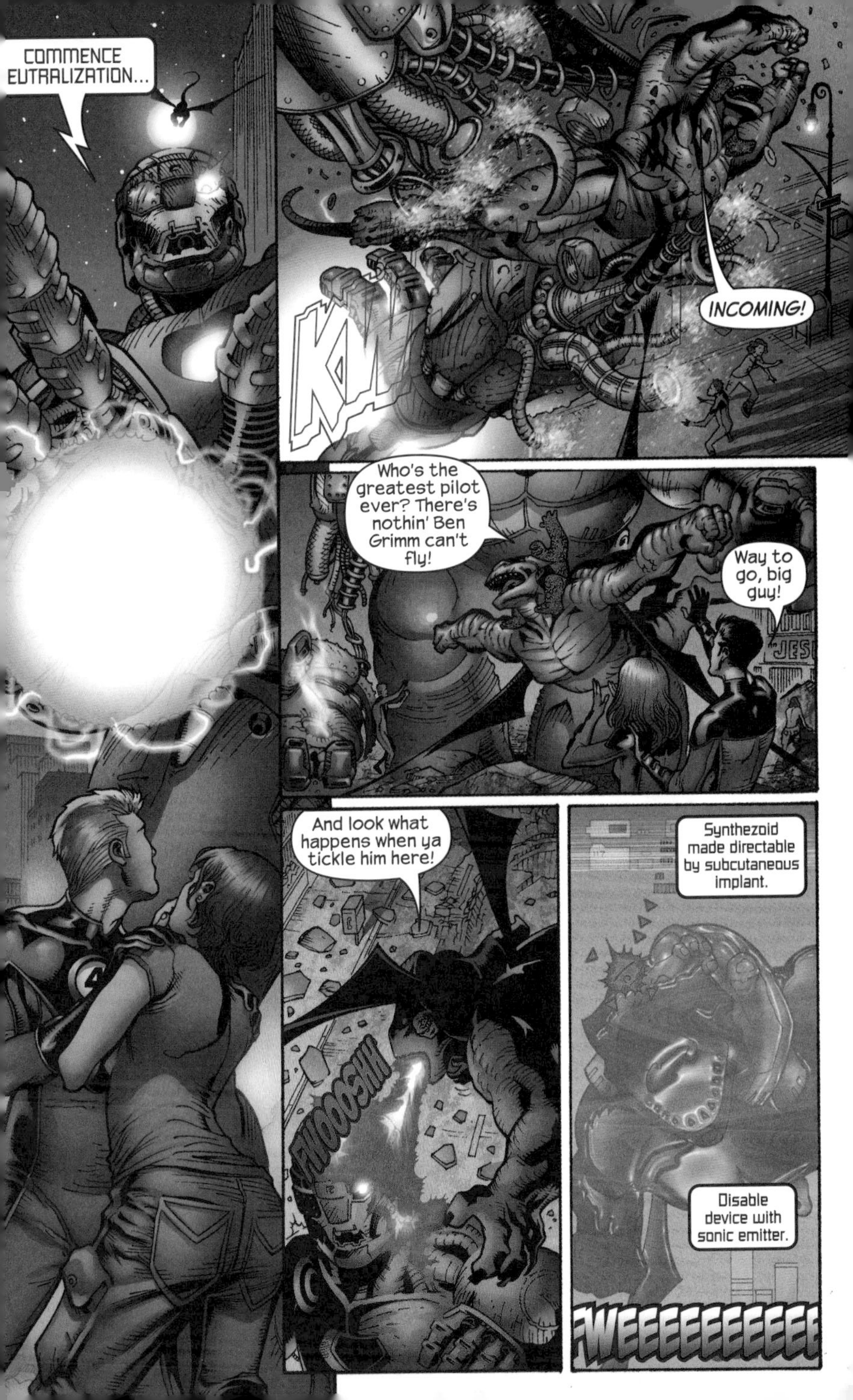
COMMENCE
EUTRALIZATION...
INCOMING!
Who's the greatest pilot ever? There's nothin' Ben Grimm can't fly!
Way to go, big guy!
And look what happens when ya tickle him here!
FWOOOSHH
Synthezoid made directable by subcutaneous implant.
Disable device with sonic emitter.
FWEEEEEEEEEE

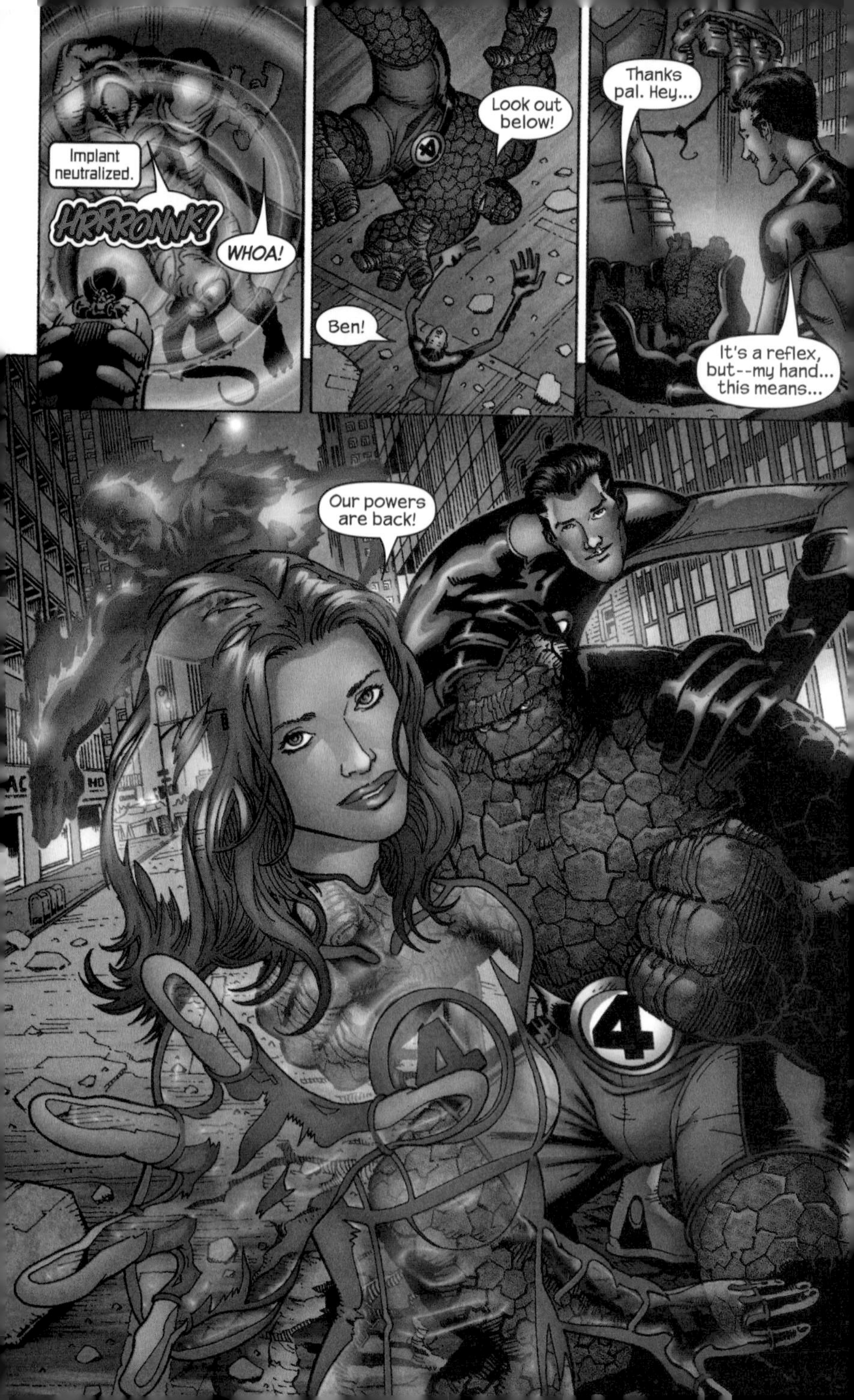
Implant neutralized.
HRRRONNK!
WHOA!
Look out below!
Ben!
Thanks pal. Hey...
It's a reflex, but--my hand... this means...
Our powers are back!

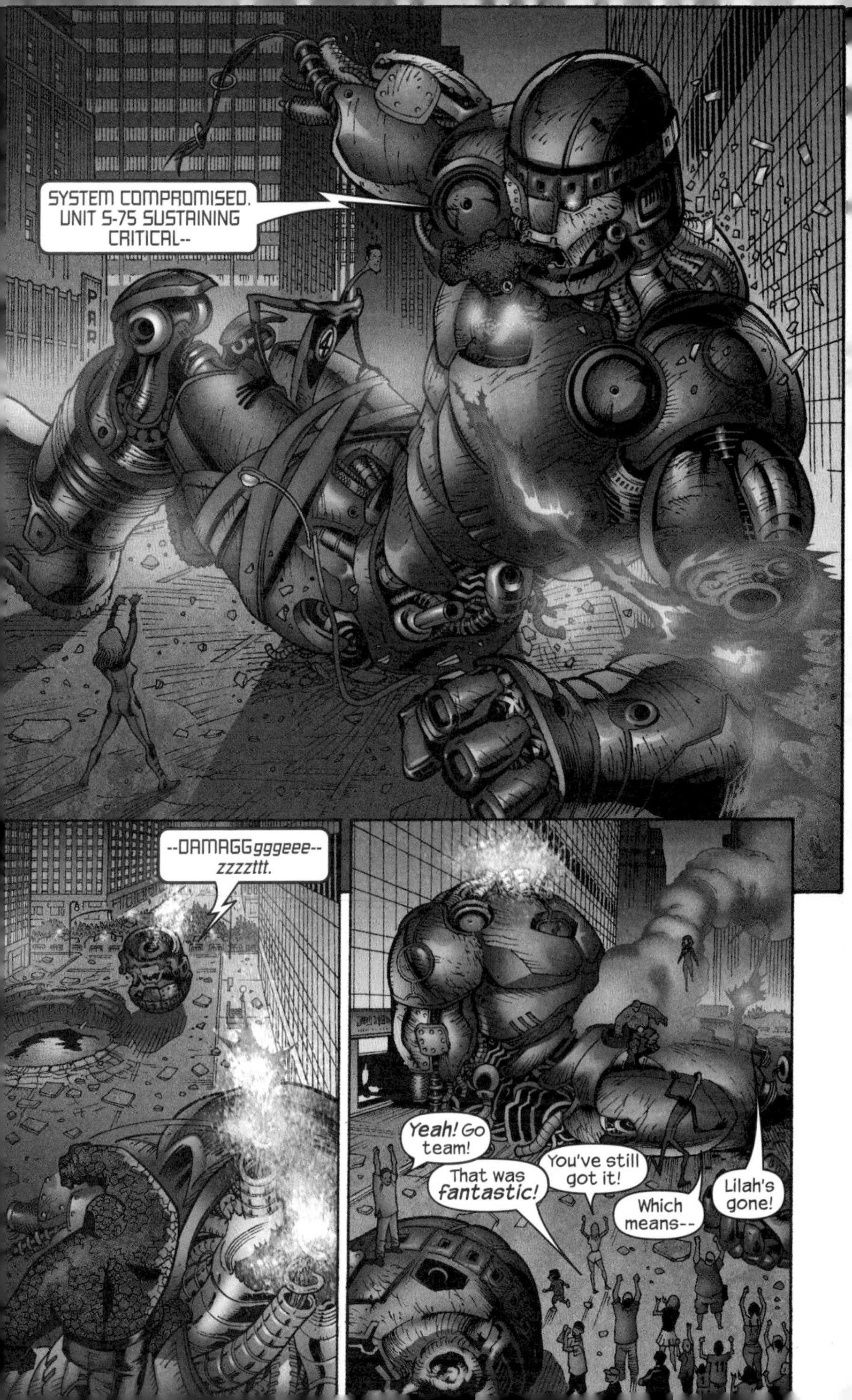
SYSTEM COMPROMISED. UNIT S-75 SUSTAINING CRITICAL--
--DAMAGG*gggeee*-- *zzzzttt.*
Yeah! Go team!
That was *fantastic!*
You've still got it!
Which means--
Lilah's gone!

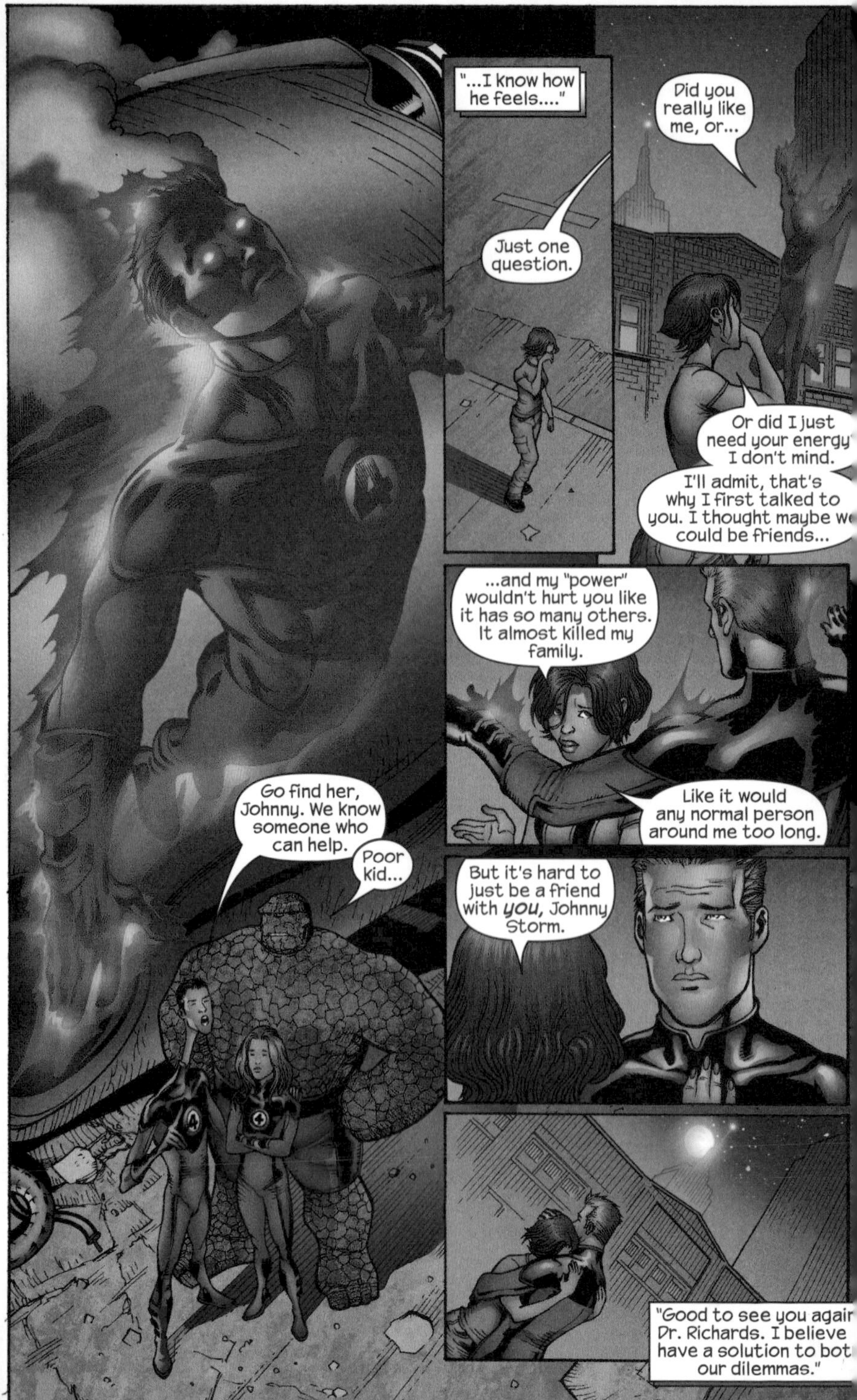
"...I know how he feels...."
Just one question.
Did you really like me, or...
Or did I just need your energy
I don't mind.
I'll admit, that's why I first talked to you. I thought maybe w could be friends...
...and my "power" wouldn't hurt you like it has so many others. It almost killed my family.
Like it would any normal person around me too long.
Go find her, Johnny. We know someone who can help.
Poor kid...
But it's hard to just be a friend with *you*, Johnny Storm.
"Good to see you agair Dr. Richards. I believe have a solution to bot our dilemmas."

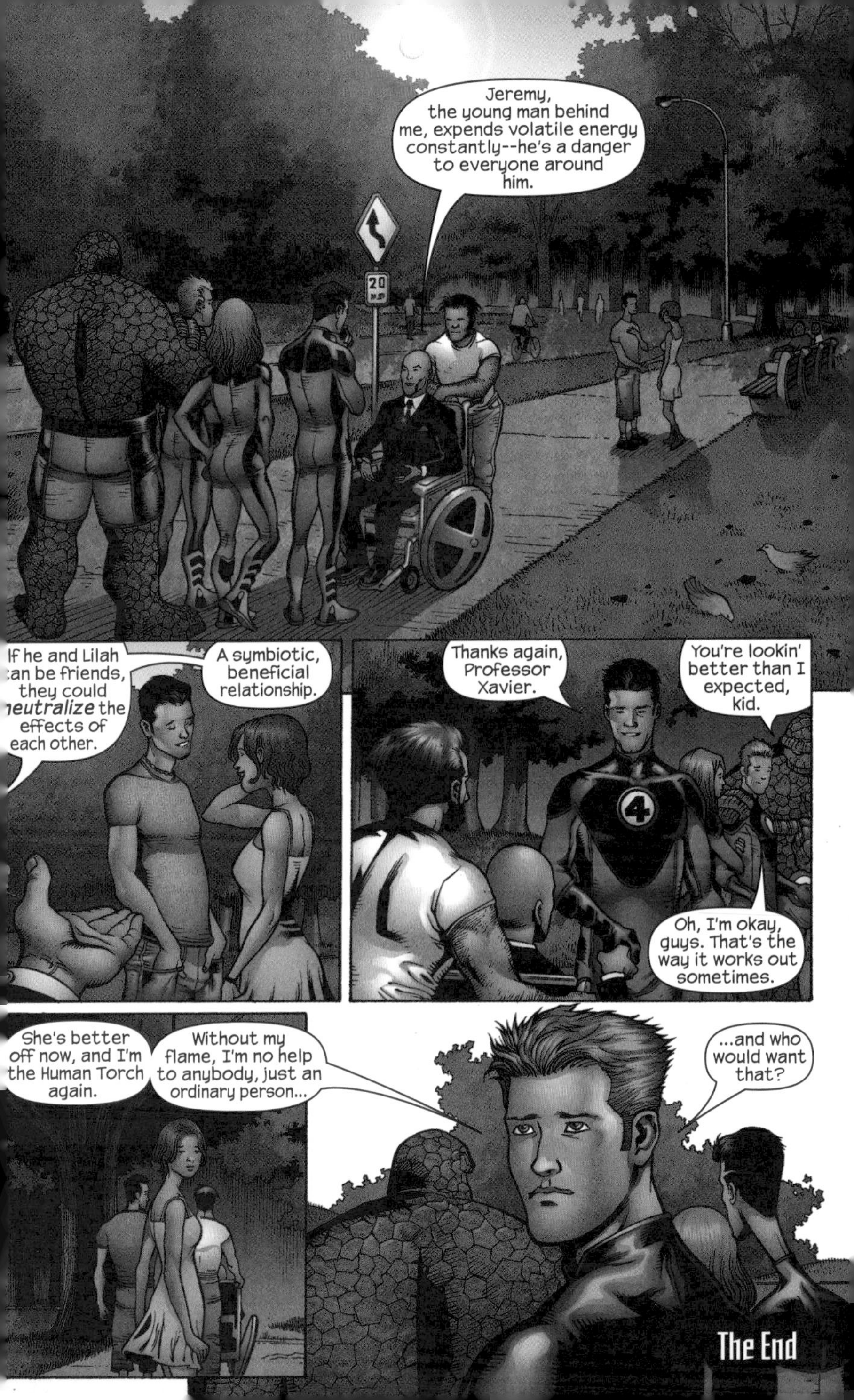
Jeremy, the young man behind me, expends volatile energy constantly--he's a danger to everyone around him.
20
If he and Lilah can be friends, they could *neutralize* the effects of each other.
A symbiotic, beneficial relationship.
Thanks again, Professor Xavier.
You're lookin' better than I expected, kid.
Oh, I'm okay, guys. That's the way it works out sometimes.
She's better off now, and I'm the Human Torch again.
Without my flame, I'm no help to anybody, just an ordinary person...
...and who would want that?
The End